Breathin
were a co
combination…

Add the two blaring, competing televisions in the gym that hovered to Janine's upper right and left sides, the mind-numbing Muzak being piped over the loudspeakers placed strategically around the large room, assorted nubile and robust young forms running around half-naked, and the huffing, panting man beside her—who could not be ignored no matter *how* much she tried—and she was on system overload.

Any minute now she was going to blow. Or trip. Both were possible; neither favorable.

She looked over at the man, hoping and praying he wouldn't keel over, based on the sounds *he* was making. Having a man die on the treadmill next to her would definitely put her over the edge.

She looked at Mr. Locomotion again, wondering how he could go out in public to make such guttural, almost animalistic sounds. By animalistic, she was thinking swine, possibly boar.

She was obviously oblivious to her own auditory articulations.

"You okay?" the man asked.

Elise Lanier

Elise Lanier is a pen name for Elise Leonard, who also writes children's books under her real name. Elise earned her undergraduate degree from LIU-C.W. Post, and her master's at SUNY Albany. After teaching for almost twenty years, she now writes full-time in the home she shares with her husband of twenty-five years and her two cool, smart, attitude-packed teenage sons.

TREADING LIGHTLY

ELISE LANIER

TREADING LIGHTLY

copyright © 2006 Elise Lanier

isbn 0373880782

This edition published by arrangement with Harlequin Books S.A.

® and TM are trademarks of the publisher. Trademarks indicated with
® are registered in the United States Patent and Trademark Office, the
Canadian Trade Marks Office and in other countries.

TheNextNovel.com

 HARLEQUIN®

PRINTED IN U.S.A.

Acknowledgments:

My heartfelt gratitude to the world's greatest agent,
Jay Poynor, for his hard work, his perseverance, his
constant attention and his wonderful friendship.
He gives far more than anyone would expect
from a man in his position.

Special thanks to the agency's V.P.,
Erica Orloff, for everything.

I'm sincerely grateful to my editor, Tara Gavin.
Your insight is pure genius, and I'm thrilled and honored
to have you as my editor. Thank you. (And just so you
know, I *really* wanted to put exclamation points after each
of these three sentences, but I restrained myself.)

To my husband, John: How does one thank another
for giving them unconditional love and unwavering
support for twenty-five years? "Thank you"
seems inadequate, but…thank you.

Michael and John. You are my sons, you are my
inspiration, you are my life. You totally amaze me.
Keep tackling life head-on. And never forget…
I've got your backs!

To my mom: You *really* lived. Thanks for showing me how
to do it. I miss you and think of you often.

To my dad: I'm so glad I got to share your best years,
however few. I really miss you.

A special shout-out to Lieutenant Colonel
M. Noyes, my first writing contact and now my friend.
Had I never been published, I still would have won.
I stayed the course, and yes, you told me so.

Finally, a word of thanks to my readers…
Honoring the light in you,
Knowing the light in me,
We are one.

This book is dedicated to all women over forty.

We've earned our wings, ladies. It's time to fly.

CHAPTER I

"Jesus, Mom! What the hell happened in here? It looks like a testing sight for curling devices."

"Don't say 'Jesus,' Craig."

"Why not?"

"Because we're religious," she said distractedly, while plucking at an errant wisp of hair, making it stand up straight.

"No we're not."

"Oh. Right. Well, it's blasphemous."

"No it's not."

"Well, don't say it anyhow. And before you ask your next question, it's because I *said so!*"

"So, what the hell's going on?" he persisted.

"Now that I cut my hair, I don't know if I need the three eighth-inch curling iron, the half-inch curling iron, or the five-eighth-inch curling iron to fit my curls. My old hot rollers won't stay in. It's too short. Oh, and don't say 'hell' either."

"How come? *You* say it all the time!"

"It's not attractive coming from the mouth of a twelve-year-old."

"I'm almost thirteen," he claimed, throwing her a sideways glance that would have weakened a lesser opponent. "And it's enchanting coming from your mouth?"

"Hell, yeah!"

Her attempt at irony didn't escape him. "Okay, Mom, I get it. Let's not overdramatize things."

She burned her finger on the hot curling iron, grimaced and cursed. "Why stop now?"

"Yeah," he said, snorting a laugh and stubbing his huge, adult-sized, boot-covered foot into the bathroom rug. "Good point. So what's for dinner?"

She could handle his mood swings—they mirrored her own. Perimenopause and the teenage years were a lot alike. Well, except for the drooping, the sagging and the bloating. On the bright side, her pimples weren't as bad as his. On the not-so-bright side, he applied his makeup far more artistically than she applied hers. But both only wore it for large-scale social occasions; another thing mother and son had in common. "Spaghetti."

"Again?" he whined.

"Well, did *you* remember to take something out of the freezer?"

"I didn't know it was my job."

"It's *both* our jobs," she said, trying the five-eighth-incher out for size.

"Why don't you just take it *all* out of the freezer so we've got it on hand?"

"Tried that once. It all went bad."

"Oh," he said, eyeing her newly made curls. "Those are too big. They look loopy. Yours are tighter. Like those springs you find in a pen."

Janine grabbed the half-inch curling iron to try out the smaller size.

"Mom, the small one! Try the *small* one," he said with abundant annoyance. "You're just wasting your time with the other two."

She put down the half-inch and grabbed the three-eighth-inch iron, watching him from the corner of her eye. "Since when are you so concerned with how I spend my time?"

"Since I'm starving to death!"

"Ah," she said, a slow smile spreading across her face. "I should have guessed. You're so good to me, my son."

"It's all about you, Mom." He grinned.

"Yeah, right." She tried the three-eighth-inch barrel and had to admit he was right. It worked the best. "Hey, do me a favor and go put a big pot of water on the stove, would ya?"

"Yeah, okay. Whatever. Anything to get some food around here," he muttered on his way out.

"And throw some salt into it," she continued. She knew he was rolling his eyes. "And don't forget to put a lid on it, or it will take forever to come to a boil." That was one of the few culinary tips she knew.

Twenty-five minutes later they were headed for their usual positions at the kitchen table.

"So why the big interest all of a sudden, Mom?" Craig said as he simultaneously pulled out and hopped onto his chair from behind. It was a slick move she'd often wondered how he came up with. It also prompted frequent prayers to the gods of the family jewel keepers that he wouldn't hurt himself. One false move and she'd never have grandchildren. Time and again she'd told him not to do that, but he always ignored her, laughing at her concern and insisting it was his signature move.

Each time he did it, she'd cringe, but with a teenage son, one had to choose one's fights cautiously. After all, motherhood was a long haul. A very long haul. It wasn't just that wonderful and all-too-swift period of cute, gurgling baby noises and patty-cake. Sure, it was that too. In the very beginning. But that only lasted a short while. Then you're given a few years to prepare yourself, ready yourself—at least as best you can—for…this: your child's unswerving, nonstop, express train ticket headed straight to puberty. Some called it adolescence. To others it was known as the "front lines." A chosen few simply referred to it as "hell."

She'd learned a long time ago, that if you fought every battle that came up, a mother—particularly an overprotective one—would be dead in no time. That clearly in mind, she decided not to comment on the hopping-over-the-back-of-the-testicle-crushing-chair move. She figured if he ever *did* miss, he'd be humbled, humiliated and racked with pain—which was far more of a deterrent by example than any "I told you so" ever was.

"What do you mean? Why, all of a sudden, my big interest in what?" She sat down with a heavy sigh. "Please pass the Parmesan."

He handed her the tall, green bottle. "All the hair-curling stuff. You've always had the equipment and never used it *before*."

Out of the mouths of babes. Her mind couldn't help pondering the depressing thought that she had *lots* of equipment that hadn't seen any use for a while. "I don't know, it just feels funny." Her hand flew to her head, and patted.

"You did a good thing, Mom," he said, while slurping up a stray strand of spaghetti.

She watched her son lick sauce off his mouth with a quick flick of his tongue. "Yeah, I know. Thanks."

"I wonder who'll get it," he said, before shoveling in another huge mouthful.

She had the urge to tell him to take human bites, but didn't. "I don't know. They handle it like an adoption."

He nodded. "Have any regrets?"

She swallowed and then added more Parmesan cheese to her mound of spaghetti before answering. "Yeah, marrying your father."

He rolled his eyes. "I meant about cutting off your long hair."

Maybe a little. "Nah. It's only hair."

"Not to the girl who'll get it," he said, hitting her reason for doing it to begin with square on the head.

"Yes," she said wistfully, imagining the joy of the sick and horrified hairless teen who would receive it. "I suppose."

They ate in relative silence, a habit they'd gotten into over the past couple of years. "So how was school?" she asked before the meal wound down. She knew he'd lock himself in his room for the rest of the night, and they'd shared such a nice moment before, she wanted to extend it.

Wanting and getting were two different things when one had a teenage child.

"What is this? Twenty questions?" he asked, his wall of attitude now firmly placed around him.

"It was *one* question."

"One too many," he said snidely.

Yes, their Hallmark moment was over. "What's the matter, Craig, did I hit a nerve?"

He rolled his eyes. "Everything you *do* hits a nerve, Mom."

A smarter woman would have quit while she was ahead. She went on. "Oh yeah, I forgot. But help me out here, a little. You're not failing anything, are you?"

"No," he said sullenly.

"Anything I should know about?"

"No."

"Any teachers want to see me?"

"No."

"Doing drugs?"

"Jeez, Mom!"

"Answer the question and it'll be the last one I ask."

"For tonight."

"So, sue me for caring about my kid!"

He rolled his eyes again.

"Well?"

"Well what?"

"Drugs?"

"No!"

"Good. And can I trust you?"

"You said that would be the last question."

She shoved a huge forkful of spaghetti into her mouth. "I did, didn't I. Okay, you don't have to answer that last one."

Like her, he shoveled a large forkful of spaghetti into his mouth.

"Just nod."

"Mo-om," he cried, spitting bits of spaghetti and sauce on his side of the table.

"Don't talk with your mouth full."

He finished chewing and swallowed hard, eyeing her mischievously. "You'll have to forgive me, my mother never taught me manners."

"Don't try to change the subject, Craig." She wasn't going to let up until she had her answer, and he must've known that, since he'd lived with her for his entire lifetime.

Capitulation was inevitable. She'd wear him down eventually. It was easier to answer and move on with life. "Yes, Mom. You can trust me. I don't do drugs."

"Okay, just checking," she said with a smile.

"Anything else you want to drill me about?" He took a swig of his soda from the can.

"No. I'm good for now. Eat your spaghetti, dear. And didn't your mother ever teach you to use a glass?"

"We don't have any clean ones."

"Oh. Okay. I'll have to buy some more."

"You *could* break down and wash some, Mom."

She opened her own can of soda and took a swig. "What? I'm the only one that lives here? Your hands are damaged?"

"It's easier to give in than argue," he said with a smirk as he pushed over the ever-present pad of paper that sat on their table, and handed her the pen that stayed permanently on top of it.

She wrote: *Buy More Glasses!*

As she pushed the pad away, the phone rang and Craig reached to get it. Janine didn't bother answering it anymore after three o'clock. It was always for him, and never for her, so why bother.

"Hey, Dad," she heard her son say after a brief pause. He listened for a while then looked at her cautiously.

Here it comes. It was another one of those conversations

that was going to make her out to be the bad guy. She could see it in her offspring's eyes. She could feel it in her stomach. Either it was that, or the half pound of pasta and tomato sauce sitting like a brick down there.

She ate too fast. Always did. It was a trait her ex-husband had pointed out frequently. Of course it didn't help that after a long while of hearing him constantly assert that she ate too fast, she responded with a concise remark of what she thought *he* did too fast! True, it's not the most high-minded or con-fidence-building thing to criticize about a man, but any man should know not to criticize a woman about her eating hab-its. *Both* were hitting below the belt, if you'd ask her. So she'd always considered it a fair comeback. He didn't.

But he was never a match for her. She'd overpowered him from the moment they'd met. When they were first together and newlyweds, he'd told her he thought her assertiveness and aggressiveness was sexy and exciting, but after a while, he'd changed his mind.

For her, when they'd first met, she'd thought his shyness and passive-aggressive, soft-spoken ways were endearing. Plus, it was easy to always get her way. But after a while, there was no way around it for her. She'd only perceived him as "wimpy."

Wimpy, but very manipulative. It was that passive-aggres-siveness that threw her off every time.

She wasn't used to that because she'd always called 'em like she saw 'em—saying what was on her mind. She was al-ways up-front. There was never a hidden agenda when Janine was involved. She let everything show. Whether the other person wanted to see it or not.

Her ex-husband, on the other hand, played so many head games she never knew what his intentions were, or what he was getting at. All through their entire marriage—and their divorce—she had never known what he was trying to accomplish. He'd always had an order of business—of that she was certain—but she was never privy to it. And obviously, by the one-sided conversation she was hearing from her son, her ex was up to his usual scheming, underhanded tricks again. Which only goes to show, she thought to herself, a leopard never changes his spots.

It reminded her of a story.

One day a man found a frozen snake in the forest. Feeling sorry for it, he took it home and nursed it back to life. He defrosted it—or whatever the hell it is you do to a frozen snake to nurse it back to life—and gave it water and food.

As soon as the thing unfroze, the man was hand-feeding it with love and care when it suddenly bit him.

The man said, "How can you bite me? I nursed you back to health! I gave you water by dropperfuls and even hand-fed you!"

The snake looked him in the eye and said, "Thanks, buddy, but you're forgetting one thing."

The man said, "What's that?"

The snake said, "I'm a snake."

She wondered what Martin was up to now.

CHAPTER 2

"Oh come on, Mom! Why not?"

"Because it's too dangerous, Craig. I said no, and I mean it."

"I can't believe I have an opportunity like this, and you won't let me go!" He stomped his heavy, boot-clad foot. "It's a once-in-a-lifetime chance to go white-water rafting with Dad! You're, like, the Wicked Witch of the East, not letting me go!"

She shrugged, not budging at all in her decision.

"You're so unfair! I hate you!" screamed her usually passive son before storming out of the kitchen, slamming the door behind him. He was basically easy-going, that is, until his father put some stupid idea in his mind causing him to rebel and rear his defiant head in a blaze of hateful challenge.

He slammed his bedroom door, too, for good measure. Or maybe because she'd followed him, hoping to work things out before they got too ugly.

"Don't you want dessert?" she called in after him.

He didn't bother answering her. She could hear him muttering to himself in his room. Being her only child, she knew he did this often—probably because he *was* an only child and didn't have anyone besides her to talk with—so she tried to allow him some leeway and privacy. "If I never saw her again, it would be fine by me! Lord knows I can barely stand living with her! She's so unfair! She's closedminded, overprotective and unfair!"

Okay, he had the right to get angry and she understood his frustration, so she let his comments go, realizing where they were coming from. He hadn't really said them to her face, anyhow, so she had no right addressing them, arguing about them, or even agreeing with them.

"And Dad's right. She's a bitch!"

Okay, now he was starting to get her hackles up. She quickly became so angry she could feel the heat of her blood as it pumped through her, but again, she tried to be understanding and realize where *that* had come from. Breathing deeply to regain her composure, and silently cursing her ex-husband for making her out to be the bad guy for the millionth time, she could only hope and pray his hair continued to recede at its blistering pace, and his premature ejaculation problem continued in its customary fashion.

Lost in her silent prayer, she hadn't noticed that Craig had opened his bedroom door again until he'd slammed it with enough force to make the windows rattle and the pictures bang against the walls. She might have tried opening his bedroom door and entering, hoping to calm both of them down and possibly calling a truce, but she'd heard him throw himself on his bed, the squeal of the bed frame's feet scratching along the wooden floor as his weight was hefted upon it. That was her first clue as to what was going on in there. The second clue that he wanted nothing to do with her came when he flicked on his stereo—the Linkin Park CD blaring through his speakers.

He knew she hated Linkin Park, so when he'd turned it up, *way* up, she got the not-so-subtle hint that he was a bit miffed and wasn't in the mood for talking. She could feel the music reverberating in her bones. And that was with the door closed. "Yeah, good. That'll teach me!" she muttered to herself. "Make yourself deaf." She could have screamed it to her son, but no one, including herself, would have heard her over the shattering volume. Obviously he didn't care if he blew his eardrums out. She had pissed him off, and now it was time for a little payback—teenage style.

She shook her head and headed to her own room, knowing they were done communicating for the night. His stereo was so loud she almost missed the incoming call, but a few months back he'd talked her into buying phones with LEDs that lit up when they rang, so although she didn't hear it, she could see it was ringing.

He must have, too, because he had lowered the volume significantly and swiped up his phone at the exact moment she lifted her extension. He was probably assuming it was one of his friends, because she heard him say, "Yeah, talk to me."

"Hello, dear."

"Oh. Hi, Grandma."

Janine knew so much about him that she could read his thoughts almost to the letter. Right now he was thinking, *Oh, great, it's the woman that spawned my current adversary. The female that gave life to the bane of my existence. Yeah, like I really feel like speaking with you at the moment!*

"Hello, dear. How is everything?"

Again, she knew exactly what he was thinking. Most likely because they had a conversation about this at least once a week which always started with him whining, "Mom, what kind of lame question is that? *How is everything?* Like *I'm* supposed to know how *everything* is doing. And Grandma asks it *every* time she calls! What is it with older people? Does *everything* they do have to be so freaking annoying?" She wondered why he thought she knew the answer to that question. Especially because—ironically—she constantly asked herself the exact same thing after each and every conversation with her mother.

"Everything's fine, Grandma. How's *everything* with you?" she heard him say, and smiled, knowing that if Craig was anything, it was predictable.

"Well, dear, I have a nasty sinus infection at the moment, but you know me and how susceptible I am to sinus infections. Every time I get a cold, it goes right into my nasal passages and I get a sinus infection. This one's a doozy! Today my discharge is green. Yesterday it was yellow, but today it's green. That's bad. A sign of infection. I can't wait until it's clear again."

Way too much information there, Grandma! Janine thought to herself, wondering if she should let Craig off the hook by interrupting here, or let him suffer a little longer. "Sorry to hear that, Grandma. I hope you're feeling better soon. If clear nasal discharge is what you wish for, I hope your wish comes true." The sarcastic little brat. She had to admire him, and would have rescued him, but his harsh words were still fresh in her head, so she let him have a few more minutes of torture.

"Me too, dear. Me too. So, how's school going?"

Janine smiled with the knowledge of what her son was thinking. *Another lame question.* She knew his insides were crying out to say, "How do you *think* it's going, Granny? It sucks! It's school!" but instead, he said, "School's fine, Grandma."

"Are you getting good grades?"

And there was worst question number three. He constantly whined to Janine, "Does Grandma have to have the *exact* same conversation *every* time she calls? She's lived, like, forever! Can't she come up with any other questions? Since she feels the need to come up with any questions at all, that is. Why does she always think that asking me the same exact lame questions will give her any different answers? Have they ever changed, yet? Does she even *hear* my responses? Does she even *care?*"

"Yes, Grandma. Mostly A's."

Janine heard her mother cough up a disgusting wad of what she could now only picture as a big glob of "snot"—in Craig's native tongue—on the other end of the phone. She wondered if Craig was picturing it too, and figured he most likely was. How appealing, she thought, as her mother went off on a hacking spree. She could have sworn she heard Craig mumble "Nice," but it was hard to tell over the amplified expectoration being spewed through the phone line. It made one glad Ma Bell had perfected the resonance of their fiber-optic lines. As the huge conglomerate promised, they made your phone connection so real, it was like you were right next to each other. There's a lot to be said for not being able to hear a pin drop. "You're so smart, Craig. Just like your mother used to be."

And there it was. She *had* to remind him of his antagonist. *Had* to bring her up. Janine knew he'd been trying so hard to forget about and ignore her—hence the blaring music to drown out her existence—and now she was right up there on his mind. Her mother was right, he was a smart boy, so Janine knew he'd make both of them pay with the one punishment he could inflict on both of them simultaneously. "I'll go get her for you, Grandma," he said before Janine heard him throw the phone down on his bed.

"Yeah, that's it. Let 'em at each other. They deserve each other! I sure as hell don't deserve either *one* of them, but they sure as hell deserve each other," he muttered to himself as he stomped down the short hallway to her room. Her bedroom door was shut, so he didn't see her leaning against it, her ear against the hollow door. "She's working—all the more reason to disturb her—she hates to be interrupted when she's working," he said to himself with the pleasure of a nefarious villain who had a deliciously reprehensible plan. With what she could only imagine was an evil smile, he pounded on her door. "PHONE!" he shouted to it.

Head rattling, she called out, "Who is it?" while covering the mouthpiece of the phone tightly with one hand and her mouth with the other so she'd sound distant. Yes, she knew it was a juvenile move, but she did it anyhow.

"Yeah, right. Like I'm going to tell you. If I did, you'd beg me to tell her you were in the shower again. And there's no way in *hell* I'm going to do that! A favor? Yeah, right. I don't think so," he mumbled to himself—yet was loud enough for an ear plastered to the door to hear—before she heard him clomp back to his room, slamming his door behind him for good measure.

She picked up her extension, clicking the button and pretending she didn't know who was on the line. "Hello?"

"Oh, hello dear."

"Hello, Mother," she said with a definite lack of enthusiasm. Her son didn't know how good he had it. He had *no* idea what it was like having a mother who was a pain in your ass. He may *think* she was a pain, but she was a *poodle* as compared to the old attack dog that was *her* mother.

"You must be working on one of your little books, because I called you three times this week, and you never returned my calls." This was great. Just what she needed. Fighting with Craig, and now her mother was sticking it to her. But, you had to hand it to Mom. In one fell swoop she had insulted her profession, her writing, her manners, and her capacity as a daughter. All with that one short sentence. Her ex could learn a lot from her mother. At least her mother ragged her quickly and efficiently. Not like Martin. He was much more slow and laborious. Quite amateurish, actually. But after a lifetime with her mother, a seasoned insult comic would appear incompetent and amateurish.

"Sorry, Mother. I'm doing an edit. It's hard for me to get interrupted. I need to keep focused so mistakes don't happen."

"What, like your little books are as important as brain surgery that you shouldn't get interrupted? Or are you trying to imply that speaking to me is a mistake?" Damn, she was good. Either way, Janine looked like an idiot. In so many words— or rather, so few words—her mother had once again reinforced that her books were unimportant, her career was insignificant, and she sucked as a daughter. If it weren't so exhausting—and directed at her—she'd probably find it impressive.

"No, Mother. I didn't say that."

"I don't know how you make your living as a writer, when you can't clearly explain yourself in a simple conversation."

"Whoa, Granny. Pull in the reins! Even *I* think that one was a little rough, and currently I'm on the warpath with her almighty highness."

Janine rubbed her temples and sighed. "Craig, get off the line, would you please?" She hadn't realized he was listening, but as the saying went, what was good for the goose was good for the gander, so she couldn't rightly say anything, could she? Plus, she really didn't mind. She had nothing to hide. Particularly from her son.

When she heard the click of the phone, she assumed he had hung up. "Mother, I've had enough fighting for one day. Between Martin and Craig, I was at my limit before you called, and to be quite honest, I don't have the energy or desire to contend with you right now. If you'd care to, you can try calling in a few days and hopefully by then I'll be better equipped to handle your hostility."

Her mother gasped.

"No offense, Mother," she said as an afterthought.

After harrumphing better than a short, round Englishman wearing a monocle, she said, "How can I *not* be offended, Janine?"

With a heavy sigh, Janine said what she knew she'd have to say to get the older woman off her back. "I'm sorry, Mother. I'm under a lot of stress lately. Please forgive me." She rolled her eyes as she said it, thankful she was on the phone and not having this conversation in person while having to keep a straight face. She couldn't have pulled it off if she had to do it face-to-face. As it were, she was smiling wickedly and the sparkle in her eye was a dead giveaway that she was not the least bit sorry.

CHAPTER 3

Her mother's phone call was long forgotten. The woman was a pain in the butt, but that wasn't anything new. The minute she'd hung up, it was off her mind. This edit was important and she needed to finish it, so she'd worked all night. When Janine finally looked at her clock, she was surprised to see it was 2:23 a.m.

"Guess it's time to call it a night," she said to herself as she shut down her computer. The eerie light it had cast no longer illuminated the surrounding space, throwing her into total darkness. Taking a deep breath, she walked out of her room, not needing any light down the short hall toward Craig's room. She'd done this a million times before.

A faint yellow band glowed from underneath his door, and she surmised that he'd fallen asleep with his light on again.

Opening the door slowly so it wouldn't creak, she gazed at her son sprawled fully dressed across his bed. She crossed the room silently, thinking he looked like an angel in repose, and knelt beside the bed so she wouldn't wake him. Carefully she untied the laces of his government-regulation black boots and gently tugged them off. God, his feet were huge. And they stank, too! Keeping those mammoth puppies penned up in those hot, festering, black leather encasements didn't help matters. The boy's feet needed air circulating around them.

With that thought in mind, she removed his wet, sweaty socks and threw a blanket over his prone body, kissing the top of his head and smoothing back his bangs as she did every night after he fell asleep.

"Mommy loves you," she whispered. It was her ritualistic mantra that she uttered to the sleeping boy nightly.

She stood for a few minutes, watching him sleep, letting the sight calm her. When she felt her body relax and lose some of the strain that seemed to be ever present in her upper back, she reached over and turned the light switch off with a click.

Closing the door silently behind her, she left his room to do the other thing she did nightly. Raid the kitchen.

Heading straight for the junk-food cabinet to check out what was left, she grabbed a fistful of strawberry Twizzlers, and popped a stray purple jelly bean she'd found on the bottom of the shelf into her mouth before realizing what she'd just done. She spent a couple minutes trying to calculate when that uncovered jelly bean could've possibly been purchased, not remembering the last time she'd bought a bag of jelly beans, then quickly drowned out any possible contamination worries by scarfing down approximately thirteen licorice sticks, hoping that would obscure or perhaps overwhelm any bad pollutants the one measly grape-flavored jelly bean might've caused. She closed the cabinet door before padding back to her room to attempt sleep. It was hard for her to un-wind when she was in edit mode. She held an entire novel in her head, and needed to make sure every thread, every action, every sentence fit perfectly. It took her almost two hours, but by approximately four in the morning she finally fell asleep.

As she'd tossed and turned, she had again been struck by the relative ease at which she could make things work out perfectly on paper, but in her real life, her existence was a mess. Try as she might, she couldn't control things as she could in her books. And anyone who knew her would agree that she always tried. It wasn't that she was a control freak. Well, maybe it was. But things just never seemed to work out for her the way they did for her characters.

For example when she woke up the next morning, she'd trodden into the kitchen, eyes crusted over with sleep, hair sticking out haphazardly on the right side and plastered against her head on the left, heading for the coffee machine. He was her only true love now—Mr. Coffee. At least at that hour. Ben & Jerry's came in at a close second, but not *first* thing in the morning. Perhaps second thing. But not first.

On her way to her beloved Señor Café—she saw him as the Latino type, deep, dark, rich, fiery, and with a kick that woke her up quickly—she passed the kitchen table with the pad. Her heart soared every morning when she read the short note from her son, which had become a tradition they'd started when he was old enough to go to the bus stop each morning without her guidance.

That decision had been more of a negotiation than an outright decision. She'd felt he was too young to go to the bus stop alone, and he'd insisted he was "big" enough. After a few dozen extremely mature instances of "are not," "am too," "are not," "am too," she'd finally confessed in her most pathetic whine that she'd miss him. That's when he came up with the note idea. "That way you'll be able to keep me with you all day, Mom," he'd said.

She'd almost cried when he'd said that because she was so proud of him. "Who's the grown-up and who's the kid?" she'd said to him that morning so long ago as she ushered him out the door before closing it. She remembered watching him through the peephole until she couldn't see him anymore. When he was gone, she'd turned, leaned against the door, and cried because her baby was growing up.

Now her baby was well on his way to manhood. In some religions and cultures, he would be considered a man in a few short weeks.

She pulled the pad to her while forcing her right eye open by prying it apart with her fingers—ripping out a few eyelashes in the process. Thankfully, her left eye wasn't also crusted shut. Just the right.

She squeezed her eyes open and shut a few times to get them to focus before trying to read his message. Nothing. Nada. The pad was blank.

So…he still wasn't talking to her.

"Damn it! And damn you, Martin, for starting this little war!" Although she was angry at her ex, her heart sank because she hadn't gotten a note from Craig. He always wrote something before he left for school, and she loved his sweet notes. They started her day and made her smile.

There'd be no smiling today. "Thank you, you rotten, selfish bastard!" she said aloud to her ex, hoping he could hear her.

On to Mr. Coffee. Once she was fully pumped up with high octane, she could begin her morning ritual.

Her morning ritual had changed dramatically these past few months.

It had all started when she hurt her back. Thinking it was a pulled muscle, she'd tried to ignore it, but within minutes it had gotten so bad she was crippled in pain. That's when she'd figured it might be more than a pulled muscle. She didn't have one ounce of medical training, but she didn't have to be a medical genius to know that if one minute she'd been fine, and the next she could barely move, things weren't right. When she could finally get herself out the door of her apartment to see the doctor, she'd begged him for muscle relaxers, hoping to ease the excruciating pain.

"Not so fast, little lady," Dr. Harvey Rogers had said.

"What? No drugs?" she'd shrieked in panic.

"Yes, I'll give you a prescription, but by the way you're standing, I'd like to get some X-rays, too."

"X-rays? It sounds expensive. Is it covered by my plan?"

"Yes, Janine." He'd rolled his eyes. "But does it make a difference? If this were Craig's back, would you ask that question?"

"Of course not! How could you even ask me that? If this happened to Craig, I would do anything he needed. No matter what the cost. And you know that!"

"Yes, I do. And you deserve the same quality of care. So don't tick me off again by asking another stupid question, Janine. If I tell you I want an X-ray, just go get the damn X-ray!"

She'd smiled at him. He'd been her doctor for as long as she could remember. "Yes, sir."

The results had come back a few days later, and instead of telling her over the phone, he'd made her come back into his office. She had no idea what to expect—and her mind had included a plethora of possibilities—but what he'd told her was the furthest thing from her guess.

If she'd been paying attention to the clues, she would have known before being told. She'd known Craig was growing, but it seemed her height was diminishing as well. Then she'd had that sudden pain—stopping her completely. It had hurt to stand, walk, sit and lie down. There was no position she could assume that would give her relief. It hadn't felt like a pulled back muscle. It had been too debilitating. In her heart she'd known it was something else, which was why she'd dragged herself down to the doctor's office to begin with.

"Osteoporosis," she'd shrieked when Harvey Rogers gave her the bad news. "How in the hell did I get osteoporosis? This is ridiculous. There must be some mistake. I don't have osteoporosis."

"You do, and it's bad, Janine. I'm not playing here. One sneeze and you could break your spine. Clip your pelvis into a counter's corner, and you could be in a wheelchair for the rest of your life."

At the time she'd thought he must be kidding, and had said, "Stop making this up, Harvey! I'm really in no mood for jokes. I've got a deadline, and stress up my ass! I don't need your stupid gags today."

"Honey," he'd said far too seriously for her comfort, "I'm sorry, but I'm not joking. Your spine is collapsing upon itself. You didn't pull a muscle, honey, you fractured your spine."

She'd remembered looking at him as if he were nuts. "Check the report again, Harvey."

"I've checked and double-checked it. I even put a call in to the lab's head technician to see if there could possibly be some mix-up."

"And?"

"And, there's no mix-up, no mistake." The look he'd given her was steeped with sadness and concern. "My dear, you've got the stubbornness of a two-year-old toddler, the eating habits of an eight-year-old child, the figure of a sixteen-year-old boy, the mentality of a thirty-year-old wildcat, the mouth of a forty-year-old sailor, and the bones of a seventy-five-year-old woman."

He'd tried to use humor to help defray the emotionalism of the diagnosis, but she'd been thrown into a state of shock when she'd found he wasn't kidding around. "How did this happen?"

He'd shrugged. "You're genetically preprogrammed."

"What the hell does that mean, Harvey?"

"You're tall, thin, Caucasian, and breast-fed a child you had later in life. You're the poster child for this disease."

"It's a *disease?*" she'd gasped.

"Osteoporosis? Sure is, honey," he'd said quietly. Too quietly.

He'd scared her. "So what happens now?"

"Well," he'd said slowly, "now you have to use that stubbornness of yours to get yourself on a regimen of eating right and exercising to get those bones as strong as we can."

"Can we do that?"

"We can try. But I have to tell you, there's no easy or magic solution to this, Janine. You're going to have to work at it. Diligently. And daily."

She'd made a face.

"Look, if you need their help, I'm willing to put a call in to your mother and also one to Martin if you feel you need support with this."

She'd gasped again, only this time, not in shock but in horror. Clutching her hand to her chest, she'd said, "You wouldn't *dare!*"

"Oh no?" he'd said, eyeing her directly. "If it's the difference between your doing as I instruct or not, you're damned straight I'll call in the troops. This is serious, Janine. I can't stress this enough."

"Okay already, I get it, Harvey. Cool the threats and theatrics."

"You need to follow my orders or I'm going to call in the hounds."

"Hounds my ass…they're more like pit bulls!"

"Like you're not one of those yourself," he'd said with a chuckle. "Now listen up and listen good…" was the start to his long list of things she'd had to eat daily, do daily, and take weekly. He'd also given her a prescription that came with a warning list so long it had scared the hell out of her. After taking the pill she couldn't lean over, bend over, lie down, eat fiber, take medicine, drink anything other than water, or ingest food, to list a few. It was scary, and had made her realize the magnitude of this whole thing.

Harvey had been right. It wasn't a joke.

After that, she'd done some pretty thorough research via the Internet, and everything he'd said was true and accurate. Everything. From her genetic predisposition, to her chances of future fractures and damage based on that current level of bone density. He was also right on the money with his ordered advice on how to fight any further damage through diet, exercise, and the latest medication he'd prescribed to help stop and possibly reverse bone loss.

Now, as he'd said, it was *her* job to follow that strict course of therapy.

That fateful day, on her way home from Harvey's office, she'd stopped at a grocery store and bought milk, yogurt, ice cream, and one of each of their stocked cheeses—Romano, Parmesan, Monterey Jack, mozzarella, provolone, Swiss, jalapeño jack, American, Muenster, white cheddar, and regular cheddar in mild, medium, sharp, extra sharp, New York, and Vermont.

The other thing she'd done that day was call a used-sporting-goods shop to find a reasonably priced, secondhand treadmill. The first call was all it took.

"I've got plenty to choose from, lady. Come on down and you can try 'em out," the man had said.

Not knowing what she was looking for, or what the differences could possibly be, she'd told him to send a good, reliable yet reasonably priced machine that wouldn't take up too much space in her already cramped bedroom.

"Ya mean the space-savin', basic model?"

Sounded good to her. "Yes, that'll be fine. Thank you."

"Ya need incline, preprogramming, or anything over ten miles per hour?"

"I don't know."

"Do you run?"

"No. I'll be walking."

"Do you want it to move up and down simulatin' hills?"

"No. I don't think so."

"Okay, lady. I've got a good, plain, basic, space-savin' machine I think'll be poifect for ya."

He'd given her the price, including shipping, and told her his guy could deliver it the next day. She'd given him her credit-card number and told him she'd be there waiting.

She'd decided not to tell Craig about the osteoporosis thing. At least not yet. Not until she'd gotten herself on the right path to making herself healthier. She knew she might not be able to make it better, but she *could* try not to let it get too much worse—possibly slow it down a bit.

That very afternoon Craig had noticed something was awry.

"What's with all the cheese, Mom?"

"I had a craving. And you know, Craig, it wouldn't hurt you if you ate a little calcium, too."

He'd shrugged. "Sure." The boy ingested anything that didn't scurry out of his reach, what did he care if it had nutrients, minerals or calcium in it? Well, now that she'd discovered the dire results of eating a calcium-deprived diet, she'd make sure her own flesh and blood didn't fall into that dark pit.

"Eat some cheese," she'd called as she tried to empty a corner of her room for the treadmill being delivered the next day. She had no idea how big the machine would be so she cleared as much space as possible, attempting to additionally free up a pathway for the deliverymen to carry it in.

"Hey, cool. What's up?" Craig had asked upon seeing her activity.

"What? Something has to be up for me to be cleaning my room?"

He'd raised an eyebrow at her. Only one eyebrow. She didn't know how he did that but was always fascinated when he did, because she thought it was nifty and creepy at the same time. She didn't have the talent, and often wondered if Martin had the one-eyebrow-raising endowment. She'd wondered, but never enough to ask the bastard when she had the divine pleasure of talking with, to, or at him.

"Okay. So maybe I am cleaning up for a reason. I've decided to go on a health kick."

Craig had laughed. "That's funny, Mom."

"I mean it!"

"I'm sure you do. But for how long this time? That's the real question."

"Forever."

"You say that *every* time, Mom. You've said that the last seventeen times you've gone on a permanent health kick."

"Well, this time is different!" she'd huffed, insulted by her son's lack of faith in her word.

He'd done the one-eyebrow thing again. "How so?"

"Because I mean it this time."

"Unlike all the *other* times you've said it in the past?"

She'd remembered getting annoyed. "Is this you encouraging me, here? Or is it you trying to talk me out of it before I even attempt to start my new healthy lifestyle?"

His hands had flown up in the air. "Hey, don't go all postal on me, Mom. I'm just trying to gauge how committed you are to this—your latest—healthy-lifestyle kick."

"I'll tell you how committed I am to it, you big doubting Thomas, you! I bought a treadmill."

He'd looked as if she'd slapped him in the face. "What?"

"You heard correctly," she'd said snootily. "I bought a treadmill. I'm cleaning my room so when it's delivered tomorrow, there will be a place for it."

He'd nodded his head slowly. "Good for you, Mom. I've been trying to get you to do some exercise for a while now, and I'm glad you're finally listening."

"Yeah, well, you've nagged me long enough, plus it's hard keeping up with such an active son. I had to start doing something."

He'd grinned crookedly. "Good for you. I'm proud of you," he'd said as he left her room so she could finish clearing and cleaning.

"Well, I haven't done anything yet," she'd called after him.

"You will, Mom. If you set your mind to it, you'll do it!" he'd yelled back.

"Hey, that's my line," she'd whispered to herself.

She shook her head at the memory. And now, months later, here she was, walking on a treadmill every day, just as she'd foretold. Who would have guessed extortion—and the threat of deformity—would be such a big motivator?

Done with her coffee, still depressed at her lack of morning, son-written note to cheer her up and start her day, she ambled back to her room and looked disgustedly at the treadmill shoved in the corner. "Looks like it's just you and me, bud," she said to it as if it were a person. It was the only thing she related to besides her son these days. And now that Craig was no longer talking to her, it was all she had left. Too bad it wasn't a man. It would've been ideal: it was hard, built, always ready for her, made her sweat, got her blood pumping, and never said a word! Their woman/machine association was probably the closest thing to a perfect relationship she'd ever had in her entire lifetime. "And you don't leave your crap all over the floor, either," she said to it as she climbed on after swiping the hand towel she'd used yesterday off the floor. She'd used it to mop up the sweat that had poured from her during her laborious exertion, but after she smelled it and found it wasn't too pungent, she shoved it into the towel-holder hole, figuring what difference did it make? She'd take a shower right after the torture session anyhow.

She hopped on and began her walking, her mind traveling in five different directions at once. Her latest book, her son, her infuriating ex, her flabby, jiggling thighs, and her pain-in-the-butt mother. When she couldn't home in on only one problem, she decided to forget them all momentarily.

CHAPTER 4

"Why can't I go with Dad?"

She sighed heavily. "This fight again? How many times can we have the same fight?"

"Until you give me a good answer!"

"You mean the answer you want to hear."

The corner of his mouth quirked up a little. "Well, why can't I go?" This time it was more of a whine than a demand.

"Because it's too dangerous, and he's not the most athletic person on earth."

"So? What does that have to do with anything?"

"If the raft goes amuck, he'll have a hard enough time saving himself, much less rescuing you!"

"First off, the raft isn't going to 'go amuck.' Secondly, there will be a guide in there with us. You don't think he's going to let me drown, do you? He'll lose his business!"

"He'll have other people in the boat with him, and he'll save them first, assuming your father will save you—which he won't because he's an inept spaz who couldn't save a drowning fly from a cup of coffee—and you'll be left, dead, floating down the river after you hit your head on a rock!"

"Mom, how do you think of these things?"

"They just pop into my head."

"Well, get it to pop out! That's not going to happen!"

"How do you know?"

"Because the odds are astronomical!"

"Don't raise your voice to me, young man!" she screeched.

Her son stared at her in disbelief; he was no longer amused and hate now flashed from his eyes like daggers.

"Oh my God. Now look at what you've done. You've got me sounding like my *mother!*"

"Another bitch on wheels," he muttered under his breath.

"That's it! Get to your room!"

"My pleasure!" The entire building heard his door slam. How did things get so heated so quickly? They both needed time to cool down. And what *she* needed was to ram a hot poker up her ex's butt for putting this maniacal pipe dream in her son's head. Martin knew damn well she wouldn't let Craig go on a trip like that. As far as she knew, Martin *himself* wouldn't want to go on a trip like that. He was probably having another of his midlife crises, which she could care less about. What *did* concern her was that he had to throw it out there, knowing their son *would* want to go, and also knowing she'd be the bad guy by putting her foot down with a resounding no. That son of a bitch.

Trying to distract herself from her ex's latest manipulative stunt and her son's formulaic response to his artful maneuver, she moved to the pile of mail and ripped open the top letter with pent-up anger. Not noticing it was from the Internal Revenue Service, she hadn't expected to read the imposing and alarming words the businesslike letter contained.

"Damnation! I can't believe it! Why this? Why now? Why *me?*"

She threw the letter on the table and immediately ran to her room to her trusty computer to fire off an emergency message to her agent.

Sid:

Help! They're after me! The stinkin' IRS wants more money! Lots more! What's up with that? They state that I couldn't possibly have made so little in the last two years. What do I do about this? They're saying I owe thousands in back taxes!

And have you sent out the last manuscript I sent you? I know Evette doesn't want it, but there's got to be someone out there who does!

—Janine

Her ire spent, she stomped back to the kitchen to grab some ice cream. That would help her mood. "The IRS! Those bloodsuckers. Does it *look* like I'm rolling in dough?" Some Cherry Garcia was what was needed right now. With chocolate syrup. Lots of chocolate syrup. Grabbing a spoon in anticipation, she opened the freezer to find a huge gaping space where they kept the ice cream. Two half-gallons were gone. Vaporized. The Chunky Monkey and the Phish Food were missing. (Phish Food being Ben & Jerry's chocolate ice cream with gooey marshmallow, a caramel swirl, and fudge fish. Not, you know, "fish" food—food for fish.)

She shook her head but dared not ask her son if he had eaten them. In his present frame of mind, she winced at the thought of his possible response and figured he must've been the one to eat it. Who else would have? Unless her former stalker was back. But she hadn't heard from him in a while. Perhaps she had *another* stalker. A new stalker. A violent stalker. The thought scared the heck out of her—worse than this IRS scare.

She thought about her previous stalker situation.

Only she, Janine Ruvacado, would have a stalker who actually broke into their stalkee's apartment, ate their food, and tried on their good lingerie and shoes. She shook her head and smiled with the memory. Fans. Obviously she couldn't live with them (if they were obsessed and touched in the head), and, as she was finding out lately, she couldn't live *without* them either (if she needed or wanted to make a living).

"How can those leeches at the IRS think I've got money flying in? I can barely afford to keep my human-vacuum of a son supplied in Cherry Garcia and Phish Food!" She slammed the freezer shut then pulled it open again. "Just look at that freezer!" There were two icicle-covered lumps that had not been touched since Hoover was president. They were there when she moved in, and Lord only knows what they were. No one ever dared to find out by defrosting the things. *If* you could pry them out of the frozen tundra to thaw! "I should invite those sons of bitches here and let them look at the opulence I live in! One look at the Taj Mahal I call home, and they'd back off pretty damn fast," she muttered.

Acid rock came stabbing through the airwaves at a Concord-equivalent level of volume. And her already pounding temples were now pulsing in 4/4 time. "Great."

She thought she'd heard the phone ring but wasn't sure. The kitchen phone was LED-less.

"Hello?" she screamed into the phone. "What? I can't hear you. Hang on a minute."

She stormed down to Craig's room, pounded her fists on the door and screamed, "Turn that down! I can't hear whoever's on the telephone!"

When the volume was turned down with no other comments coming forth, she stomped back to the kitchen to pick up the extension she had left on the table.

"Hello? I'm sorry. My son…"

"Can't you control that boy, Janine? Letting him listen to stuff like that will send him right on the road to drugs and alcohol!"

She rolled her eyes heavenward. *Thank you, God. This is exactly what I need right now. My mother, Attila the Hun, spouting off childrearing advice with the authority of Dr. Spock.* "Mother," she said softly, taking a deep breath while trying to fight the urge to scream. *Will you please be quiet and mind your own business, you insufferable witch!* "It's always a pleasure to hear from you, but Craig will not start drinking and doing drugs by listening to rock music. All the kids listen to this stuff."

"And they're all doing drugs! Don't you read the paper or listen to the news?"

"Yes, Mother, on occasion I read the paper and listen to the news. But you can rest with assurance that Craig's not doing those things because he listens to heavy metal."

"Don't patronize me, Janine. I watch Oprah! And I've seen him when he goes out to his druggie concerts with his cronies!"

Cronies? Who refers to preteens as cronies? "He and his friends have fun dressing up when they go to concerts, Mother. That's all."

"He wears more makeup than you do! Well, anyone wears more makeup than you do. You really should take more pride in your looks, Janine. You weren't born with much, but you can remedy that with some makeup. Just ask your son! He'll show you."

She took another cleansing breath. It wasn't working. The urge to scream *Will you please be quiet and mind your own business, you insufferable witch!* was still upon her. "It's a little black kohl around his eyes for the funny effect of it, Mother."

"Well it looks ghastly. And you shouldn't let him do it. Any caring mother would not let their son go out of the house looking like that."

Will you please be quiet and mind your own business, you insufferable witch! "Thank you for your support, Mother, but it's really harmless, and to be honest, I have to choose my fights with him now that he's a budding teen, and that's not one fight I want to waste my time or energy on." She sighed audibly, hoping her mother would get the hint.

"Speaking of wasting your time and energy, Janine, as I was saying, you probably should take your son's lead and think about wearing a little makeup yourself. You're not getting any younger, dear, and no offense, but you can use all the help you can get in the looks department. You get your looks from your father's side you know, not mine."

Will you please be quiet and mind your own business, you insufferable witch! "Yes, I know, Mother. You've been telling me for over forty years now."

"Which goes to prove my point, dear. You're getting older and you're still unattached. And what man in his right mind will want an old, reclusive, irritable woman who doesn't even attempt to make herself look attractive? Or at least as attractive as she could possibly make herself look—*if* she'd take some time and do something with her hair and her makeup. You can't change what God gave you, dear, but there's certainly enough beauty products and makeup out there that can help you take a shot at fixing what you weren't born with."

Janine smiled. *This ought to get her.* "I cut my hair off a few days ago."

"What?" The older woman gasped. "Why would you *do* such a thing? Your hair was one of the *only* appealing things about you!"

"Why, thank you, Mother. And now I don't even have *that* in my favor."

"Oh my God! I know! Why would you *do* that, Janine?"

Will you please be quiet and mind your own business, you insufferable witch! "I gave it to Locks of Love."

"Who's Loxa Luv? She sounds like a porn star. Why are you giving a porn star your hair?"

"Locks of Love, Mother. It's an organization that makes wigs for teenage girls who lose their hair from medical problems."

"But your hair was down past your waist!"

"Yes, Mother. I know."

"How much did you cut off?"

"All of it."

The older woman choked on her gasp.

"It'll make a nice, long wig for some girl," Janine added.

"You don't even know who it will go to?"

"Nope."

She heard her mother tsk a few times. "How could you do such a thing?"

Will you please be quiet and mind your own business, you insufferable witch! "I was being generous and giving, Mother. A notion you may not be familiar with."

"What do you look like now? Without your hair, you have nothing left. Nothing!"

"Why, thank you, Mother. As a matter of fact, you're probably right. It's short, cropped close to the head, and now that the weight is gone from it, it's sprung like a thousand demented pogo sticks on crack."

"Oh my God. It sounds gruesome!"

"Yes, Mother. I'd have to say that's exactly how it looks."

"Well, it's a good thing you're reclusive. No one has to see you."

"Yes, Mother, I'm saving the world by staying indoors."

"You don't have any awards ceremonies or anything coming up do you, dear?"

Will you please be quiet and mind your own business, you insufferable witch! "No, Mother. But thanks for pointing that out for me. It makes me feel a hell of a lot better to know I won't be offending anyone while *not* getting any attention or accolades for my work."

"Yes, dear. Glad I could help."

Sarcasm was lost on the woman. "Do you have anything else to say to me, Mother? I've got a lot on my plate right now."

"Oh, please, Janine. Don't start overeating, too. Between your hair, your plummeting career and your difficult son, you don't want to add to your misfortune by making yourself overweight!"

Will you please be quiet and mind your own business, you insufferable witch! "I was talking metaphorically, not foodwise. I've got a lot of *problems* on my plate right now, Mother. And Craig is not difficult, Mother. He's the perfect kid. So before you start ripping him apart like you do me, my advice is to say goodbye and hang up the phone before I give you a little piece of my mind on *your* parenting abilities."

"No reason to get yourself in a huff, dear."

"Yes, Mother, there is. You can say whatever you like about me, but when you cross the line and talk about my son, you're overstepping your bounds, and you'd be wise to back off."

"But I…"

Will you please be quiet and mind your own business, you insufferable witch! "Back off, Mother, and say goodbye."

The older woman sighed. "Okay, Janine. I don't know *why* you have to turn everything into a fight. I was only trying to give you advice based on some of my many years as a—"

"Goodbye, Mother," she said as she hung up the phone on her mother, mid-sentence.

She hadn't noticed that the music had stopped. Nor did she see Craig come out of his room, sliding along the hallway to the kitchen in his socks; so she was startled when he spoke. "You okay, Mom?"

Janine nodded. "Yes. I'm fine."

"I heard everything," he said gently. "I didn't mean to, but when you knocked on my door, I thought the phone was for me so I listened in."

"It's okay."

"Thanks for sticking up for me."

She nodded.

"I'm sorry about what I said before."

"It's okay."

"No, Mom. It's not. You're nothing like Grandma."

A snort of air came from Janine's nose. "That's a relief."

They stood in silence, neither knowing what to say next.

"Why do you let her talk to you that way, Mom?"

She shrugged. "Why fight it? It just extends the conversation. I've learned long ago to let her have her say and not argue. Arguing only prolongs the agony."

He nodded.

She looked at her son. Really looked at him. "I don't want you to ever think that way about me, Craig. I want you to be able to talk to me."

"I can, Mom."

She smiled sadly at the most important person in her world—the *only* important person in her world. "Will you let me know if I ever get too overbearing and you can't express yourself to me? Because the day that happens will be the day I've destroyed the best thing in my life."

He looked at the floor, stubbing his toe at some invisible mark. "Yeah, I'll let you know."

CHAPTER 5

The sunlight streamed across her face, and the sound of an ambulance screaming outside her window woke her up from her troubled sleep. Looking around, she saw that she wasn't in prison for tax evasion, but was still in her own home. Thank God it was only a dream. A nightmare, really.

She pulled herself out of bed, threw on a robe and stumbled to the kitchen for her morning jolt of caffeine. Passing the table, she looked for the pad and found her morning note from Craig.

Not yet, Mom. I can still take ya!☺
Don't let Grandma get you down.
You're smart, talented, and beautiful in my eyes!☺

Smiling, she was glad he couldn't see her at that moment. She looked down at the old, worn terry-cloth robe with pulls and stains, and fingered her dirty hair. He wouldn't find her so beautiful right now. But perhaps she was wrong. When *he* had bed-head and crusts of sleep in his just-wakened eyes, she found him quite adorable. Beautiful. The only time she found him more beautiful was when he was sleeping. Because when he was asleep, he was without any defenses. He was her son, her child, the being she had given life to—pure and open. He was still her baby when he slept.

She looked down at the pad again and smiled. How could her mother think this boy was anything but terrific? Look at the sweet message he'd left her, knowing she was stressed and tired and feeling crappy about herself.

She shuffled over to Mr. Coffee, measured out some coffee and thought of her son as she stood there waiting for the pot to fill. The heavenly aroma filled the small, drab kitchen, and she found renewed strength in the blissful fragrance. When the trickling sound ended, she poured herself a cup and padded back to her room, mug in hand, to get her e-mail messages. Once she'd responded to anything urgent (like hopefully the response from her agent Sid), she'd get to her walking.

She logged on and brought up her e-mail program, sipping the hot coffee while waiting for the messages to come through. Looking for anything important, she was a bit miffed that she hadn't heard from Sid. "Damn it! When I was making money hand over fist for the man, he answered my e-mails within minutes!" Lately, if she heard back from him within a week, she felt honored. "Has my latest work been *that* stinky?" she wondered aloud as she deleted the mortgage offers, the porn-site insertions, and the other nonpersonal spam that flooded her in-box. Feeling depression start to sink in, she put on her mannish-looking walking shoes and sports bra—no use having anything droop further, time and gravity were doing enough to help in *that* department—and climbed aboard her treadmill.

She popped in the videotape of *Family Feud* that Craig had recorded for her daily and started walking. *Family Feud* was on twice each weekday, which made one hour of tape. If she timed it right, she could walk about forty-five minutes worth in an hour. If she was lucky. The time discrepancy was due to her usual pit stops—which she took every ten to fifteen minutes or so. Having a bladder the size of a thimble, she could only get about a quarter mile done—tops—before she needed a bathroom break.

"House! HOUSE, you moron! How can you not say house?" she yelled at the doofusy-looking man on her TV screen. "Where do you live? In a cave?" she shouted, gasping for breath. "In an island hut? In a cell? You moron!" She shook her head. "People are idiots!" she sputtered. "Where do they *find* these people to go on this show? Under a rock?" she muttered, and made a face that was a cross between severe pain and the immediate aftermath of finding out your son has head lice while you're lying with him on his pillow to talk about his day. "You don't deserve to win the twenty thousand dollars. You're too stupid!" she told the man on her screen.

When she had first started walking, Craig tried to show his support by sometimes sitting on her bed while she walked, watching *Family Feud* with her as she plodded along. The television volume needed to be way up to be heard over the noise the treadmill made, so he'd join her, casually saying it was so loud in the apartment, there was nothing else he could do without hearing it anyhow. He'd laugh at her disbelief at the answers people came up with on the show, and funny as it first was (watching his mother tromp like a hamster in a wheel while screaming obscenities at a taped game show), it lost its appeal pretty quickly.

One day, when he was in his room doing his homework,

she was screaming, "Now, now! NOW!" and he'd thought she was screaming, "Ow, ow! OW!" He came running in to help his poor mother, only to find her not lying in a crumpled heap at the base of the treadmill as he'd expected, but red faced and screaming at the TV, her hands balled up in fists, as her sneakered feet pounded away. It was just as well she hadn't hurt herself, because he'd wondered how he was going to carry his mother—who was wearing her usual workout attire of nothing but old panties, a sports bra, and ugly walking shoes—to the hospital.

After he complained that he couldn't hear himself think over her pounding feet, the squeak of the treadmill, her screaming at contestants, and the blaring television, she tried to get her walking done first thing in the morning while he was at school. This way he would have no excuse to not do his homework; nor could he ever say he didn't have the peace and quiet to do it well. Plus, she figured in case she *did* hurt herself or keel over and die, it would also save Craig the embarrassment and logistical problem of getting her to either the hospital or the morgue. In the "getting hurt" case scenario, she'd have all day figure out a way to get herself to a hospital independently, and in the "keeling over and dying" case scenario, well, she'd be dead, and there's not much anyone could do about it.

The afternoon after making that momentous decision to walk mornings while he was at school, she'd instructed him to dress her adequately before calling the police should he ever come home to find her lying dead in just her sports bra, old, big underwear and walking shoes. When she'd tested him, by asking him to choose an ap-

propriate outfit for the situation, he'd failed miserably.
Who'd get caught dead in an olive-green velvet blazer and
old, faded gray sweatpants one had worn during a pregnancy more than a decade before but kept and still wore
because they were comfy? Yes, he was right, they'd be easy
to slip on her prone, stiff, dead body. But to be caught *dead*
in that outfit! So ever since, she kept a neatly folded pair
of black slacks and a fresh, crisp blouse on a chair nearby,
so he would dress her appropriately should the need arise.
The black slacks were slimming, and the blouse was supposed to be wrinkle free. It was truly the perfect outfit to
be caught dead in. She also threw out the olive-green velvet jacket.

So now she walked in the mornings. Currently, she was
alternately screaming "Brad Pitt" and "Tom Cruise" at a
woman with a foot-tall, bouffant hairdo from Idaho who had
just given the answer "Fred Astaire" to the question: Name
a famous actor. Who did she think they polled? One hundred
people from a nursing home? When her husband, wearing a
light blue polyester suit, said "Charlie Chaplin" she decided
to take her second bathroom break. "Will Smith, Russell
Crowe, Keanu Reeves, Mel Gibson," she muttered to herself
as she walked to the bathroom. "Or, if you wanted slightly
older—which it seems you *do*—how about Robert DeNiro,
Paul Newman, Harrison Ford, Clint Eastwood!" she huffed.

Upon her return, she climbed onto the treadmill and
started again, disgusted by the couple who obviously lived
under a rock in Idaho. Suddenly she heard a terrible clunk
and was almost thrown from the treadmill when the walking tread came undone and the front bar that held the tread

part in place arced up and lifted on the right side—perpendicular to the walking platform.

"Hmm. That can't be good." Not good at all. Now what the hell was she going to do?

She tried stepping on the bar to push it back in place, but it didn't budge. It just stood there, poking out, the tread all wavy and askew.

"Damn it! This sucks," she muttered as she got off, no longer thinking about how badly the Idahoans were playing, which had been all consuming mere seconds ago.

Not knowing what else to do, she thought of her maintenance man.

Throwing on some clothes, she steadied herself for the trip down to the building's basement.

The basement was where the tenants kept their stuff in small, partitioned cages. In their particular compound, Craig kept an assortment of sporting goods and miscellaneous stuff he'd collected that she'd insisted were not to be kept in the apartment. Her particular donation to their assigned pen was her clothes from the off-season, stored in large, rectangular containers.

She hated going to the basement. Her self-assigned, floor-specific claustrophobia always made her overactive imagination envision the entire building collapsing on top of her with her not being able to get out. Needless to say, just hitting the B button in the elevator brought feelings of suffocation for her.

This wasn't the only outlandish visualization she had. She had *lots* of peculiar Janine-induced mental pictures. Quite a few were rather inspirational. But as unlikely as they all probably were, they freaked her out nonetheless. If the basement brought impressions of asphyxiation, the *sub*-basement brought more atrocious visions of terror. For below the dreaded basement…was the *sub*-basement. The sub-basement was a totally creepy, dark, dank place where the building's maintenance man, Mr. Franklin—a friendly enough old coot—could usually be found. Rumor had it that his office was there, but she'd always had a sneaking suspicion that the strange old man lived down there, too.

Janine shivered with fear and repulsion as the elevator doors opened to that floor.

"Mr. Franklin?" she called, a slight echo following her words.

Taking a few steps into the sub-basement, she could smell the mold, and hated the look of the rusty, exposed pipes traversing over her head. The ceiling was low, as though the building had already settled or had a mini-collapse, squashing the space originally designed. Was that water she heard dripping? Maybe the pipes had already broken with the pressure of the building that was surely starting to collapse.

The sooner she got out of there, the better. "Are you down here, Mr. Franklin?" She heard the panic in her voice, but was too creeped out to disguise it. Try as she might, she couldn't stop picturing the rats that were probably scampering around her feet at that very moment. *The Black Plague started here, I'm sure*.

"May I help you, ma'am?" A young man appeared out of nowhere, scaring her to the point where what little was left of her hair almost stood on end. He wiped his hands on the dirty rag hanging from his shoulder.

"I'm looking for Mr. Franklin."

"I'm he. I mean him. I'm him. Mr. Franklin."

She stared at him. "Unless you've taken some kind of youth elixir, had hair plugs, and dyed whatever little tufts were already there from gray to black—you're not Mr. Franklin."

He laughed. "Oh. You must be referring to my grandfather. Gramps retired to Florida."

"He did? When did that happen?"

"Eight months ago."

"Oh." *Shows how observant I am.*

"I'm Mr. Franklin, too, but I think that sounds so officious, don't you? Please, call me Ben."

"Okay, Ben," she said, trying to recall if she'd ever heard a maintenance man use the word *officious* before. She might not acknowledge their presence—or lack thereof—but she *did* notice their speech patterns and chosen vocabulary. Her job made that a habit and a necessity. "So, Mr. Franklin, I mean, Ben." She stopped speaking. Something was off, amiss, but she couldn't put her finger on it. "Wait a minute. Your name is Ben Franklin?"

"Ironic, huh?" His smile was lopsided.

"Well, yes."

"I've yet to invent anything useful, although I've spent my lifetime trying to come up with something."

She felt sorry for him. "Most of the good things are already invented."

"Don't I know it," he said with a huff, looking totally dejected.

"Keep at it, Ben Franklin. You'll think of something."

"Thanks." He grimaced. "It's a hard name to live up to."

"I'd imagine so. It must feel like a curse for someone in your line of work."

"Yeah. Welcome to my world." His head hung low for about three seconds before snapping up with new life. "So, how can I help you, Miss Uh…"

"Ruvacado. Janine Ruvacado. Fifteen D."

"Fifteen D." He thought for a few moments. "Oh, you must be Craig's mom."

She smiled. Everyone knew Craig. "Yup. That's me. Craig's mom."

"He's a great kid. He was one of my first customers when I got here. I changed out some worn skateboard wheels for him."

Her smile widened. "Yes, his skateboard. He loves that thing."

"It's a beauty!"

She'd gotten it for him when the money was still pouring in. It's a good thing she bought it when she did, because now she couldn't even afford the replacement parts for it. "Thanks."

"So what can I do for you, Craig's mom from Fifteen D?"

"Janine, please. Well, I seem to have broken my treadmill."

He looked from her left side to her right, then twisted his neck as if peering behind her. "I don't see it here, so I guess it's still up in the apartment. Want me to take a look at it?"

"I thought you'd never ask. Your grandfather was a real love. He'd always fix anything that went wrong around here, even if it wasn't building related."

"Yeah, Gramps is a fixing wiz. If he can't fix something, it can't be fixed."

She laughed. "Yes, it was his motto. 'If I can't fix it, no one can,' he used to say."

"Some may take that as being cocky, but with Gramps it was true," Ben Franklin said seriously.

Biting the smile that wanted to creep across her face, she replied with equal seriousness, "Yes, I know. He fixed many a broken thing for me."

Ben nodded, solemnly.

They walked to the elevator and Janine sighed with relief as they got in and started for the "surface" floors. Her sigh wasn't lost on Ben.

"Glad to be out of there?"

"Yes!" Then she realized she might have been rude. "I'm sorry. How did you guess?"

"Besides the look on your face as we entered the elevator?"

"That bad?"

"Well, no. The horrified look on your face for the entire time you were down there might've also given it away. And I didn't think it was because you were alone, in the middle of nowhere, with a stranger."

"I'm sorry. It's nothing personal. I just have a fear of basements and sub-basements."

"Taphephobia?"

"Excuse me?"

"Do you have taphephobia?"

"What's that?"

"The fear of being buried alive."

"Oh. No. Not really. I don't think it's that bad. I'm not afraid of being buried alive." Although now that he mentioned it, she was upset by the thought. Being buried alive *had* to be horrendous. "It's just a fear of being in basements and sub-basements. I've got an overactive imagination."

He nodded. "I understand."

She snorted a laugh, trying to push aside the thoughts of a predeath burial. "You'd be the first. Everyone else thinks I'm nuts."

The elevator stopped at her floor and they got out, walking to her apartment. She pushed open the door that she'd left ajar.

"You really shouldn't leave your door open like that. Anyone can walk in."

"So I've been told. But I figure, what are the odds of some lunatic walking in the opened door of the fifteenth floor of this building at the exact moment I'm down in the sub-basement, looking for your grandfather?"

"Pretty slim, I'd suppose."

"Yeah, and it gave me the added incentive to hurry back up from the dungeon. I couldn't sit around with your grand-dad shooting the breeze. I could honestly say, 'Gotta run, Mr. Franklin, I left my door open.'"

He followed her through her apartment. "Yeah, Gramps sure can shoot the breeze when he's in the mood."

She opened her bedroom door. Normally she wouldn't allow anyone in there, especially with the mess that was the usual decor, but this was an emergency. She hurried to pick up the stray panties that hung off the lamp. She hadn't both-ered to clean up, assuming old man Franklin would take his time getting his arthritic body up to her apartment. She'd also had the added bonus of knowing his glaucoma-riddled eyes weren't as sharp as they probably once were.

"So that's it?" the young Ben Franklin uttered, pointing to the treadmill.

Considering it was the only treadmill in the room, *and* had the upper bar-thingie poking out perpendicular to the walking belt, she hoped his fixing talents were sharper than his observational gifts.

He was still looking at her for an answer.

"Yes. That would be the one," she said, trying to remain calm.

He shook his head slowly. "Doesn't look good," he said.

"Ya think?" she said, feeling her sense of calm sliding away.

"Yup. Doesn't look good."

That's all he had to say? Even *she* knew it didn't look good! Why else would she have gone down to that horrifying dungeon in search of his grandfather?

"So what are you going to do about it?" she asked, trying to leave the challenge—and hysteria—out of her voice.

He shrugged. "Don't know for certain till I look at it."

"You *are* looking at it!" The hysteria was creeping in. She'd promised Harvey she'd walk every day to help fight the osteoporosis, but how could she do that if the damn thing was broken?

"And it doesn't look good," he said again.

"We've already ascertained that chosen tidbit of information," she said with impatience. "Is there anything else you can say or do to get it fixed in—" she looked at her bedside clock "—the next half hour?"

"Nope."

Great! "So what am I supposed to do?"

"About what?"

"My *walking*. I'm supposed to walk every day for at least a half hour."

"Sorry, Ms. Ruvacado, but you won't be doing that on this machine anytime soon."

"So what am I supposed to do?" she demanded shrilly. At the look of fright on the poor man's face, she realized she needed to tone it down a bit. "I'm sorry, Ben. I shouldn't shoot the messenger. But, really, what am I supposed to do now? I have to walk daily, or my doctor will pester me. He's already threatened to tell my mother and ex-husband to get them involved in making me walk if I didn't do it voluntarily. Plus I'm afraid that if I stop doing it, even for a few days, I'll never start doing it again."

"Can he do that?" Ben asked with astonishment.

"Can *who* do *what*?" She was way beyond her frustration level.

"Can your doctor call your mother or your ex-husband like that?"

"Not ethically. But they're both listed as my emergency contacts, so he figured he'd extort me."

"I thought a doctor had to take a Hippocratic oath?"

"He must've stepped out to the bathroom or something during that part of the ceremony. He has no qualms about blackmailing his patients if he feels it's in their best interests."

"That's not right!"

"Yeah, tell me about it. But he holds the strings, so I've got to dance his little dance like a marionette."

"Or walk his little walk."

"Yes. You're catching on to my dilemma."

"How about a gym?"

"Are you kidding? Do *that* in public?" Her hand waved at the broken treadmill.

"Sure. Lots of people work out in gyms."

She looked sideways at him, her disgust clearly evident on her face. "I'm not 'lots of people.'"

CHAPTER 6

How were people supposed to see that? It was hard enough to hear the damn thing, but to see it, you had to crane your neck at an absurd angle. That's not mentioning the fact that there were two different channels competing for your attention on each side. A talk show on one, and the morning news on the other.

She could've possibly watched one, but couldn't decide if she should wring her neck to the right and give her full attention and allegiance to the news, or contort her neck to the left to catch the casual, witty repartee of the talk show. Either way, she'd end up deformed for the rest of the day—if not longer—with a stiff neck. Plus, both shows were at equal sound levels, thereby drowning each other out, making either one impossible to hear easily. So instead, she looked straight ahead while miserably listening to the man beside her gasp, huff and grunt.

She wasn't used to all the added stimuli. It was hard enough for her to do this without having any other action going on around her, taking her attention from the task at hand. Breathing and walking was a complicated enough combination for her to handle. Add the two blaring, competing television sets hovering to her upper right and left sides, the mind-numbing Muzak being piped over the loudspeakers placed strategically around the large room, assorted nubile and robust young forms running around half-naked, and the huffing, panting man beside her who could not be ignored no matter *how* much she'd tried, and she was on system overload.

Any minute now she was going to blow. Or trip. Both were possible; neither favorable.

She looked over at the man, hoping and praying he wouldn't keel over based on the sounds *he* was making. Besides having a man die on the treadmill next to her, the fuss and upheaval that would ensue would be quite annoying. Plus, on top of all this noise, the loud, blaring ambulance siren sure to follow Mr. Locomotion's collapse would definitely put her over the edge.

She looked at him again, cyclically thinking that his utterances were horrendous and wondering how he could go out in public and make such guttural, almost animalistic sounds. They were disgusting! By animalistic, she was thinking swine, possibly boar. The snorting, gasping, huffing and panting were quite annoying and disturbing.

She was obviously oblivious to her own auditory articulations.

"You okay?" the man asked.

She looked around to see whom he was talking to. Considering no one else was at the bay of treadmills, she assumed he was talking to her. *Me? He's asking if I'm okay? He's the one who sounds like an angry bull making an obscene phone call.* "I'm fine, thanks," she said haughtily, not wanting to add yet another action—talking—to the breathing and walking she was already juggling.

"You seem angry," he said succinctly, between gasps.

She knew she walked like a horse, but angry? Why would he think that? And so what if she was? It wasn't any of his business. And who the hell was *he* to intrude on her almost spiritual level of clarity and concentration by drawing attention to her clomplike walking style? What did he expect her to do? Tiptoe? Sashay? Undulate provocatively? Do a frigging catwalk?

He was the one making strange noises she found totally repellent while he was sweating like the fat, bearded lady at the circus, but you didn't see *her* telling *him* about it or drawing his attention to it, did you? No! That's because she wasn't *like* that. She reserved sharing her *real* thoughts with the people who knew her best. Like her beloved son, or her abhorrent ex-husband, or even her pain-in-the-butt mother. Not some strange, panting man she'd never seen before.

"I'm fine. Thanks," she said pointedly, hoping to end this exchange. There, conversation closed.

More breathing, more huffing. "You don't seem fine."

Who did he think he was? Her mother? Her keeper? Her shrink? Okay, she'd been patient with the man long enough, but now he was starting to tick her off. She waited until her own breath was strong enough to talk before making her response. "Well, I am," she procalimed, knowing full well she was *not* fine, but she sure as hell wasn't going to share it with him—a complete stranger.

But then she heard the words Martin had spit at her during their phone conversation last night. Well, *conversation* was a pleasant word for what it really was. It was more like a screaming match, but that was neither here nor there. "*You have serious trust issues, Janine. I don't know how I can help you with that. Lord knows I couldn't help you while we were married, but maybe now that we're divorced I can prove it to you through actions that people—mankind—can be trusted and believed in. I do think you believe and trust me, but you won't admit it! In what situations will you trust me with our son? Who knows, Janine. But he is my son too. And I deserve the right to do with him what I'd like to do. Your attempt to stop us from being together is wrong, and will only turn your son away from you. You've got problems, Janine. What do I feel is the best way for me to help you? Hell, I don't know, I'm no expert. But what else can Craig do except eventually walk away from you? Over time, you'll see that I'm telling you the truth."*

They weren't the last words of the screaming match, but they certainly led up to them.

"Who the hell do you think you are, Martin? I know you like to think of yourself as the male version of Mother Teresa. But you know what, bud? You're just a passive-aggressive bastard who uses this new age mumbo jumbo to try to sound as if he's got things under control. But let's not forget, little man, I've lived with you and know you're just a sniveling little wuss who wishes he were otherwise! You are not taking my son river rafting, and it is because I don't trust you to care for him properly. So go have your midlife crisis without involving Craig. And for the record, I'm not stopping you from seeing him. Go right ahead, see him till your eyes bug out, but you are not, Martin, NOT taking him rafting."

She was reliving the conversation as the man beside her kept making his disgusting sounds. In a way, Martin was right. She did have trust issues. So what? She felt she'd always had them. But to her, it was understandable. Look at her parents, her life, her past. She lived with her past. Always. Maybe it was baggage, but as far as she knew, everyone had their share of baggage. If you were human, and you had lived a few years, you had baggage.

She looked at the panting man beside her. He probably had baggage, too. Sweat was dripping into his eyes, his face was red with exertion, and there were lines of agony on his face. He smiled at her. Or grimaced. She couldn't tell which, but she thought he might have meant it to be a smile.

She only had the gym pass for a week, while her treadmill was being repaired, and once the damned machine was fixed, she'd be back home in her safe environment where no one could reach her or hurt her. *Listen to me! I do have trust issues. Oh hell.*

She looked at the man again and saw that he looked harmless. At least he looked harmless to her now. The poor guy was so exhausted he couldn't swat a flea at this moment. So what could it hurt? He *was* a complete stranger. Why not tell him? In a week's time, she'd never see him again.

"I'm sorry," she said, hoping he'd realize she was apologizing for her rudeness but was a bit breathless at the moment, so she needed to keep things pretty concise. She took a deep inhalation to compensate for the breath she'd used to apologize.

Normally, at home, she'd be in her panties and sports bra, watching her taped programs of *Family Feud*. It was much harder doing this while fully dressed with no distraction of Richard Karn and the two five-person families from around the country saying completely stupid things. At home, she didn't have to have a conversation, she just had to occasionally shout at the contestants when she felt like it. Like the other day, she was yelling "No cheese!" repeatedly before muttering to herself that the contestant was a moron. The question had been, "Why wouldn't a mouse want to live in your house?"

Who the hell, in their right mind, answers "Because it's a brick house and there are no holes to get in." What was that lady implying? A *wooden* house has holes in it for mice to get in? Where was the logic? Janine could possibly understand "I own a cat," or something else that made *some* sense as to why a mouse wouldn't want to live in your house, but "It's a brick house and there are no holes to get in?" What the hell kind of stupid answer was that? Did the woman live with the three little pigs?

Or how about the guy on the show a few days ago, whose question was "Why would an airplane not take off on time?" She screamed, "the weather, the weather, THE WEATHER" to him. But did he listen? No. He said, "Because it was delayed." That wasn't an answer. It was the question! Repeated! She'd been totally disgusted, concluding that that's the problem with the world today— nobody listens.

She looked over to the sweating, panting man and wondered if he really cared to hear what she had to say, or if he was like everyone else in this world today and didn't listen. He was still looking at her and was still smiling. Or grimacing. She still couldn't tell which.

Oh well, what the hell. It wasn't like she could hear the TV or anything, and she had to do her walking, even if it was in public, or Harvey would call Martin or her mother. Plus, she had to pass the time *somehow*. "I've had a bad couple of weeks," she blurted out.

At first she didn't know if he had heard her, because he didn't answer, but when she stole a sideways glance at him, he smile-grimaced again.

"What happened?" he said between huffs. Apparently he too had trouble breathing while doing this torturous contraption. The only difference was that he was running while she was walking.

Looking at him, measuring whether she should she tell him or not, she let the question war within her head for a while. Should she tell him? Shouldn't she? On the one hand, why should she? On the other hand, she'd only be there one week, tops, so what difference did it make? Once her treadmill was fixed, she'd be back home again. Alone. At least that's what Ben Franklin had promised. She'd thought a week to fix the thing seemed an exorbitantly long amount of time, but he'd said something about getting a special part, which might take a while, so what could she do? That's when she'd called the manager at the closest gym and arranged to do her walking there for a week.

The manger had tried to sell her a full membership, but when she remained adamant that she only wanted to use the treadmill, and that was all she wanted to do at the gym, he gave her a quote for a price that she felt was reasonable, and asked him to put it in writing, saying she'd be there early the next morning to sign it and pay him in advance for the week's treadmill use.

The manager had laughed when she arrived that morning. "I thought you said you'd be in here early," he'd said with a teasing gleam in his eye. He was a young man, built like a brick house (no mice getting in there!) with arms like Arnold Schwarzenegger's.

"This *is* early!" she'd said as she yawned for emphasis.

"We're open at four in the morning for the early birds," he'd said before laughing at her horrified expression. "But this is a better time. It's much less crowded now. Most people are off to work by now, so it'll be easier for you to get a tread-mill."

He was right. It was easy. Besides Grunting Red-faced Man, she was the only one interested in the treadmills.

"So, what's happened these last two weeks," the heaving, crimson-cheeked man puffed out, drawing her attention back to the present.

She looked at him again, noting his flaccid cheeks boun-cing with each step, his thinning wet hair plastered against his scalp, and the sweat pouring from him like Niagara Falls. Oh, what the hell! What could it hurt? "My son's getting at-titude," she blurted then inhaled. "My agent is ignoring me—" another breath "—my treadmill broke—" another gasp "—I've got osteoporosis—" a gulp "my stalker may be back," another wheeze for breath, "—the IRS thinks I'm cheating them—" some panting "—my mother thinks I'm raising my son wrong—" a small hiss of air "—oh yeah, and I have a bastard of an ex-husband who is trying to make my life a living hell."

"Wow," he said, slowing his machine to a walk. "I'd call that a bad couple of weeks! Want to talk about it?" His breath was becoming lass ragged now that he was walking instead of running.

"No. That's okay." She breathed. She was still hoofing it at an alarming pace (for her). That was quite typical of her. No warm-up, no cooldown, just jump right in at the maximum speed until she got it done and hit her goal, then stop. It was the way she had done everything her whole life.

She'd like to say that she admired people who warmed up and cooled down as he was doing, but honestly? She didn't have the time for that. For her, life had always been "get in, do it as fast as you can, and get out." It's how she shopped, worked, played, ate and even now, as she'd recently discovered, exercised.

Martin used to say, "There *are* shades of gray, Janine. Everything's not always black or white," but she seemed to see everything as one way or the other. Good or bad. Love it or hate it. Take it or leave it. Black or white. On or off. She'd never been wishy-washy about anything. Anything.

She looked up at the TVs and winced. Talking, walking and breathing were causing enough problems for her; trying to ignore all that noise, when she was used to only one form of stimulation at a time, was really grating on her nerves.

"You want them off?" he said, following her gaze, his breathing now regular since he was cooling down.

"You can do that?"

"What?"

"Shut them off?" she said with amazement.

"Well, sure," he said with a hearty chuckle.

His deep chuckle unnerved and annoyed her. She hadn't noticed the deep timbre of his voice before, which might have been because he was gasping, snorting, panting and making other disgusting noises, but now that she'd noticed it, she wasn't too pleased. She was more comfortable with him when he was offensive and disgusting.

And also, who had died and left him boss of the gym televisions? And more irritatingly, why, in God's name, hadn't he offered sooner?

He picked up a remote, turned his back to her—a nice back with broad shoulders, she noted for the first time—pointed the remote at the left-hand set and pressed. With a blip of static, it shut off. Ah.

And now there was one. He turned to her and held out the remote.

It must be some kind of gym etiquette thing. The person on the side of the television got to decide what to watch or when to turn it off.

"The power button's on the top right," he offered while still holding the little device out to her. "The channel buttons are on the lower right. And the volume controls are on the lower left," he said, without looking at the remote control. He'd obviously used it before.

Truthfully she would have grabbed the thing and shut it off in an instant, but at the moment—as with all the moments when she was aboard a treadmill—she was hanging on for dear life and couldn't let go of one hand without spinning out of control like a demented top gone berserk before falling off the damn machine.

Think of rowing a boat with only one arm. You would just spin in a circle. Except on a treadmill, you would spin for a millisecond before you got thrown like a rodeo rider off a bronco. Don't ask how she knew this. She just did. She still had the black-and-blue marks to prove it. Although they were a purplish-yellow by now. So she shook her head. "No. You do the honors." Unquestionably in system overload, she choked on her last breath. "Please."

He smiled. She didn't know if he smiled *at* her, *because of* her, or *in spite of* her, but she knew this time it was a definite smile and not a pain-induced grimace. She checked him out and noticed that since he'd slowed the motion to a snail's pace—but was still walking faster than she was—and his face was no longer the color of red cabbage (thank God), he seemed pretty athletic, and she figured that for him, watching her must be like when she had to sit through Craig practicing the baritone last year.

That had been excruciating. His one rotation for band had been torturous for her, even though her son seemed to enjoy it. His dedication was admirable. Every day, like clockwork, he'd take that huge thing out of its coffinlike case, and he'd practice what he said were scales. She didn't have the heart to tell him what she thought of his baritone-playing ability. But he'd enjoyed it, and from what the band teacher said, he was good at it. In the end, she was glad when he'd decided—on his own—that it wasn't for him.

She'd breathed a huge sigh of relief when he'd declared his decision, and was grateful they hadn't been evicted before the semester finished. Obviously it took time to draw up the paperwork for evicting a tenant for making sounds that sounded like a fat man with a flatulence problem. For once, time and luck had been on her side.

"Do you want to change to something else? Or would you like to shut it off completely?" the man asked politely.

He was thoughtful; she had to give him that. "Off," she said between loud, massive gulps of air.

He nodded. Pointed. And blip.

Heaven. Silence. All that remained was the hum of Muzak in the form of a violin version of The Beatles' "Hey Jude," and the whirring of the treadmills.

She could deal with that. Nauseating as it was.

CHAPTER 7

"These must be good machines. They merely hum." She paused for breath. "At home, mine roars, squeaks, clicks and makes a grinding noise reminiscent of an old-time train."

He laughed appropriately.

"Sometimes I half expect big puffs of steam to come out of it."

He turned off his machine and grabbed a towel from the rack nearby, wiping the sweat from his face and neck. Once the towel was moved aside, his smile was evident. He had a nice smile, now that all that other stuff—like his tomato-hued face and his loud coughs—were gone. Gone and almost forgotten.

Almost.

"Sometimes, I expect big puffs of steam to come out of *me*," she went on, laughing at her own goofy sense of humor.

He put the towel around his neck and hung on to the ends with both hands. "You really attack that treadmill," he said with a crooked smile, leaning against the treadmill he'd just vacated.

"I hate it," she blurted.

"It's obvious." He chuckled. "Why?"

She tried to shrug but couldn't let go of the support bars

to get the height needed for her shoulders to make a fully realized shrug.

"So why do you do it?" he asked.

As Craig would say, *What was this—twenty questions?* What did he care? It was none of his damn business why she did this god-awful torture. Did he think if she didn't *have* to, she'd be doing it? She had other things to do! Books to write and edit. Kids, mothers, agents, government officials and ex-husbands to fight with. Cheese to eat. There were plenty of things she needed to do besides this. She looked at the guy, who was starting to become annoying.

Was he annoying? Or was it her *life* that was annoying and he was just standing in the way as she'd discovered that?

He smiled back at her, his gaze steady, making her feel bad for wanting to be left alone to get this chore over with. "I do it because I have osteoporosis."

"Yes, you mentioned that. I was surprised when I heard you say that."

"Join the club. So was I when I found out."

He scrutinized her carefully as she kept clomping and huffing. "You seem too young to have that."

"Yeah, right. My sentiments exactly. But I'm the poster child," she said between huffs.

"What?" He looked confused.

"Tall, thin, small boned, Caucasian, breast-fed my kid who I had later in life, not a big milk drinker. Apparently I was born to get this."

"Oh. I didn't know that." He nodded his head in thought.

"Me neither. I only found out all this after I was diagnosed, and did some research on the Internet."

He nodded again, still leaning on his treadmill.

The seconds stretched between them. She knew this because she was watching them on the timer part of the treadmill's readout. A good twenty-three seconds passed.

"My name's Tom. Tom Kennedy."

She eyed him with distrust. Names? He wanted to exchange names? Wasn't it bad enough that they'd semi-shared sweat, weird noises, and other bodily fluids? He wanted to cross the line and exchange *names*?

It was too much, too soon for her. Well, definitely too much. To indicate that it was too soon would imply that she'd expected to exchange names eventually. She hadn't.

She had no intentions of giving out her name to a stranger. For all she knew he was a pervert or a rapist or a pedophile. Okay, so the pedophile thing would sort of rule her out, but she had a child to consider, too. She wouldn't lead him straight to her home and her son!

"Nice to meet you, Mr. Kennedy," she said simply as she kept up her vigorous pace.

He smiled knowingly. Obviously it wasn't lost on him that she didn't share or offer her name in exchange. Yet, it didn't seem to bother him, which annoyed her, too.

"Thanks," he said with a smile that was starting to grow on her. "I've got to run and shower now. Maybe I'll catch you around here again sometime," he offered good-naturedly.

"Maybe," she said, trying not to show either her annoyance or her *slight* interest.

He laughed heartily as he turned and left, and she could hear his rumbling laughter above the piped-in Muzak while he made his way across the large building's expanse, heading for the locker rooms.

Her annoyance level went up a few more notches, which she pondered for a while as she continued her walking. That wasted some more time, and she had only about ten more minutes to go, and was at the tail end of her session. Her eyes were closed with concentration, her hair soaked with the sweat that also slicked over her entire body. She was trying to ignore the feel of her wet T-shirt clinging to her overbearingly hot body and the feel of her soggy panties as they hung from her. The added shorts seemed to hold in the heat more than when she merely wore panties, causing what could only be imagined as the picturesque look that she'd wet her pants.

She was deep in thought that wearing clothes while walking was *the* most uncomfortable thing she'd ever done besides childbirth, when she heard the voice of Mr. Huffing-Red-Face.

"Well, have a nice day."

Her eyes snapped open to see a *gorgeous* man in an Armani suit, leather briefcase in hand, and killer smile plastered on his stunning, masculine face.

Where were the flaccid cheeks? Where was the red, blotchy skin? And that hair! It was fantastic. Very sexy! It was gelled into a spiky, funky do that made him the spitting image of James Brolin—*pre*-after-marriage weight gain. You know, Barbra Streisand's new husband? But before he put on the added pounds. Did anyone but her remember James Brolin as the sexy Dr. Steven Kiley from the old *Marcus Welby, M.D.* series from the sixties? And this guy certainly wasn't making piggish, snorting noises now! Wow. Talk about an extreme makeover. Damn. He sure did clean up nicely.

Which, for some reason, threw her head-on into *total* annoyance. Wouldn't you know her pig man would turn into a prince? And here she sat, or stood, well, tromped really, in all her sweat-soaked, flabby, gasping, matted-hair, jiggly-butted glory, looking like she had just peed her panties. Great!

"Yeah," she muttered, "you have a nice day too."

He chuckled again, before turning on his polished wingtips and striding confidently out of the gym.

That bastard! How dare he falsely represent himself like that! If she'd known she was walking next to a James Brolin look-alike, she would've possibly not told him about her crappy life. Not that it mattered. But she wouldn't have let her guard down and let him in. She was so pissed off by the sudden turn of events, she would've thrown her sweat-doused rag at his retreating back, but realized that he'd done nothing to actually warrant such a cruel and repulsive act. But he *could* have somehow let her know she wasn't sweating with the oldies as she'd assumed. She liked him *much* better when she thought he was an old, worn-out, harmless, unattractive bystander.

She finished the last few minutes of her walking, stepped off and then gathered her stuff that she'd left piled next to the treadmill. When she'd called, she'd told the manager that she wouldn't use his locker room or shower facilities, and she was a woman of her word. Plus, she didn't shower in public places. Lord knows what germs or fungi one could pick up, and she didn't like the thought of people watching her cleanse her naked body. In her opinion, her body was a temple. An asymmetrical, sagging temple that was systematically falling apart at the seams, but a temple nonetheless. She'd shower at home.

Bustling her sweat-soaked body back home took no time at all. It actually took longer for her shower's hot water to heat up. She peeled off her wet, smelly clothes and hesitated before throwing them in the hamper. Better to let them dry first. Otherwise the mold would infiltrate the hamper and breed further damage.

So she threw her workout clothes on the floor. Right next to the pile of crusty socks Craig threw there during the week.

"Other mothers would freak that I throw my socks all over the bathroom floor," he'd said, while shaking his head at her reminder not to bury his damp socks in the hamper with his dirty clothes. "But *my* mother? *She* insists that I throw my clothes on the floor so the smelly germs will aerate and dry before putting them in the hamper to accumulate mold and fungus!"

Little wiseass. Well, who asked him? And what did he know? He was only a kid.

She smiled at her thoughts as she stepped into the shower. Yes, he was only a kid, but he was a good kid. She'd loved his note from that morning.

Mom, you'll be the belle of the ball.
Um, I mean…the belle of the gym!☺
Good luck and try to have fun!

Her gym experience hadn't been so bad, but it hadn't been all that great, either. She'd much prefer to do her walking in the privacy of her own home where she could wear— or more importantly, not wear—whatever she felt comfortable in.

The warm water felt good on her tired muscles, and she

was rethinking the incredible transformation of Mr. Pathetic to Mr. Esthetic when the shrill ring of the phone interrupted her thoughts.

Hoping it was her agent, she jumped out of the shower and ran for it—dripping water in foot-sized puddles across the hallway to her room. "Yes," she barked into the phone, hoping to answer before they hung up.

Nothing. Just the empty sound of someone on the other end listening to her breathe. If they'd say something she could return it with a cutting response…but the silence creeped her out because she had no idea who it was. She'd tell them to knock it off, but knew her panic-laced voice would give a stalker pleasure. Before realizing she'd had one, Janine never knew the distress or the feeling of great vulnerability being stalked could impart to a person, but now she knew firsthand how frightening it could be. Until she had actually met him. Then she was less frightened.

It wasn't the constant phone calls, or the feeling that someone had been in your house, or even the damage done to your property. It was the notion that one human being could possibly harm another, and how easily and swiftly it could be done that bothered Janine the most.

She wondered again if this was a new stalker—which would make her worried and anxious—or her old stalker—which would make her annoyed but not nervous.

If they'd only *say* something, she could lash back at them. But by not saying anything, she couldn't fight back. How did you fight a ghost? How did you outmaneuver someone you didn't know and therefore couldn't fathom what their next move would be? It was impossible.

And exhausting and frightening. Especially wondering if this was a new, not-so-passive stalker. No offense intended, but her previous stalker-guy, although weird, was spineless.

She hung up the phone with wild thoughts coursing through her. She pictured herself lying dead on the floor, a bullet hole seeping with blood. No wait. Worse. Stabbed. That's gotta hurt! Not just once, many times. Brutally.

She ran back to the shower, jumped in and pushed her face under the flow of the showerhead, letting the warm water soothe her frazzled nerves. Her mind was too active, her imagination too vivid and colorful.

Yes, she'd had a stalker. But her stalker hadn't wanted to kill her, or even hurt her. Her stalker wanted to *be* her. Or so he said. He was found by New York City's finest, sitting in her closet, wearing nothing but Janine's best black suede pumps and black lace panties, eating what was left of her almost finished pint of Chunky Monkey directly from the container, wearing her most garish red lipstick. (All of which Janine threw away as soon as the policemen told her what they'd found.)

Discarding the lipstick was no biggie—she'd never liked that shade to begin with. The ice cream was almost done anyhow, and the panties were a gift from Martin that she'd never worn. So chucking those were no big loss. In fact, she got a kick out of thinking that the only flesh to be encased by Martin's little self-satisfying gift was the big, hairy butt of a weirdo with a massive beer belly. But the pumps? They were hard to toss. The wacko freakazoid *had* to pick her favorite! They were the only pair of shoes that fit like a glove—she never felt a pinch, they *never* snagged her stockings, and of course, they went with everything. She had Louis Vuitton,

Prada, Salvatore Ferragamo, Ralph Lauren, Sergio Rossi, Ann Taylor, and even a pair of Yves Saint Laurent he could've picked. But could the idiot have chosen one of *those* to have his stalker meltdown in? No! He had to choose her favorite, Nine West, mid-heel, black suede pumps she was hoping to be buried in. It was just her luck!

Mrs. Goldman, her next-door neighbor, had spied the guy breaking into the apartment when Craig and Janine were out at his school band concert. They figured the only reason Mrs. Goldman knew they were out and the noises in their apartment were not made by either Janine or Craig was because they weren't loud voices that were either screaming or laughing, nor were they flatulentlike sounds emanating from a brass instrument. Doors weren't slamming, and/or ear-deafening rock music wasn't blaring, either. Pretty much, she and the rest of the building instinctively knew that if any noise other than those listed were heard, the tiny little Ruvacado family wasn't making them.

Which was exactly what Mrs. Goldman had confirmed when Janine had asked her—after thanking her profusely—why she'd called the police.

At the advice of the police officer who was first on the scene, Janine had a restraining order drawn up on the kook, and for at least seven months hadn't heard from him.

So she honestly didn't know if *this* was him, but the constant calls with no one on the other end were what had started the man's compulsion with his "favorite author of all time" according to his confession on the police reports. The police had also shared that he'd kept mumbling—almost maniacally—something about her "long, beautiful hair."

Finishing her shower, she threw on a robe and ran to her closet. Just in case it *was* him stalking her again, she figured she'd hide her Easy Spirit low-heeled black leather pumps. Better safe than sorry. She couldn't replace the perfect Nine West shoes she'd felt the need to throw out—and Lord knows she'd tried to replace them every time she passed a shoe store!—but these were her next best pair of pumps that went with everything, and she would *not* lose her runners-up. If the nutcase broke in and wore those, she'd never have another pair of comfortable pumps to wear for interviews or dinners or gala anythings! Not that there were any gala anythings planned for her near or distant future, but, well, she'd better be safe than sorry.

She hadn't understood what he was thinking about when he had his mental breakdown the first time, but if he tried it again, she'd be prepared for him this next time. She went to her lingerie drawer and pulled her favorite panties from the bottom and shoved those in the foot area of the pumps she was about to hide.

The panties weren't her prettiest by far, but they must've been cut wrong, because they were the only pair she'd ever owned that covered her ample butt and didn't give her a wedgie, and she wasn't about to give those comfy babies up without a fight!

Now that her call-induced panic was dissipating, she tied her robe tightly around her and went to her desk to start her editing. Leaning down, she turned on the computer and waited for it to warm up or load up or whatever it did.

Sid had said he wanted her to cut thirty-five thousand words from the latest book she'd sent him to read. "Take out all the fluff and internal agonizing" were his exact words.

She'd been working on the edit for days now and, as much as she'd tried to cut the words, she'd ended up *adding* five thousand.

"I'll get to the cutting later on in the story," she assured herself as she sat with her left hand on the keyboard and her right resting on the mouse. She closed her eyes and willed herself to focus on the story at hand. She needed complete concentration to remember each thread, each story line, each nuance of the book in order to decide what to cut and what to leave in. She had reached her perfect place of immersion when the phone rang, shattering her mind-set like a hammer smashing a mirror.

"I can't get a minute's peace!" she muttered to herself before lifting the receiver. "Hello," she barked into the phone.

CHAPTER 8

"Janine, why do you answer the phone in such a manner? What if I were a prospective man?"

Great! Are you testing me, God? Because if you are, I deserve a medal, and if you're not, please give me strength. "Is there something you're not telling me, Mother?"

"About what, dear?"

Add humor to the list of things that are lost on that woman. "Nothing, Mother. Now how may I help you, so I can get back to my work."

"Oh, okay, dear. You're still writing, then?"

Janine felt her jaw ache, and tried to relax and stop grinding her teeth. "Yes, Mother, I'm still writing."

"I'm only asking because you haven't come out with anything in a while, dear."

"Yes, Mother, I'm aware of that. But thank you for reminding me."

She laughed gaily. "One wouldn't think you'd need reminding of *that*, dear."

Where's the strength, Lord. Where's the strength? "One wouldn't think."

"I tried calling this morning, but you didn't answer. I was

hoping you'd be at a salon somewhere, getting a makeover or something."

"That's where I was, Mom."

Her voice brightened like the sun coming from behind a cloud. "You were at a salon? Did you do something with that hair, dear?"

"No. I was doing the 'or something.'"

"Now what on earth does that mean, Janine? Were you getting a makeover or not? Because you really do need one, dear. I can only imagine that hair. It was the *only* thing somewhat feminine about you, and now you went and chopped *that* off. Have you viewed yourself in a mirror lately?"

How could a woman that resembled sweet, cute Betty White have such an abrasive personality? You'd think a cute old lady like her would be sweet and loving. But looks were deceiving. Instead, her mother had the warmth and tact of Simon Cowell talking to a pimply faced, knock-kneed, horrendously tone-deaf kid. She enjoyed bestowing her little tidbits of advice, as much if not more than he did.

Her loving words of wisdom floated out toward everyone privileged enough to cross her path. No one was off-limits. She would bust Gandhi's chops. *"You're too thin! Why don't you eat something? That whole ridiculous vegetarian phase of yours isn't wearing well on you. You look scrawny. Here, have some meat, maybe some beef."* Or maybe, *"How are you going to find a decent woman when you insist on wearing those diaper-looking clothes? They don't show you to your best advantage, dear. How about a nice double-breasted charcoal-gray suit with a red power tie? You'd look much more authoritative in that, dear."* Or possibly, *"You mean you're still doing that religious, peace-lov-*

*ing thing? You really should give that up, dear, there isn't any
money in it."*

"Are you even listening to me, Janine?" she shouted.

No, Mother. "Yes, Mother."

"Well then, what do you think?" she said with exasperation.

Considering that she had no idea what her mother was
presently dissecting, she took the easy way out. "Look, I've
got to go. This edit's not going to do itself."

Her mother harrumphed before surrendering. "All right,
dear. But think about what I said."

Yeah right. Like that was going to happen. She didn't
know or even care what her mother was referring to. "Of
course I will, Mother," she said, before hanging up the phone.
This time she'd remember to get online and stay online so
no one would bother her. Although, in reality, the only people who could bother her were her mother and her stalker,
and now that they'd both called, she was free to leave the
phone line alone. Her ex would never call her when Craig
wasn't home, so she wasn't worried about him.

The rest of the day passed quickly as she attempted to cut
words from her latest tome. It was hard—like lopping off her
own limbs—which after cutting off one, you'd see the difficulty of cutting off the remaining limbs. What would be left
to cut off the last one?

When she heard Craig come home, she was relieved.

"Hey, Mom," he called as he slammed the front door.

"Hi, babe. I'm in my room."

"Like where else would you be?" he said as he lumbered into
her room. He looked at the treadmill, which still had the bar
thingie sticking out of the front of it. "Still broken?" he said.

"Doesn't it look that way?" she said. After staring at it on and off throughout her day, Janine's active imagination had started to wonder if it were trying to flip her off. It kind of looked like it was—with its bar protruding straight up from its middle.

He held his hands up before him, "Hey, chill, Mom!" He bounced onto her bed. "Bad day?" he asked, squirming around to get comfortable.

She looked at him to see if he sincerely wanted an answer. When she couldn't decide, she told him anyhow. "The pits."

"How was the gym?"

She looked at him sideways through slitted eyes.

"That good, huh?"

"Better."

He laughed and looked back at her treadmill. "When's Ben going to fix it?"

She sighed. "He said within the week."

"It looks like it's giving you the bird," he said, and laughed.

She gave him her full attention. "Wow, that's weird! I thought the same thing all day today."

"Oh, crap! That's not good."

"What's not good? And don't say 'crap.'"

"That I'm starting to think like you."

She looked at him directly. "Worse things could happen," she said with mock irritation.

"Yeah, according to Grandma, I could start looking like you, too." He got off the bed and walked to her, punching her on the shoulder. It was the closest thing to a hug she'd gotten in a while.

"Gee, thanks."

"Anytime, Mom."

The little wiseass. She wondered where he got his wry sense of humor—but didn't wonder too long—knowing Grandma would say, "Like mother, like son, dear. You should really watch what you say in front of the boy. He picks up your every bad trait."

"So what's for dinner?" he said as he jumped back on her bed.

"Oh *damn* it!" she said.

"Forgot to take something out again?" he asked with a cynical smirk.

She sighed heavily. "Yes. Sorry."

"Pot of water?" he asked as he moved off the bed, shoulders sagging, to get out the big pot for spaghetti again.

"You know? I'm getting sick of spaghetti. Aren't you?"

"I've been sick of spaghetti for eight years, Mom."

She laughed despite herself. He didn't need to be encouraged, but the kid *was* funny. "What do you say we go out tonight?"

"You mean it?"

"Sure. I'm not making any headway with this edit, and it looks like Sid's not going to call me anytime soon. Lord knows we're spaghettied out, and whatever money I do have left, we'd better spend before the IRS comes in and takes it from us anyhow."

"Now there's a good attitude!" he said cheerfully.

It was hard not to love her son. He was a great kid. Dripping sarcasm and all. "So, where do you want to go? Tonight, my son, *you* can choose."

Thinking first, he said, "Anything but Italian. I don't want to even catch a glimpse of spaghetti tonight."

They sat in silence, imagining the possibilities of a spaghetti-less dinner.

"Greek?" she threw out for him to consider.

"A possibility. What else?"

"Mexican?"

He made a face. "Nah. Not tonight."

"Steaks?"

He didn't look impressed. "Too much work."

She laughed. "What is? The chewing, the cutting or digesting."

"All of it."

Teenagers. They could get very lazy but were at least honest enough to admit it. A thought popped into her head and she jumped out of her chair. "I've got it!" she exalted.

"Jeez, Mom. Chill out! What are you, mainlining speed or something?"

Exuberance wasn't cool when you were almost thirteen. "Sorry. But I think I've got it."

"Got what? Dementia?"

"No. Well, maybe," she said, and grinned. "How about Japanese?"

"Japanese," he repeated, letting it roll around on his tongue and in his head.

"They chop it up for you, so you don't have to worry about the cutting. The pieces are so small, the chewing is easy, and as far as the digesting…like Chinese, we'll be hungry again in an hour, so we can buy a couple Ben & Jerry's flavors on the way home."

He was nodding slowly, an impressed look on his face. "You know what? I think you *did* get it! That's almost genius."

"*Almost* genius? Like hell, my boy. It *is* genius!" she said, puffing her chest out like a peacock. Her son was duly impressed until she placed her hands under her armpits and started flapping her elbows like a bird, and doing a strange cataleptic dance while chanting "I still got it."

"Mom, Mom, MOM!" he shouted over her chanting.

"What?" she stopped, turned and looked at him, removing her hands from under her arms.

"Anything you *might* have had, *if* you ever *did* have anything at one time or another, you can rest assured…you no *longer* have." He shook his head with mortification and disgust, and blinked his eyes as if he'd just spent the past fifteen minutes staring with his naked eyes at the sun. "Shit, Mom!"

"Craig! I do not want the S word spoken in this house!"

"Sanity?" he asked.

"Don't be a wiseass. You know what S word I'm talking about."

"Schizophrenia?"

"Craig!"

"Simpleton?"

"Okay, that's it. We're staying home and having spaghetti!"

"Shit!"

She nodded her head. "Yup. That's the one. Now don't let me hear it again!"

He saw he'd been punked. "So we're still going out for Japanese?" he asked cautiously.

"You think I want spaghetti again? Hell no! Of *course* we're going out for Japanese." She put her arm around him and squeezed, knowing he'd only let her do that because he really, *really* wanted to go out for dinner. "In fact, let's not just go to Japanese, let's do Benihana. What do you say?"

He nodded, mega-impressed. "Let's do it!"

She locked her arm through his and turned toward the door to leave.

"Um, Mom?"

"Yeah?"

"Are you going to wear that?"

She looked down at her attire. "Oh, yeah. I forgot. The benefits of working at home. You get to lounge around all day in stuff like this."

"But you're going out in public now, Mom. And with me."

She looked at her son's men's extralarge T-shirt with, of course, spaghetti stains splattered across it, his humongous black pants that could be easily worn by the hugely sized man his baritone playing reminded her of, and his ever-present black leather military boots. "Yes, I see how you wouldn't want to be seen with me. I might embarrass you."

"Thanks for understanding." He patted her shoulder.

Was that consolation? "Give me five minutes. I'll be right out."

He looked her over carefully. "Take ten."

"Thanks, Grandma."

He threw up his hands. "Hey, I'm no Grandma. If I were like Grandma, I'd have told you to take a couple of hours. Or—" he thought about it "—I would've made some snide crack about how you could take forever and still wouldn't come out looking presentable."

"Gee, thanks. When you put it that way, I guess I should be thankful you only allotted me ten minutes."

He shrugged. "That's the most it ever takes me."

"Really?" she asked, looking him up and down sardonically. "You'd never tell."

"Touché, Mom. Take as long as you need. I mean, take as long as you'd like."

Before thinking, she leaned over and kissed the top of his head. "You'll make someone a good husband someday, son."

He pushed her away. "Mo-om, watch the hair! I worked hard on it this morning."

Who would've known that mop of bed-head was prearranged. "Sorry."

He looked at his watch pointedly.

"Okay, I'm going. Knock it off before I take back my good-husband compliment."

He rolled his eyes before turning to leave her room. "Yeah, like I really give a shit about that right now. I'm a kid" was the last thing she heard before he closed her door behind him.

"Craig!" she screamed.

The door opened and he stuck his head in. "What?"

"Your language. Watch your language!"

He sighed heavily. "Yes, Mother," he said, before silently closing her door again.

Eight minutes later she came out of her room dressed to the max. She even had on stockings, and had taken her Easy Spirit pumps out of hiding, thinking if her stalker was back, and *did* break into their apartment again, she'd have the best stuff *on* her this time. Including the panties that fully covered her ample keister.

"Hey, Mom. You look great." He checked her out thoroughly, and she felt fantastic at his flattering remark. "You know, for an older woman."

Okay, so he needed work in the compliment department. "Thanks for clarifying."

She noticed that he'd changed his T-shirt, but didn't comment on it, knowing he'd be annoyed or embarrassed if she did. The less said, the better around him lately. His mood swings, like hers, could wreck an entire evening.

The cab ride there was typical. Smelly and dangerous. But Craig loved it.

He had a whole cabbie rating system figured out, and enjoyed playing it each time he was in a cab. He gave them two points for scaring old ladies trying to cross the street, five points for near-missing bicycle messengers (they were harder to frighten than the old ladies), and added a point for each blaring horn honk (but only if it extended more than three full seconds. Anything less than that wasn't noticed in New York). Flipping someone off used to be worth more but was now lessened since he saw it so frequently, and foreign curse words (even if he didn't understand them, or even fully know if they *were* truly expletives) earned a full six points. "For the educational value they imparted," he'd explained to her once.

Embarrassingly enough, she'd gotten used to his game, and played it herself each time she entered a taxi. She said it was to keep her mind off the fact that she was taking her life in her hands by getting into a cab to begin with, but the truth was, she got a kick out of his game, and it passed the time while she was in a situation where she had no control.

Only in *her* game, she took off points for every time the cabbie said the word *lady*. Not as in, "Please enjoy the ride, my lady." But more like, "*Lady*, I know how to get to the Upper East Side! I didn't get here yesterday. I got here three months ago." Or, as they sat in bumper-to-bumper traffic, roasting in the heat while smelling her own overheated body odor adding to the plethora of stale body odors permeating the cell-like back of the taxi: "Don't tell me to go through the park, *lady*! Everyone knows you'll get stuck in traffic at this hour if you go through the park!"

Over the years she'd found that salesgirls and cabbies used the word *lady* as a replacement for the word *bitch*. Once she figured this out, she started taking off points for its usage while taking a cab.

"Turn at the next light, would you, please?"

"Listen, lady. I know how to get to Benihana's. This is afternoon rush hour. We're going to sit in traffic no matter how we go!"

"Since I'm paying—" she leaned forward "—why don't we do it my way."

The man inched through the intersection and did *not* turn at the next light.

Craig looked at her to gauge her reaction.

"He just lost his tip," she said softly with a hard face. "In fact, you know what? We'll get out here, thanks, and walk the rest of the way," she said louder to the cabbie. "What do I owe you?" she demanded.

Craig registered shock. Not because she demanded to get out when the cabbie didn't follow her request or got pissed about his not listening to her. He'd spent enough time with her to know her reactions. He was shocked she wanted to walk. "We'll *walk* the rest of the way?"

She shoved the exact amount flashing in red on the meter through the little glass partition. "There you go," she'd said casually. "Oops, wait a minute, I forgot your tip," she added after making sure he'd received the full amount for the fare. Then she added one nickel to the empty little glass cup thingie to let the cabbie know he'd messed with the wrong "lady."

As they got out, they heard a steady stream of what they assumed were Arabic swearwords.

"He gets extra points now, Mom."

"Yes, but you have to take them off for the two 'lady's' and the one 'bitch.'"

"That's the way *you* play. Not me. The points stay."

She made a face at her son. "You're so supportive."

He blushed.

They walked in silence for a while before Craig spoke again. "I don't mind the walking. I like it. But I'm expecting you to start complaining about your feet any minute. Want me to get another cab?"

"How gallant of you," she teased.

"It's not gallant, Mom. It's self-preservation."

She raised her eyebrows at him. *Both* eyebrows. She couldn't do the one-eyebrow thing. "How so?"

"I really don't feel like spending the whole meal hearing about how your feet hurt."

"Not to worry, I've got my Easy Spirits on."

"I can't keep track. Are those the ones that hurt?"

"No. They're the only ones that *don't* hurt."

He nodded. "Good."

They walked along and finally caught sight of the restaurant.

"You know, Mom. I'm impressed. Your exercising must be doing something. You're not out of breath, you're not complaining, and I hardly needed to slow down for you."

"Why thanks, son. Looks like you can save the cane idea for *next* Christmas."

"A cane? Mom! How poorly do you think of me? For you—because I love you so much—I'd get a *walker*. Not a mere cane!"

"Ah, thanks. A walker."

"Yeah, and not just some cheap, sleazy walker. I'd get you the top-of-the-line walker. You know. With wheels, and a basket on the front, to hold your stuff."

"Maybe I'd give you a ride in the basket."

Disgust etched his face. "No way, Mom! Don't even think about it!"

They opened the door to the smells and sounds of sizzling chicken, steak, and vegetables. "Oh God, I'm so hungry," she said as she inhaled deeply.

"Me too," he said, breathing in. "I hate to say it for fear you'll break out in your chicken dance again, but this was a great idea, Mom."

"Eat your fill, babe, because tomorrow it's probably back to spaghetti."

The maitre d' came over and hustled them to a table where they instantly became mesmerized by the chef that banged things, tossed knives, chopped efficiently and cooked their meals before them as they watched with amazed eyes. Benihana wasn't just a place that served great food; it was an entire dining experience.

An experience, she was pleased to admit, that wasn't lost on her or her son.

CHAPTER 9

The next morning found her plodding to the kitchen for her much-needed caffeine.

She reached for the pad as she passed the table.

Thanks for dinner, Mom.
It was great!☺
All that ice cream should give you something to
walk off today.
Have fun at the gym!
Catch ya later.

He never signed his notes. But why should he? Like there was someone else who would leave her a note each morning?

Their recent truce regarding the trip Martin had suggested for Craig's birthday hadn't been mentioned for a while, but not because she didn't think it was on the boy's mind. She knew him well enough to know that it was right up there, swirling around.

She also knew him well enough to know that the only reason he was *not* mentioning it was because he hadn't come up with a good reason for her to change her mind. Yet. But he was working on it diligently, she was certain.

Never being one to look a gift horse in the mouth, she appreciated her reprieve, no matter the reason. Although admittedly, she'd be curious to see what he would come up with in his response. His justification would be entertaining.

Knowing she'd have to do her walking at the gym again, she padded back to her room to ready herself for her second ordeal. But before she left, she decided to put a call in to Ben Franklin.

"Ben? It's Janine. Did the part come yet?"

"I only ordered it yesterday. You've got to give it a couple of days, Janine."

"Oh, okay. Just trying to keep up with things. Wouldn't want anyone to drop the ball or anything. The sooner I can do this at home again, the happier I'll be."

"Yes, I figured as much. You don't strike me as being a gym rat."

"A what?" She wanted an explanation before she decided to become offended or not.

"A gym rat. Someone who hangs out at the gym all day."

"Well, you can be assured I'm not that. I get in, do what I have to do, and get out."

"I bet you do," he chuckled. "But don't worry, Janine. I won't disappoint you or Mr. Iacocca."

"Mr. Iacocca?"

"Yeah, Lee."

"You *know* Lee Iacocca?"

"No, but I follow the good man's mantra."

"Lee Iacocca has a mantra?"

"Well, I don't know if you'd call it a mantra, but he was quoted as once saying, 'Your legacy should be that you made it better than it was when you got it.'"

"Hmm," she said, not knowing what else should be added to that.

"I plan on doing just that, Janine—making your treadmill better than it was when you got it."

"Hmm," she said again. "I don't want you to make it better than I got it, Ben, I just want you to make it work."

"I'll attempt to do both."

"Okay then. Goodbye."

"See ya, Janine."

After hanging up the phone, she realized she'd exhausted all excuses to stay home, so she turned on her ugly walking shoe heel and hiked the two blocks to the gym.

She was in luck today. No one was at the bank of treadmills. Everyone in the gym was either jumping and bouncing in an aerobics class or working with the weight machines. She didn't bother looking to see who was there, because she didn't care.

"Hey, girl," the cute manager called to her as she passed the front desk.

"Hey," she called back as she headed straight for the treadmills before anyone else arrived.

"Happy trails," he called to her back.

She waved her hand, not turning or wanting to slow down and chance having someone join her.

Throwing her stuff on the floor nearby, she hopped on and turned the speed up to her usual, immediately hanging on as the tread hurried up to speed.

"You should really warm up," she heard a smooth male voice comment.

You should really keep quiet, she wanted to reply.

"That wasn't nice," he said, before laughter rumbled from his chest.

Had she said it out loud? She didn't think so. Her eyes darted to the mirror in front of her, and she saw Mr. Brolin casually standing behind her treadmill, his foot up on the table that held the towels as he tied his shoelace.

At her look, he laughed again. "No, you didn't say it aloud, but I could read your face."

She nodded, already starting to lose her breath. More, she figured, from the good-looking man standing behind her watching her flail around like a spastic windmill, than from her workout—because it usually took about four minutes before she started to gasp for air, and she'd only been walking for two minutes so far.

"Face reading. Good trick," she huffed out.

"Not really a trick, more like a business necessity."

She only nodded, hoping he'd go away. No such luck.

He got on the treadmill next to hers and began a slow walk. It figured he'd follow the rules and do a warm-up before he ran.

"Do you want the TVs off again?" he asked as he took the remote from his shorts pocket.

What, he brought his own remote? He must be one of those gym rats.

She nodded, gasping.

He turned the televisions off and turned to speak to her again. "Better?"

She nodded again. Panting. Now she was up to the four-minute mark, so the lack of breath was attributed to her workout, not to Mr. Good-looking. She hoped he knew that. "Thanks, that's much better."

He smiled a disarming smile at her.

For lack of anything else to do, and hoping to get her mind off the man next to her, she let her thoughts wander to her earlier encounters of the day. It was only nine o'clock in the morning, so she didn't have that much to peruse. She thought of the sexy kid who managed the place, but that wasn't a productive thought, so she focused on her morning conversation with Ben.

"Your legacy should be that you made it better than it was when you got it," she said aloud.

He laughed. "Thanks for the kind words, but it was only turning off some televisions."

"No," she said, panting and shaking her head. "Ben Franklin said that."

"Ben Franklin? I thought it was Lee Iacocca."

What, everyone knew what came out of the mouth of Lee Iacocca but her? What was she, living under a rock? "It *was* Lee Iacocca, but Ben Franklin said it to me this morning."

He looked at her as if she was nuts. "Ben Franklin, huh?" he asked as he raised the speed of his machine.

"Yeah," she spit out. "He's my maintenance man."

He looked around before speaking. "Ben Franklin's your maintenance man?"

"Yeah. His grandfather retired."

He smiled and nodded slowly, as if patronizing a child. Or placating a wacko. "Oh. That explains it."

She nodded, knowing it *did* explain it.

After a few minutes a huge-breasted blonde came prancing over to the treadmills.

"Tom?" she asked Mr. Still-Warming-Up.

"Yes, Bunny?" *Bunny?*

"I went to get a bikini wax yesterday and the bimbo working on me got carried away, and now…well…I'm bald. Wanna see?" she asked while striking a pose.

There was so much wrong with that little tirade, Janine didn't know where to begin listing all the erroneous bits and pieces.

Maybe she did.

First of all… Bunny was referring to someone *else* as a bimbo? Secondly, why, pray tell, was she telling this to *him?* And third, but nowhere near last, why would she offer to *show* him?

"Do you think I can sue?" Bunny asked her good friend Tom.

Sue? For what? Improper hair removal? Punishing her pubics? Depriving a dimwit? Wiping out her womanhood?

Janine cracked up at her own inventive legalize. But really, did the ditz think she had a leg to stand on? A hair of a chance of winning?

Once again she laughed (actually choked) and had to stop her machine for fear of falling off. Since it was less noisy, she listened to Uncle Tom's response.

"No, Bunny, I don't want to see it, and I don't think it's a good idea to sue."

"Why not?" she pouted, thrusting out her gigantic breasts and folding her arms underneath them in a huff.

"Well, for one, will it grow back?"

Oh my God! Was he really asking her this?

"Yeah," she whined, pursing her lips and moving her hands to her hips. "But…"

He waited for the rest of Bunny's response, but when none

came forth after thirty seconds, he continued. "So by the time it gets to court, it will have all grown back. You will no longer have a case."

Bunny sulked prettily and once again asked, "You want to see it?"

Threesome-Tom looked over at Janine, who was still staring at the two conversationalists.

"Don't look at me," she said, throwing up her hands before starting her machine again. Full power. "I sure as hell don't want to see it," she muttered to herself.

Out of the corner of her eye, she saw Bunny eyeing Tommy Tenderloin and licking her lips seductively. He, on the other hand, seemed palpably uncomfortable. Which he should. What—in God's name!—kind of conversation was that for a grown man to have with a young woman?

True, he wasn't the one who had brought up the subject, but she could count on one hand the number of times she had spoken about her pubic hair with a man. Let's see, she thought to herself, trying to stay amused and occupied so she wouldn't have to hear his response to Bunny's offer, there was the time she…nope. That wasn't about her… Or the time she, um, spoke with…no, that wasn't the topic of conversation with him, either.

In fact, she had *never* spoken about her pubic hair with anyone. No one. Not even with her husband. Not that she couldn't or wouldn't have discussed it with Martin, but for some reason, in all the years they were married, it just never came up.

She was pondering that thought when Mr. Mediator turned to her and spoke.

"I'm sorry about that."

"What for?" *Mr. Mammary-Man.*

"For Bunny. I hope she didn't make you uncomfortable."

"Why would she?" *Because you're a disgusting creep, you breast-loving cradle-robber?*

"Well, the topic of conversation didn't seem all that appropriate," he said, raising his machine's speed to allow him to run.

"No? I hadn't noticed," she said haughtily.

He shook his head and laughed. "You're a different kind of woman, aren't you."

Because it wasn't a question, more like statement, she didn't respond.

Now that he'd started running, he started making those weird noises she remembered from the day before. Must *everything* at a gym be grotesque and weirdly bizarre?

"Well, I'm just sorry," he said on the exhalation of a breath.

They did their walking and running in silence. Well, relative silence. Everything's relative.

"Are you her father?" she finally asked. She was angry that she'd said it, but wanted him to know he was a pervert for ogling a girl young enough to be his daughter.

"No."

"A women's privates' hair specialist?" *What was the matter with her? Couldn't she keep her big mouth shut?*

"No."

"A doctor?" That might somehow explain the conversation.

"No."

"A lawyer?" That too might explain it.

"Not really."

"Then what *are* you that would warrant that conversation?" She shouted for some unknown reason. *Oh for God's sake! What the hell do you care?* she asked herself.

"I have no idea why she asked me that. Yes, I have a legal degree and can practice, but I'm not really a lawyer. I'm a businessman. I only have the law degree to help with my business. It's not like I practice or anything."

He was pleading his case well, but she had no business caring what he did for a living, what he did with his life, or with whom he did it. She had no idea why Bunny's comments had bothered her so much. Maybe because she was growing older and realized that it had been a long time since she'd pranced around and flirted and pouted so outrageously. Oh, who the hell was she kidding? She'd never pranced, rarely flirted, and although she knew she could frown like a pro, didn't remember ever pouting like a sex kitten. And that's not even acknowledging her jealousy over the young woman's breasts. Twenty years from now they'll be sagging down to her knees! But today? They weren't! And that really pissed her off! "Look, it's none of my business. So let's just forget it, okay?" she hissed between gasps.

"Okay. I just didn't want you to think I responded to stuff like that."

That did it. Why was he telling her this? And what made him think she gave a damn what he responded to. "It's not my concern," she replied between gasps for air.

"I know," he said.

She looked at his now flabby, red, blotchy cheeks and wondered how she had thought he was handsome. Did she really think he looked like James Brolin? At the moment, he more closely resembled a pig. And not a cute little pink pig, but one of those ugly, potbellied varieties. Not that he had a potbelly. He had a tiny paunch, not really very noticeable, but at his age, it was a given. In fact, she preferred a man to look his age. Possibly because deep down she felt that if the man looked *his* age, he wouldn't mind her looking *her* age.

He must've been thinking along a similar line of thought—how Bunny was young enough to be his daughter—because his next question seemed fitting to follow with that train of thought.

"Tell me about your son."

She was a little taken aback. Although she wasn't a household name anymore, she used to be a bit of a celebrity, and swore she'd never let the filth of publicity and falsehoods creep into his young life.

But she was no longer a bestselling author. Her name was no longer on the tongues of the elite literary community. Her own stalker wasn't even giving it his best effort anymore. Yeah, he'd call every now and then, but he wasn't as obsessed or enamored with her as he used to be. He was just going through the motions.

But, she could never resist talking about her son. He was the best kid on the planet. He was her strength—her heaven. The best thing she'd *ever* done in her life. The best thing life had ever given her.

She looked over at Tenacious Tom. He wanted to talk? Well, what could it hurt? She'd be gone in less than a week, ne'er to see him again. "He's a great kid!" she blurted between puffs. "Smart as hell."

The man nodded and grimaced. He was at his full pace now.

"And funny! He's got a great sense of humor."

The man nodded again.

"He's the best thing that ever happened to me." She snorted a laugh. "But I guess all parents think that about their kids. Do you?"

"What?" he asked in jogging shorthand.

"Feel that way about your kids?"

"Don't...have any," he said.

She was surprised. He was a good-looking man (pre-jogging) and she was amazed to hear he didn't have kids.

"Not...married," he added.

"Oh," she said, starting to understand Bunny's little conversational request. "And you say you have your own business?"

He nodded, sweat dripping from his chin.

"Ah. And I'm assuming it's a thriving business?"

"Quite successful," he added with pride, between huffs, groans and other assorted noises.

Bing, bing, bing. We have an answer. Bunny's a little gold digger!

She wondered if this man knew the reason Bunny had come on to him so forcefully? She'd blown over him like a hurricane. But maybe he liked that, the opportunistic bastard. Although, in his defense, he *had* made a point to tell her that he didn't respond to Bunny-type advances.

CHAPTER 10

"You're very interesting. Do you know that? You're intriguing," he said plainly.

Intriguing? She looked at her reflection—at her sweat-stained clothes and her short, skull-plastered hair. She took in the lines on her face and noted the uneven skin tone, the brown age spots sprinkled over her face like freckles, and eyes that were too small for her head. She had no response.

"It's been…a long time since…a woman intrigued me," he said between gulps of air.

If this was what intrigued him, then it was understandable why he'd be waiting so long between moments of intrigue.

As if he read her mind, he added, "It's been a long time since anything intrigued me."

How did he do that? Read her thoughts like that? He must be a kick-ass businessman if he could read all his clients and customers like that.

He laughed aloud, as if he heard her thoughts again. "You're bright, articulate, funny, attractive, and most importantly, you don't seem to be impressed by money."

"Keep going," she said as breezily as she could while stomping away on a treadmill.

"Yes, you walk like a horse, have a mouth like a sailor, and from what you said yesterday, have a list of problems and issues longer than Santa's list of good kids, but you intrigue me."

"Okay, now you're losing me."

"You know, right now I think of you as 'the angry, sarcastic woman stomping away her miles on the treadmill next to mine.' Strangely, I don't even know your name."

"What's in a name anyhow?" she asked cryptically, still not comfortable sharing that bit of information.

"Do you *have* a name?" he asked her, once again lowering the speed of his treadmill to do his cooldown.

"Yes," she said informatively.

"Want to share it?"

"No," she said abruptly.

"Okay, I can deal with that. I don't mind doing a little work. Hell, I built my entire business up from nothing to the prosperous, thriving company it is now. Work's never been an obstacle I've shied away from. If anything, I love rolling up my sleeves and getting into things."

He was losing her again. "Rolling up your sleeves and getting into things?"

"Yes."

"Like how?"

"Let's see. First, I'll let my mind catalogue what I already know about you."

She snorted in challenge.

"You have a teenage son, whom you obviously adore."

She rolled her eyes, unimpressed. "That's a given."

"Okay. Well, from what you said yesterday, you have an agent for some reason."

Hmm. A good listener. That's unusual. "Okay. So you think…you've got me…all figured out by that?"

"Maybe."

She snorted again.

"Having an agent might indicate that you're possibly an actress. But I've never seen you before. Not that *that* means anything. I rarely go out, and haven't my entire lifetime—always putting my business first. So you *could* be an actress."

"Well, despite your busy social schedule…you wouldn't have seen me…working as an actress anyhow." *Doesn't the man have eyes? How could he think I'm an actress?*

"A social life? I'd waited *years* to get one, and once I had one, I found out it wasn't all it was cracked up to be."

She grunted. "Yeah. Don't I know it!"

He smiled. "Okay, so you're not an actress. Possibly a singer? Or perhaps a dancer maybe?"

"*That's* your logical conclusion? I'm a singer or a dancer?"

"Well, I've never heard you sing, but I *can* see your legs. You've got great legs."

"Can't sing a note," she supplied breathlessly.

"So you're a dancer."

She raised her eyebrows. "You think so?"

"Yes. You also said you had a stalker. So that would fit. And you mentioned the IRS was hounding you. Which would also fit."

"Your powers of deduction leave a lot to be desired, buddy."

"So even with those killer legs, you're not a dancer?"

"Nope."

"Okay. So I'm back to square one. Let's see." He thought

for about a minute. Well, it was more like forty-nine seconds. She was watching her display.

"I got nothing!" he said, shaking his head with disappointment.

She smiled and nodded. "Yup. You've got nothing."

"Look. You don't have to tell me your name, but at least tell me what you do for a living."

She eyed him suspiciously.

"Add neurotic and guarded to your list of qualities," he said with an impish smile.

His words hit home again and she thought of Martin's accusations. Maybe she could let him in a little. What could it hurt? He didn't want her name. Just her occupation. Without her name, it meant nothing. He'd *still* have nothing. "I'm a writer," she blurted between huffs, then switched off the machine with a flourish, grinding to a halt.

"Done?" he asked.

"God, I hope not! My last two books didn't sell well, but I hope my career's not *completely* down the toilet."

He looked pointedly at her treadmill. "You're just stopping?" he waved to her quieted machine.

"Oh, you mean walking?" She laughed. "Yes, I'm done."

"Don't you want to cool down?"

"No."

"Not at all?"

"No."

"You're just going to stop?"

"Yup. Looks that way. Doesn't it?"

He turned his treadmill off, too. "Well, I guess that's enough of a cooldown for me."

"How long's enough?" she asked.

"For you, little Miss Doesn't-cool-down-at-all? Any amount of time would do." He gave her a reproachful look. "But the standard is about five minutes before and after running."

"Oh. I learn something new every day."

He rolled his eyes. "You're a smart aleck, but you're cute. So. You're a writer?" he said, while wiping the sweat off his face.

"Yes. I wanted to be a nuclear physicist, but MIT turned me down when I couldn't put the application pages in numerical order."

He barked out a laugh. "Dreams die hard," he said, smiling.

She nodded, enjoying his dry wit.

"You're funny and quite smart."

"Did you deduce that from my inability to get into MIT?"

"Don't sell yourself short, Writer-lady. Only a smart person could come back so quickly with such a reply."

"Yeah, right," she said, taking a towel from her pile of stuff. "In my defense, I remember it was a very large packet."

He watched with interest as she dabbed at her pinkened face. "They ask for a lot at those big-time colleges," he offered.

"Yeah, don't I know it! I ended up going to the local community college. Where did you go?"

"I'm wondering if I should tell you the truth," he said shyly.

"Why?" she asked.

"Because I figure that if anything *should* happen between us, I want things to always be truthful and honest."

"That's a big 'if.'"

"So I've been told," he said boldly.

"Are you going to tell me where you went to school or not? Because personally, I could care less. *Don't* tell me if you don't want to," she said defiantly.

"Harvard Law and Business School."

"Oh," she said, somewhat deflated. All of a sudden she was tired. Or maybe she was just exhausted from her all-out, no-holds-barred walking session.

"But I had help with my application packet," he said, smiling a thousand-watt smile her way.

"See?" she quipped, "that was my whole problem. I tried to do it alone." She felt better. This man had a way of making her feel renewed strength.

"You tried to do it alone, huh? That seems to be *my* problem, too. I always try to do things alone."

"Things are never as much fun done alone," she said provocatively. Was she flirting? It had been so long since she'd done it, she didn't even know if she was doing it presently. And if she *was* flirting, was she doing it correctly? Had the rules changed?

"Would you like to join me for something at the fruit bar? Coffee? Fruit shake? Pineapple boat? Water?"

Obviously she was doing it correctly. Hit and snag! As much as she didn't need another complication in her life right now, at least she could feel good about herself. *I've still got it!* "As much as I love coffee, I'm too hot for it, but the fruit shake sounds refreshing. And the water sounds fantastic."

"No pineapple boat?"

She laughed. "Maybe. Let's check the prices first, before I commit." *Did you hear that you scum-sucking IRS bastards? I*

have to check the price of a pineapple boat before I consider or-
dering one! Does that sound like the plan of a money launderer?
An abundantly rich woman of means?

"It'll be on me."

"Well, then. Maybe I'll have *two* pineapple boats," she said
flirtatiously.

"Eat a whole fleet for all I care."

Oh yeah. I still got it!

"In fact," he said, raising his voice so everyone in the entire place could hear, "I'm buying pineapple boats for everyone in the house."

The remaining die-hard gym rats called out their thanks.
Which brought her attention to the six people left in the
building since the aerobics class had let out.

"Thanks, Tom," they all shouted, waving at him and smiling between grimaces.

The manager was now wearing an apron and slid his way
behind the "fruit bar."

"Did I hear correctly, Tom? You want to supply each one
of these hardworking guys and gals with pineapple boats?"

"Yes siree, Matt. A round for everyone, and put it on my
tab."

"Thank goodness the aerobics class has already let out. I'd
run out of pineapples!"

"Well, hopefully you've got ten on hand," Tom said lightly.

"Ten?" Matt asked.

"Yeah, one for everyone in the house, including yourself,
and two for the little lady."

"Ah, Ms. Treadmill-Only," he said with a smile. "How's
that working out for you?" he asked Janine.

"Okay," she mumbled.

She sat and listened as Tom chatted with Matt while he made the pineapple boats. "So how's business been, Matt?"

"Okay. A little slow but good. How's things by your other place?" He must have meant Tom's workplace. Maybe Tom *was* a gym rat.

"Good. Busy. Working long hours, but, what else is new?"

"Hey, you gotta do what you gotta do," Matt said cheerfully.

"Yes. That's true." Tom looked at her and smiled. "How about getting Miss Treadmill-Only some water, Matt. She looks parched."

She looked parched? She wondered what *that* meant, but before she could get too insulted, Matt opened a bottle of water and handed it to her saying, "There ya go. Drink up. Want one too, Tom?"

She let the cold, clean water run down her throat. It felt great. Maybe she *was* parched. She usually drank while she walked at home, but here at the gym she didn't. For a couple of reasons. The biggest one being that she couldn't get off the treadmill every ten minutes to go to the rest room at the gym, so it was best not to fill up on water. No matter *how* thirsty she got while she walked there.

"Sure. Why not."

Matt handed Tom a bottle, too, then went back to making his pineapple boats.

"Hey, you need one more, Matt. You're only making nine."

"You don't have to buy me one, Tom. I get them free all the time." Matt turned to Janine and puffed out his wide chest comically. "Unlimited fruit shakes and pineapple boats. It's the prime benefit of being the manager."

"Manager *and* part owner," Tom said, making Matt blush.

"Yeah, I keep forgetting. I've been the manager for so many years, the 'part owner' thing is new," he said to Janine in explanation.

"Well, congratulations," she said with enthusiasm.

"Thanks," he said, looking more at Tom than at her.

Matt finished the assembly line of pineapple boats and, when he was done, shoved one in front of Tom, two before Janine, and put the remaining six on a tray to deliver about the gym to the people working out.

"These look yummy," she said.

"And they're good for you, too," Tom said while piercing a melon ball with his plastic fork.

They ate heartily.

"You do so intrigue me, Ms. Writer-lady."

She tried to smile over her mouthful of melon, but she'd taken too big a bite. It was so refreshing and sweet, she couldn't help it. "How this time?" she said with a full mouth.

"I notice that you eat in batches," he said, watching her intently. "Intriguing. Very intriguing." He took a bite of pineapple before continuing. "That you ate all the strawberries, then all the pineapple, then the melons—by type—and then the kiwi. When you ate the kiwi, you closed your eyes and groaned."

She wiped her mouth with a napkin, embarrassed that he'd been watching her so carefully.

"You like those kiwis, don't you?" he asked nicely, obviously trying to let her know that she had nothing to be embarrassed about.

"They're my favorite."

"Hmm. Interesting. So why didn't you eat them first?"

"I always save the best for last," she said, as she watched him eat his pineapple boat, trying to see if he had a pattern when he ate. "And you?"

"No rhyme or reason. I just eat from the top down," he said before giving her his best lascivious smile.

She laughed a throaty laugh, enjoying this whole flirting thing immensely.

"Your laugh. It's tempting," he said softly, which made the atmosphere suddenly a bit too intense for her. Light flirting was fine, but he'd upped it a notch, which made her lose her balance and her comfort level.

As if he sensed it, he changed tack. "Do you always eat in preferential order?"

"Usually," she said with embarrassment, while looking at the next pineapple boat before her. The first one was empty.

"How do you eat peas and carrots?"

"With much difficulty."

He threw back his head and laughed. It was a nice, masculine sound. "You're charming. Smart, beautiful, vibrant and charming."

She looked away so he wouldn't see her discomfort. Insults she could handle. Compliments were much harder for her to swallow.

"Hey," he said, eyeing her directly, changing his tone completely. How did he do that? How did he know he was making her want to run away? "Why not try messing up the system, and doing something totally crazy!"

She looked out from the corner of her eyes. "Like what?" she asked gingerly, wondering what he'd say next.

"Just eat the next boat willy-nilly."

She laughed. "Willy-nilly?" she teased.

"Yeah. It'll be a new experience for you."

"A new experience! It'll be chaos!" she gasped in horror. "Sheer chaos."

He placed his hand on her fork-holding hand. "You can do it. I have faith in you. Give randomness a try."

She shook her head. "I don't know about this."

"I'll be right here. Next to you. Supporting you. Giving you needed backing and extensive praise. Comforting you, if you need it."

She looked at her second pineapple boat, hesitating. "It's just too hard!" She shook her head as if distraught.

"Go on. I'm here," he nodded to her reassuringly. "You can do it!"

She winced. "I don't know," she said shyly. "I don't think I can."

"You can!"

"Willy-nilly?" she asked uncertainly.

He nodded.

She closed her eyes and stabbed her fork in the boat's direction. When it made contact, he said, "Excellent!"

"I don't know if I should open my eyes or just shove whatever is on the end of my fork into my mouth," she said, eyes still closed.

"Be bold! Be daring! Be the daredevil I can tell you are!"

She smiled, her fork wavering in midair.

"I like the small sprinkling of freckles across your nose, and the laugh lines etched at the corners of your eyes. You've laughed a lot in your lifetime, haven't you?"

"Ah. You're trying to deduce things again, aren't you?"

He laughed. "Am I way off?"

"Well, let's just say that every woman wants to hear that a man likes her laugh wrinkles."

"I said laugh *lines*, not laugh *wrinkles*."

"By my laugh 'lines,' either I've spent *many* years laughing hysterically, or I've spent a *lot* of time squinting in the sun."

"Considering you have the pale complexion of a typical New York City girl, I'd have to assume my first guess was correct. You've smiled a lot."

Smiling now, she said, "Okay, you win. I'm *not* an outdoorsy kind of girl, and I *have* smiled a lot in my lifetime. Although I have absolutely *no* idea why."

"Your life's been that tough?"

"Not that tough. But not that easy, either."

"Okay, so be bold. Take a chance. Be an adventuress!"

Was he talking about taking a chance on him? Or being a bold adventuress with him? Oh, wait, he was probably talking about the pineapple boat. "Okay. I'm going all the way. Just make sure I don't poke my eye out," she said as she slowly brought the fork up to her face.

"Spoken like a true mom," he reassured her, guiding her hand so the fruit morsel would hit its mark.

"Are you watching?" she asked, nervous that she really would poke her eye out. She wasn't the most coordinated woman on the face of the earth.

"I'm watching," he said, as she opened her mouth and slid a pineapple square into her mouth.

"Mmm. Pineapple. You know, it's much more flavorful when you eat with your eyes closed. It's like your other senses compensate for the lack of sighted anticipation. I didn't know what to expect, and the pineapple flavor just burst in my mouth."

"See? Living dangerously, taking chances, might be a good thing," he said.

"I'm going to do it again," she said, enjoying their game. "You should try it."

He guided her hand back to the boat, and she pierced another piece of fruit. Helping her guide it to her mouth again, her lips parted and she slid the round piece of coral fruit into her mouth. She sucked on it for a brief second before laughing. "Cantaloupe," she said. "Mmm," she moaned. "Delicious."

"Glad you're enjoying it," he said in a voice that cracked.

She chewed the melon, enjoying the intense sweet flavor.

"So, tell me more about yourself," he said gently.

His voice was nice. Reassuring. As if you could trust him with all your secrets. But that wasn't going to happen. Her secrets were remaining just that. Secrets. "There's not much to tell," she said as she stabbed at the boat again, lifting the fruit to her mouth. "Mmm. This time I got a piece of kiwi," she added.

He laughed. "Changing the subject. That would be a good ploy if you were dealing with an amateur."

"And I'm not?" she asked, raising both eyebrows.

She wondered if he had the one-eyebrow-raising gene.

"No," he said with certainty.

"Can I ask you something?"

He nodded seriously. "Sure, anything."

"It's personal," she warned, smiling shyly.

"Shoot," he said, "but if it's too personal, I'll have to decline," he said coyly.

She laughed at his antics, not believing for one minute that he was telling the truth.

She looked at him sideways. "Can you raise just one eyebrow?"

It took about two seconds, but he finally responded. He threw back his head and laughed. "*That's* your personal question?"

She shrugged. "Yeah."

He thought about it. "To tell you the truth, I have no idea."

"Try it," she said.

He laughed with embarrassment and shook his head.

"So you don't know, you won't try, and that's that?"

"I'll try it when I'm alone, then will report my findings," he said imperiously. "Would you like me to type up a report? Or can I call or fax in the results."

"An oral confirmation or decline will suffice," she said as she laughed.

"So I'm not getting your number, am I?"

She shook her head, eating another piece of kiwi. "Nope."

"Okay, how about I go to the locker room—because at some point today I have to show up at work—and while getting showered and dressed I'll do the, ah, experiment in front of a mirror, and will get back to you on this matter."

"Okay," she said. "Sounds like a plan."

"Don't leave while I'm in there, all right?"

He looked like a little boy afraid he'd lose his puppy. She smiled. "I won't. But only because I still have more pineapple boat left."

He held out his hand to shake. "Deal. Enjoy the rest of your boat, and I'll be right out," he said before he walked away.

CHAPTER 11

Strolling leisurely as if he owned the joint, he headed across the gym slowly to rejoin her back at the fruit bar, calling out cheerfully "You're welcome" to the smattering of appreciative gym attendees on whom he'd bestowed the refreshing snack. His slow approach allowed her some time to study him. He walked with confidence, a clear indication that his business must be successful. A man who walked like that usually was a high achiever, definitely type-A, and almost always found success. He had "winner" embossed all over him.

Unlike her, who had "loser" stamped indelibly across her forehead.

His suit was well-made and expensive. And it fit him as if it was made for him. It probably was. Grudgingly, she admitted that he looked great. *Too* great if you asked her. And as she sat in her sweat-stained shorts and T-shirt, she felt every bit the ugly duckling her mother always implied she was. Those negative slams had never really registered before, but today, now, at this very moment, she heard each and every jab and crack her mother had ever thrown her way. And suddenly, it hurt.

Somewhat attracted to this man, yet also annoyed that he could be so damn striking and secure—certain of his effect, she did what she always did when confronted by anything she found threatening or alarming. She threw up a wall and barely acknowledged his presence.

Which was mighty hard, considering he sat down next to her and finished his pineapple boat with great gusto.

"Well?" she asked. "Can you or can't you?"

He smiled at her, which temporarily knocked her off balance. "Why do I get the feeling that a lot rides on my answer?" he said, looking cautious.

She shook her head. "It doesn't. I'm just curious."

"It's not a test?" he asked, showing that the man was very competitive by nature.

"No. Not at all."

"So why do you want to know?" he asked. She could tell the question came from his own curiosity, and decided to tell him.

"Well, you see, my son can do it, but I can't. And though I was married for a long time, I have absolutely no idea whether my ex-husband can do it or not. It kind of bothers me that I don't know."

Tom smiled widely and shook his head. "You are one very different kind of woman, Treadmill-Only," he said, cuffing her shoulder gently. "And, by the way, I can," he added with a proud smile.

"Let's see," she exclaimed with excitement.

He turned his head to look at the mirror behind the counter and did it. "See?" he said pretentiously.

"Show-off," she hissed.

"You're just jealous," he returned.

"Actually, it grosses me out when my son does it," she said with defiance.

"So I'll never do it again. I've lived this long without knowing I could, and now that I've tried it three times, the thrill is gone anyhow."

"Three times, huh?" she asked with a slow smile.

He blushed slightly. "I tried it twice in the locker room, just to make sure the first time wasn't a fluke."

"How very methodical of you," she teased.

"If I'm anything, I'm methodical."

"So do you think it's hereditary?" she asked seriously.

He shrugged. "No clue."

She looked at him expectantly. "Hey, you're the one who went to the big, fancy college. You should know stuff like this."

He laughed. "You know, you're right. I'm sure one of my schools—either Harvard Law or Harvard Business—had a class on the 'one-eyebrow trait.' I must not have been paying attention that day," he said.

She laughed lightly. It was a long time since she'd been so relaxed for such a lengthy stretch of time. It was a new experience. But not all bad.

"Yesterday you said you've had a couple of bad weeks. How so?" he asked.

Her guard was down, so she answered. "How *weren't* they bad!" she snorted, trying to itemize her list of troubles from most important to least. Problem was, there were too many vying for the "most important" title, which was probably what was making her not want to deal with any of them. Hoping she could just stick her head in the sand, and they'd all vanish or resolve themselves didn't seem to be working. "On the shit scale of one to ten, these past two weeks have been a twelve."

His steel-gray eyes softened slightly as he smiled. She hadn't noticed that his eyes matched his hair nicely, making his face blend appealingly. She also observed that what she thought were slack, flaccid cheeks weren't loose at all. It must've been the jarring movement of the running that made his face seem so flabby, because as she could plainly see, his face was strong and commanding. Pleasing. "There's a shit scale?"

Blinking so as not to be caught staring, she replied. "Yes."

"I didn't know that."

"Well," she said arrogantly, "there is."

"What's the key to it?" he asked with interest.

"The key?" She thought about it for a moment. "Well, I'd have to say the key to it is not to get *on* one or *develop* one to begin with!"

He threw back his head and laughed. "No. I meant what is the scale's key, since you said it goes from one to ten. For example, what constitutes a one?"

"Oh. I get it. Let's see. A one on the shit scale would be— I'm regular, and I eat a lot of fiber."

He laughed, and nodded knowingly. "What's a ten?"

"I drank the water in Mexico."

His laughter rumbled around them. Then he sobered as his eyes returned to hers. "And you had a twelve these last couple of weeks?"

"Yup," she said, trying not to stare at the man she was becoming more attracted to by the second.

"That's bad," he said stridently.

"Tell me about it," she replied.

"Why don't you tell *me* about it?"

"Do you have all day?" she asked, grinning lopsidedly.

He cleared his throat and nodded. "Okay. Let's start with one thing."

She thought a minute. One thing. Oh the choices, the choices! Should she try to let one of the top contenders come out? Or should she start from a small one and work up? She looked at him and decided to go for the least personal. She was already ticked off with the way her traitorous body was drawn to him, she didn't need to throw all caution to the wind and give out any personal information that would come back later and smack her in the face. Or bite her on the butt.

"Okay, one thing," she repeated his words.

She looked at him again and saw his chiseled face directed wholly at her, his eyes trained on her unswervingly, a look of strong determination etched on his features. Damn, the man was intense. He must be a great businessman.

"Well, my agent wants me to cut thirty-five thousand words from my latest manuscript."

He nodded efficiently. "How's that going?"

She smiled sheepishly. "Well, I'm not too good with cutting words. I'm great at spewing them out. But once they're out there, it's hard for me to cut them. I'm so prolific and poignant!"

"Understandable." He nodded quite seriously before smiling at her last crack. "Do you have a deadline?"

"Not really, but the sooner I get it done, the sooner he can possibly sell it."

He nodded, back to serious mode. "I understand. How long have you been working on it so far?"

"About a week."

"And how many words have you cut so far?"

"None. I've *added* five thousand."

He blinked twice, then threw back his head and roared before getting a grip, holding up his hands and mumbling a brief apology. "I can see where that would be a problem," he said seriously.

"Ya think?" she asked with a flurried grin.

He obviously couldn't contain himself anymore, and broke down and chuckled, shaking his head. "I'm sorry. You just caught me off guard and blindsided me. I wasn't expecting that."

Yeah well, join the club, buddy! You caught me off guard and blindsided me, and I wasn't expecting that, either!

"You know, Ms. Treadmill-Only, I've been in business a long time, and have seen a lot in my day, but you certainly do surprise me."

She made a face. "I have that effect on people."

"It's been a long time since I've been surprised by anyone or anything."

"You sound like a cynic," she said coyly.

"I've been burned before," he replied honestly.

"Well, welcome to the neighborhood, Mr. One-Treadmill-Over."

He smiled engagingly. "I like the local residents, Ms. Treadmill-Only."

This was getting far too serious for her. Sputtering, she looked at the clock on the wall, and muttered, "I'd better go. I have a lot of work to do," before she gathered her pile of things and fell off her stool.

He crossed his arms across his broad chest and chuckled. "Then get to it!"

"Bye," she said, without turning back as she started running toward the exit. "Thanks for the fruit."

"It was my pleasure," he called after her, "and don't forget to *cut*...not add!"

She nodded her head and waved her free hand, "Got it. Cutting good...adding bad."

The last thing she heard as she left the building, immediately before the glass door closed behind her, was the deep, rumbling sound of his laughter.

Determined that today was the day she would finally start cutting, she headed straight home and right to her computer after a brief stop in the kitchen to grab a mug of coffee.

Once comfortably seated in front of the bright screen, she decided to pull up her manuscript to have it ready, and logged on to her Internet server so she wouldn't be disturbed or distracted while she was having her Edward Scissorhands fest. She pictured a young Johnny Depp as Eddie, whipping out his two, bizarre scissor hands, and in a riotous, dramatic flourish forming her overly worded novel into the literary version of a topiary masterpiece.

Before she started, she knew enough about her working style to plan a quick run back to the kitchen to get some food. She went with the intention of getting a bowl of high-fiber cereal with calcium-rich milk, and some fruit for a mid-morning snack.

She came back with a huge bowl of Chunky Monkey ice cream slathered with aerosol-generated whipped cream, and a box of cheddar Goldfish crackers.

According to her, this was an exceptionally good breakfast. The ice cream was high in calcium and had bananas as its base, which were high in potassium—whatever that did. The whipped cream was *also* high in calcium, as were the cheddar cheese crackers. Her snacks were chosen purely with an osteoporosis mind-set. And *everyone* knew that Goldfish crackers were the one snack that's okay to get hooked on! Plus, it was the "snack that smiles back." What more could you want from your food? Where else were you going to find such a perfect breakfast?

There was only one thing that could make it *more* perfect.

She grabbed another mug of coffee and added a gargantuan scoop of Cherry Garcia instead of milk and sugar. This particular mug was a gag gift from her agent, Sid. He'd bought it for her years ago—it was the size of a punch bowl.

Proud of her nutritious choices, she wrestled the humongous cold bowl, the awkwardly large box, and the gargantuan yet blazingly hot arena-sized mug back to her room.

Not being the most graceful of souls, she ended up with whipped cream on the box of crackers and some cherry-flavored coffee spilled in her ice cream. Life was a bitch, but she'd survive, she thought, as she licked the whipped cream off the orange-colored cardboard box with a smile.

She placed all items within arm's reach and quickly checked her e-mail before starting her topiarylike creation. Once again she was disappointed not to see a response from Sid, but thought it was fantastically ironic that she had mail hawking all-nude pictures of Orlando Bloom and Johnny Depp. For a brief second she was tempted by the thought of clicking on it and opening it up—just for curiosity's sake, of course—but then she remembered she was a professional, and a respected author, and deleted it instead. Though, her heart did lurch during the flash that made it disappear.

Now that the significant dilemma of whether to open—

or not open—her spam mail was over, she clicked on her manuscript file and started on page one, this time ready and able to do what needed to be done.

Once again she pictured poor Eddie Scissorhands and his malformed hands, then added her face onto Johnny Depp's body. Shaking that horrific picture from her mind—because it really *was* horrendous—she kept her original feel for what she was about to do. "I'll whittle down this sequoia into a frigging toothpick!" she muttered to herself as encouragement.

By the time Craig came home, it wasn't quite a toothpick, but she was deliriously happy that *some* words were cut, and she hadn't added any. It was a start.

"I see you had the breakfast of champions again, Mom," he commented easily as he perused the dirty dishes piled around her.

"Hey, I *almost* had high-fiber cereal," she enlightened him.

He did the one-eyebrow thing. God that was creepy when she didn't expect it. Plus it made her think of Tom. "Did you?"

"No. But I came close."

"So how's it going?" He nodded to her screen.

"Not bad today. I actually cut a few, and didn't add any," she said with a proud smile.

"Well, good for you, Mom! That's like a first, huh?"

She gave him her evil eye. It didn't work. He just laughed.

"And how was the gym?"

She made a face.

"Was Mr. Sweaty there?"

Her memory flashed to Mr. Tom Kennedy in a suit, realizing she might have to adjust his nickname from Mr. Hot-and-Sweaty to just Mr. Hottie. On day two, which was today, he'd certainly turned her from Ms. Sweaty-and-Annoyed to Ms. Hot-and-Bothered. Which *totally* annoyed and bothered her!

"Yeah. He was there."

"And? Did he make his gross sounds?"

"Yes, he did."

"And did they make you want to puke again?"

"Craig! That's such an ugly word. It's so…gross."

"What? Puke? Everyone says puke! Geez, Mom! Now I can't say puke?"

When he put it that way, she had to remember to choose her battles, which was probably why he *did* put it that way. He was a lot smarter than she gave him credit for sometimes. When had he become so sharp and clever? Where was she when all this maturation was happening? Only yesterday he was a cute, chubby toddler in diapers. Now he wore a men's size-ten shoe, and could win their verbal bouts easily! He seemed to have exploded into manhood overnight. Where the hell was she when this had happened? Sleeping? Sitting at her desk?

"I don't like you swearing, Craig. I've already told you that."

"What about 'puke'?"

She let out a heavy sigh. "That's negotiable."

He nodded, knowing he'd won another battle.

"And don't call him 'Mr. Sweaty.'"

"Why not? You did yesterday."

"That was yesterday."

He caught on quickly. Yup, he was fast approaching manhood. "What did you do, Mom…make friends?"

Again, she made a face. "For your information, although it's none of your beeswax, yes, we did make friends. He bought me a pineapple boat." She lifted her chin with confidence. "*Two* pineapple boats, actually," she nodded curtly, like the Queen of England.

"First of all, what's 'none of your beeswax' really mean, Mom?"

"It means it's none of your business."

"Well, what's that got to do with bees and wax?"

She thought about it for a few moments. "I don't rightly know. But it's a popular expression."

"Is it? I've never heard it."

"It's an old expression," she said with annoyance.

"I'd have to say, Mom, I don't think anyone but you says it anymore. Even old man Gottlieb, my geography teacher, who must be a million years old by now and says the lamest things you've *ever* heard has never said it. And *he* comes out with some pretty stupid sayings!"

She threw him a dirty look.

"And secondly, Mom, I'm a little disappointed in you. You sold out to some guy for something called a pineapple boat?"

"I didn't sell out, Craig. I truly liked him. And it was *two* pineapple boats," she said proudly, and without her pending aggravation shining through.

"And what the hell's a pineapple boat anyway?" he asked.

She glared at him.

"I mean, so what's a pineapple boat? A boat made of pineapple?" He snorted with hysterics at his own joke. Maybe he had a few more days to go before reaching manhood.

His silly laughter was infectious. "It's a snack of fresh fruit, served in a carved half-pineapple. Like a boat."

His laughter ended with a few giggles. "Actually, it sounds good."

"It was." She smiled guiltily. "I mean, they were."

"So, since I can't call him Mr. Sweaty anymore, does he have a name?"

"Yes. Tom Kennedy."

"Is he nice?"

Her son's desperation to match her up with a man was as pathetic as her lack of prospects. "Yes, but I wouldn't get your hopes up."

"Oh. Bummer. I was hoping to get you out of my hair."

"With all that mousse in there, I'm surprised there's room for me to fit!"

"It's gel, not mousse," he said caustically.

"I stand corrected."

"So why shouldn't I get my hopes up?"

"Because I think he goes for younger women. You know, like most older men. They don't feel good about themselves unless they're seeing a blonde named Bunny, young enough to be their daughter, with huge breasts."

"They're all named Bunny?" he quipped.

"Or something like that."

"Hmm. Too bad. There are no Bunnys in my school that I know of."

She smiled at her son. "Don't worry, by the time you reach your fifties there'll be plenty around."

"Who wants to wait? I want to see 'em now!"

There he goes, oscillating back to the brink of manhood again.

"I noticed that you said he was interested in younger

women, Mom, but you didn't mention if you were interested in him," he said, pushing the empty cracker box off the bed so he could plop his gangly body there.

"Hey, careful! What do you think this is? A pigpen?" She needed to change the subject. Fast. She had no intentions of discussing her love life, or more accurately her pathetic lack thereof, with her buttinsky son. He didn't need to know that she'd been a *tad* interested in the "sweaty, snorting, opinionated runner turned mature GQ cover model once he showered" man. It was none of his beeswax! *She* was the adult, *he* was the kid. They needed to remember that.

He laughed. "Oh yeah, I forget how particular you are about neatness," he said while looking at the food-encrusted dishes, the dirty clothes, and the crumpled notes to herself strewn all over the floor, bed, desk and any other available surface. There was a trash basket right under her desk, but did she ever use it? No! In fact, momentarily the said trash basket was turned upside down and she was using it as a footstool.

"That's right! I'm known for my neatness in the highest of places. Did I ever tell you about the time they wanted to hire me to clean the White House?"

He rolled his eyes dramatically. "It wasn't like that, Mom. Your interpretation of that is completely wack!"

"It is not."

"Is too!"

"Is not!"

"Mom, you were invited there to speak with the First Lady about her literacy program, and to help arrange a consortium to address the literacy problem."

"*Invited*," she stressed, "to the White House."

"Yes, and after the meeting in which you threw your crumpled notes all around you as you always do while in your creative mode, the men in black came forward and straight out asked you 'if you wanted those.'"

"Yeah, so? What did they think? I carried around a shredder? Not like there probably wasn't one in every room at the White House. Did they think my notes were classified? Confidential? Top secret?"

"Mom, once again, that wasn't the point."

"Well," she huffed, realizing it was getting harder and harder to impress her son, "in my defense, it wasn't like *she* was taking any notes! The First Lady just sat there and listened."

He laughed, though clearly it was despite himself, and walked from the bed to kiss her forehead. "I don't think I'll ever understand what goes on in there," he muttered under his breath.

"I heard that!"

"Yes, Mom," he said as he left her room, "but did you understand it?"

"You're getting too damn fresh!" she yelled after him.

CHAPTER 12

The phone rang as they sat eating dinner. Craig whipped it from the wall.

"Hello?" he said into the receiver. "Oh, hi Dad," he said cautiously, eyeing her from beneath lowered lashes.

When their eyes met, he quickly looked away. As if that would somehow make her incapable of hearing him. She shook her head, knowing the light, breezy rapport that had been between them all afternoon and evening was suddenly over thanks to her ex—his father—Martin Ruvacado. *The slimy bastard!*

"Um, no. She didn't change her mind yet," her son said softly into the mouthpiece.

The son of a bitch loved this. He knew she and Craig would fight again now. And if Martin didn't know they'd fight (which he did!), he'd know his son would be angry with her once again for saying no to the cockamamy rafting idea he kept feeding into his young son's head.

"Yeah, okay, Dad. I'll talk to her again about it."

See? That bastard! He was getting predictable in his manipulations lately. He was such a stupid man, he couldn't even come up with something new or unforeseeable. Well, except the rafting trip. That was new. But, she once again chalked it up to one of Martin's bizarre midlife crises.

The thing that bothered her most was that she felt Martin sometimes used their son as a pawn. The divorce was between the two of them. It had nothing to do with Craig, and she hated that Martin wasn't smart enough to realize that. The man was a moron. How she had ever fallen for him to begin with amazed her more and more every day. Each day he lived, she swore he got more hateful and vindictive. And stupid.

Plus, he took no responsibility for any of his shortcomings. What? Like it was *her* fault he'd never advanced in his job? Like it was *her* fault he couldn't find love? Like it was *her* fault his hairline was receding at an alarming rate and he had that unfortunate premature ejaculation problem? He even blamed her for the fact that he couldn't obtain Yogi Rosenblum's ultimate level of divine peace. Which was totally ridiculous. He should be *thanking* her! After all, if it weren't for Dr. Harvey telling Martin he needed to relax and calm down or his heart would explode, or his shrink telling him he needed to find an outlet for his pent-up, repressed anger toward her before he had a nervous breakdown, Martin never would have *found* yoga. He should be thanking her for being the unsung object of his nervousness and repressed anger. If it weren't for her and his hateful feelings toward her, he never would have *met* his beloved Yogi Rosenblum!

She left the kitchen so her son could trash her openly, without feeling guilty that she was in the same room listening to the mother-bashing.

She flipped on her television set to drown out the sounds of her son getting pumped up for battle by his father. *The Apprentice* was on. That strange reality show where kids vie for corporate attention by doing outrageous things. "Why don't they just work hard?" she muttered to herself, not believing the stuff America was watching, or their fascination with it. When Donald Trump came on the show, she instantly turned off the set.

"What the hell's up with that man's hair? He's got more money than God. Can't the man spend some of what he's got on that hair?" she muttered to herself in disgust. True, she was just angry that she would now spend the rest of her evening fighting with her son, but really, couldn't the man see his hair's not normal? She knew he had less money than Bill Gates now that the market had swooped down, but for God's sake, if he was going to get everyone's attention by contributing to the garbage presented to the common man as nightly entertainment, couldn't he at least find someone who could do *something* with his hair? Geez. It was scary!

"Mom?" Craig said as he entered her room gingerly. "Can I ask you something?"

"Does it have to do with Donald Trump's hair? Because if it does, I honestly can't give you any answers, Craig. I have no idea why it looks like that."

He stared at her then blinked. "No. It has nothing to do with Donald Trump."

"Well, it's a good thing, because I wouldn't have a definitive answer for you if it *did* have anything to do with the man. Especially regarding his hair. It's like finding the Holy Grail. No one knows where it is, or what it really looks like, but everyone is thinking about it and not saying anything. Yeah, everyone's seeking it. But we all know it'll never be found. Or the mystery solved." Of course she was just stalling for time. Trying to prolong the inevitable. But how long could one talk about Donald Trump's hair? Or compare it to finding the Holy Grail? Once the basics were said, it was pretty much a moot point. Plus, after the initial mysteries of wondering "What the hell is it? What is it doing? and How can it be undone?" are solved, there's not much else to ponder.

"Mom!"

"What?"

"Forget Donald Trump's hair!"

She shook her head. "It's not easy."

"How come I can't go on this trip with Dad?" he jumped right in.

"Because I said so!" That was always a good starting point. Rational and unarguable.

"But, Mom. That's just a stupid defense. Give me a good excuse why I can't go."

Okay, so maybe it wasn't so rational. And as he easily pointed out, possibly not all that unarguable either. "I've told you already, it's too dangerous."

"Mom, it's not like we're hitting any class fives."

She looked at him as if he was nuts. "What?"

"The rapids. They're not even class fives, they're like, twos."

"I have no idea what that means."

"It means they're easy, Mom. They're for beginners. Babies. A six-month-old could go down these and wouldn't even crap in his diaper."

"That makes no difference to me, Craig. The answer is still no. And don't say crap!"

"Crap!"

They were both frustrated, so she decided to change course. "Craig, you're such a smart kid. Don't you see your father is manipulating us?"

He stood glaring at her, hands on hips. "How? By offering to take me on a cool trip for my birthday? If that's manipulation, he can manipulate me all he wants!"

She sighed heavily. Martin should rot in hell for this stunt. Instead, she was the one living in hell.

"No, Craig. I'm sorry. My decision is final. You are not going rafting. End of discussion."

He twirled on his big, black boot and stormed out, slamming her bedroom door behind him.

Peace at last.

Yeah, right. Like living with this huge pit in her stomach was peaceful. There was nothing left to do but hole herself up in her room for the rest of the night and work until the wee hours of the morning, when she'd finally need to pass out from exhaustion. "Sounds like a plan, Janine ol' girl."

She woke up tired with the same pain in her lower back that was had been throbbing when she fell into bed a few hours before. Grabbing the half-eaten Twizzler stick lying on her pillow, she shoved it in her mouth as she wandered to the window. Great. It was dark and rainy, which mirrored her feelings and made it hard not to let the eerie tentacles of depression engulf her.

Not expecting a note that morning, she hardly glanced at the empty pad as she walked through the kitchen on her way out the door. She didn't want to spend any extra time in the same room with the empty pad, and wasn't in the mood to check for the e-mail from her agent that wasn't waiting for her in her server's in-box. So she hurried out the door, already dressed for her walk.

She didn't care that her newly cropped hair made her look like Medusa or that her eyes were so swollen and tired she looked like Methuselah. She was in a bad mood and just wanted to get out and be left alone to tromp through her hour of pain—hoping to sweat the pissy mood out of her brain and body. Hopefully, she'd die of overexertion. But no, she wouldn't give Martin the pleasure. Because it was only over her dead body that she'd allow her son to go on that trip. And if it *killed* her, she wouldn't die, just to put the kibosh on Martin's boneheaded plan.

She waved to manager Matt, and headed straight for the bank of treadmills, relieved to see they were unused. She wasn't in the mood for analysis or witty banter or even a fun-filled morning of flirting over fruit concoctions.

Hopping aboard, she cranked it up and immediately started at her goal speed, staring blankly ahead, not seeing her reflection in the mirror that stared back at her. Nor did she notice Tom Kennedy take his usual position to her immediate left. She was so engrossed in grandiose thoughts of murder, she hadn't noticed his presence until he spoke.

"You're really going at it today," he said calmly.

She turned her head and was surprised to see him. "Oh, hi. I didn't see you. When did you get here?"

He turned up the speed of his machine to a run as if to punctuate his next words. "Exactly five minutes ago," he said, and smiled.

"Wow. That long? I must've been completely lost in thought."

He nodded, starting to breathe heavily. "You were. I didn't want to disturb you because you looked like you were contemplating something serious."

"I was," she panted around a sly smile. "Murder would be considered serious, wouldn't it?"

He laughed between gasps. "Yes. I'd consider murder serious."

She nodded, too winded to speak.

"Who's the unfortunate victim? One of your characters?"

"I wish," she said between pants. "My ex."

"Ah, yes. I remember." he said, thinking back. "The bastard of an ex-husband who is trying to make your life a living hell."

Wow, if she wasn't mistaken, those were the exact same words she'd used a few days before to describe Martin. "How nice," she breathed. "You remembered." She gasped a few more times. "Almost exactly."

He started to chuckle but got choked up, and ended up having a coughing attack instead. "Yes, I have a good memory for things which are said. It's a beneficial skill to have in business."

"Yes," she panted. "I'd assume it would be."

They respectively ran and walked in silence for the next few minutes.

"So what did this bastard of an ex-husband who is trying to make your life a living hell do?"

"It's not anything he's done," she puffed, "yet." She tried to inhale for the next sentence. "It's what he's attempting to do."

"And what's…that?" he said, running at full speed now.

"He's invited my son on—" she gasped for breath "—of all things—" she gasped some more "—a rafting trip."

"And?"

That was it? *And?* That was his response to her biggest nightmare? "*And*...Martin doesn't swim well. Plus, I don't want my son to get killed!"

"What class are the rapids?"

Did *everyone* know that rapids had classes but her? She needed to do some research on rapids. And Lee Iacocca quotes, too! Her son, Ben Franklin, and this man made her feel like an idiot. "I don't know!" she said with more anger than the question deserved.

Tom Kennedy nodded.

"My son said something—" she paused for breath "—about not being a class five." She gulped for air. "Whatever that means."

"Well, that's good," was all he said between huffs.

They did their workout side by side, both lost in thought.

It actually took him less time to go more miles than she did, because he ran instead of walked. He was already cooling down as she was doing her last few minutes. When he turned off his machine, she only had two minutes left. They were both covered in sweat, hair matted, and out of breath. They looked like two old, ruddy raisins in the bottom of a box of raisin bran. Pathetic, even to her eyes. Her old, tired, swollen-from-not-sleeping eyes.

"So, tell me more about this proposed trip," Tom said easily as he wiped the sweat from his neck with a towel.

She was finished, and turned off her machine with a triumphant flair. She was happy to have gotten through one more day of this torture. Every day she walked, she could picture her brittle bones getting stronger and less frail. That probably wasn't happening, for her research clearly indicated that although it was not totally unheard-of, reversal of bone loss could be extremely difficult to achieve, but she pictured it anyhow. It sure as hell beat the picture Doc Harvey put in her head of her breaking her spine with a sneeze!

Catching her breath, and grabbing the bright orange towel she'd brought with her, she shook her head in confusion. "I don't even know why Martin, that's my ex, wants to go on this trip. He's not an outdoorsy kind of man—hates it, from what I know of him—and can barely swim. Why on earth he'd want to take our son rafting for his thirteenth birthday, I have no idea."

Tom listened quietly. His stillness made her go on.

"He knows I'm overprotective. I've been overprotective since the day Craig was born. That's my son—Craig."

Tom Kennedy nodded again, ruffling his short, gray hair with the towel.

"Anyhow, so now it's like World War III in my house, with Craig and I at each other's throats over this rafting trip."

Tom nodded again. "So you say your ex doesn't like the outdoors?"

"Picture Woody Allen at a campground."

Tom Kennedy laughed, his chest expanding with each bubble of laughter.

Once again Janine was caught off guard by the reaction she had to this relative stranger. Her body seemed drawn to him, which was totally absurd considering they stood there all out of breath, and blotchy, with sweat-soaked hair and sweaty old clothes clinging to their hot bodies. She took a gander at his sweat-soaked shorts and T-shirt, and liked the way his T-shirt clung to his broad chest. She wondered if he had chest hair, and if so, wondered if it was gray.

His wet shorts clung to his thighs, too, she noticed. He had nice thighs. Strong looking. Martin had chicken thighs. Martin looked like a Perdue Oven Stuffer roaster. Only paler, and less buff.

This guy was tanned and sturdy. More like pork. You know. The other white meat. You didn't imagine pork to be spindly, or pasty, or lily-livered like you imagined chicken. No. Pork was strong and hearty, and much more manly.

Oh great, she thought to herself. First you call the guy Mr. Piggy because of his unfortunately regrettable puffing noises, and now you're comparing him to pork. Why not just combine the two and call the man Porky Pig? She eyed him circumspectly. He sure didn't look like Porky Pig to her! She let out a nervous giggle, hoping he'd assume she was still laughing over her "Woody Allen at a campground" crack.

"And he knows you wouldn't allow your son to go on the trip?"

"Maybe when hell froze over."

"Hmm." He stroked his chin with his fingers, drawing her attention to the sexy five-o'clock shadow that peppered his jawline. How had she ever thought he had flaccid cheeks? His jawline was chiseled, and sexy as hell. "I don't want to cross your familial boundaries by this suggestion, but I think you should tell your son he can go."

"What?" she sputtered. "Are you listening to me at *all?*" How could he even make that suggestion based on what she'd just told him? Was he insane? "Are you insane?"

Laughter rumbled from his chest again. "No. I am *not* insane," he mimicked.

She shook her head and gathered her stuff to leave.

"Wait." He shook his head, reaching for her arm at the same time. "Don't go. Let me explain."

"Don't worry," she huffed. "I've heard all opposing arguments, thoughts and threats. I'm all talked-out about this subject. Why I even bothered to tell it to anyone—especially a man—I have no idea. What was I expecting? Someone to see *my* side of this? It's dangerous, it's unsafe, and I don't want my son to get hurt." She tore her arm from his hold and started for the gym's door.

"Look, I don't even know your name. Please, calm down. Sit with me a minute. Let me explain. I doubt your son will even *go* on that trip. Just hear me out," he said soothingly, lowering his head to make eye contact with her. "Okay?"

She stood still, not progressing to the door but obviously not in such a hurry to leave anymore.

"Please?" he asked gently. He took her hand and walked her to the fruit bar. "Would you like some water?"

She shook her head negatively. "No thanks, I'm not hot any longer, but I haven't had my coffee yet this morning," she said, eyeing the full pot sitting on the coffeemaker.

"No?" he said, a sparkle in his eye. "I would never have noticed."

Sarcastic little thing, wasn't he?

"So, Ms. Treadmill-Only, I now know you're a bear until you've had your first cup of coffee."

"I'm a bear even *after* I've had my first cup of coffee," she said with a lopsided grin.

He smiled back warmly. "So what eventually soothes the bear?" he asked with a growling whisper that made the hairs on the back of her neck rise and her pulse quicken.

She broke their eye contact and looked away shyly, not sure she should tell him the images that he'd just forced into her mind's eye. Of course, in her mental depictions, her hair was still long, her body still lithe, and her effect on men still potent.

He cleared his throat and moved himself quickly behind the counter. "Matt, we're going to get some coffee," he called to the manager, who was spotting some guy who looked like Mr. Universe on the weight machine. When he saw Matt was about to walk over, Tom called to him again. "I'll get it, Matt. You stay with Eric."

What, did he know everyone at the gym?

She watched as Matt nodded and turned his attention back to the muscle-bound kid who was lifting more weight than was plastered to her hips.

Turning back to Tom Kennedy, she watched him pour out two cups of coffee. Regular, not decaf.

"I'm assuming you need high-test, not unleaded," he said easily.

"You assumed correctly. What gave me away?"

"Your laid-back personality."

"Yes, that fools everyone," she noted with a wry smile, not totally disliking his sarcasm.

He placed the cup before her, then went looking underneath the counter for the sugar. "Do you take cream?"

"I prefer Cherry Garcia, but if you're out, I'll suffer and use cream or milk. Or even the powdered stuff."

He smiled. "I'll see what I can find," he said as he walked

to the gym's refrigerator and peeked in the freezer section. "No Cherry Garcia, but they have chocolate, vanilla and fudge ripple."

"That'll do."

"Which one?"

"Oh. I thought you were offering all three."

Laughter burst forth as he pulled out all three vats of ice cream. "I could get used to you, Treadmill-Only."

What could it hurt to tell him her name? In less than a week, she'd never see him again. Unfortunately. "Janine Ruvacado."

"What?" he said as he removed his head from the fudge-ripple vat.

"My name. It's Janine Ruvacado. Like rude avocado. Ruvacado."

CHAPTER 13

"Cute!" he said, trying not to laugh.

"What's cute?" she asked, eyeing the huge vats of ice cream.

"You are. I could really get used to having you around. You're funny and know how to have a good time."

"I do? That's news to me!"

"Well, I don't have much experience with many women, but my ex-wife wouldn't eat three scoops of ice cream if she'd starved herself for an entire week beforehand—much less arbitrarily start her day with it lacing her coffee."

"She probably didn't sport my thighs, either."

"There's nothing wrong with your thighs," he said dutifully.

"Look, I wasn't fishing for a compliment. Just stating a fact."

He nodded thoughtfully, turning his full attention on her. "You know, since I met you, I've tried to discover what makes you so intriguing. I think it could possibly be your opinionated outspokenness. I'm not used to opinionated women. Most of the women I've known throughout my adult years have worked for me, and they yessed me and kowtowed to me at every opportunity." He stopped there and tilted his head slightly as he stared at her. "You're not like that at all.

It's refreshing. *You're* refreshing. I hate yes-men, and in my opinion, yes-women are equally disappointing."

"Me too," she said, wearing a face that showed her distaste for yes-people in general.

He smiled. "I doubt you, Janine Ruvacado, would agree with anything someone else said if it didn't strike you as right."

"You've got that right!"

"And something tells me I'm going to put that to the test and will find out how right I am soon enough."

She wondered what that meant, but didn't have long to ponder the thought because he spoke again so quickly.

"Pleased to meet you, Janine Ruvacado, as in rude avocado," he said, holding out his hand.

"Likewise," she said, clamping her hand in his.

"So, let's cut to the chase here, shall we?" he asked.

"I didn't know we needed to, but please, go ahead," she said, nodding her head.

He trained his eyes on hers, obviously trying to gauge her reaction, which made her internally brace herself. "I should probably protect my vulnerable parts, after seeing the way you responded to my idea, but I think I've decided that the family jewels are probably safe for the time being."

Now there was an interesting start to a conversation. "You only *think* they're safe? One would figure you'd want to have a definitive answer to that possibility."

"Don't try to change the subject. I know stalling when I see it."

"Touché. Proceed," she said, waving her hand in the air.

"You say your ex-husband's not the rafting–trip type. Right?"

"Right."

"And he can barely swim?"

"He doesn't like the water. We'd go to Jones Beach in the summer and he'd never take Craig into the water. I had to take him when he wanted to go in."

"What would Martin do?"

"Sit fully dressed under the umbrella with zinc oxide covering his nose."

He laughed. "Sounds attractive," he said, and winked at her.

"Yeah. Right. I even had to put up the umbrella myself, because whenever *he* attempted to put it in the sand, it would blow over at the first puff of a breeze," she said, rolling her eyes.

He laughed. "You've won me over with the image of you setting up a beach umbrella for your inept husband. You're no shrinking violet, Janine Ruvacado! In fact, I think you're magnificent. But I wonder if you know that. From what I can tell of you, I figure you're clueless."

His praise was more than she could handle. She wasn't used to it, and it made her feel uncomfortable. "You just said all that, and you think *I'm* clueless?"

Unaffected, he went on. "Okay, so here's a man who hates the water, is not an outdoorsman, and knows his ex-wife is a bit overprotective."

"A *lot* overprotective."

"Correction. A *lot* overprotective. So he tells his son—who is probably as vibrant and exciting as his mother—that he wants to take him on a rafting trip for his thirteenth birthday, knowing full well that said vibrant, exciting, *overprotective* mother will say no, causing a huge rift between the vibrant and exciting mother and son."

He thinks I'm vibrant and exciting? "You got it. See? He's a bastard. Right?"

"No. Well, yes. But what I see is a manipulative weasel who is using his son as a chess piece in a game the son never asked to play."

"That's what makes me so mad. If Martin's decided to go on a trip like this to prove something to himself—or possibly to satisfy a whim of his to help ease the midlife crisis he seems to be stuck in lately—then great for him. He should go for it. But not with Craig. And I believe he knows I wouldn't want Craig to go. If what you're saying is true, he's using his own son as a pawn to get at me, and I can't believe he'd really do that to Craig."

"I think you're right, Janine, that Martin knows you won't allow the trip. I haven't known you for very long, but I can tell you're a very, ah, decisive woman." He looked at her and shrugged apologetically, but continued speaking. "Now in business, that would create a stalemate, *if* one side didn't want to play or thought the stakes were too high."

"They *are* too high. Getting Craig killed is not an option."

"But think about it, Janine. If Martin never took Craig into the water as a *child*, what makes you think he'll go on a careening race down a fast river in a rubber boat?"

She lifted her eyebrows at his implication. Her gears started spinning, and she didn't like where her thoughts led her. "No, I can't believe that. Yes, Martin wants to hurt me, but this would crush Craig. Martin's not the sharpest tool in the shed, but I'd hope he wouldn't do such a thing to his own son…just to hurt me."

Tom sat there silently.

"You think he's bluffing?" she said plainly.

"I do."

"No," she said, shaking her head. "It's too cruel."

Tom sat quietly, letting her sort this through.

"I think I need to talk with Craig about this. He needs to be prepared," she said more to herself than to Tom. "Thanks," she said as if she'd come to a conclusion. "This needs to get resolved, and in order for that to happen, I need to take a risk."

"What kind of risk?" Tom asked.

She took a deep breath and let it out slowly. "I've got to start letting go. I need to talk with Craig about this, and hope, for his sake, that it's not a ploy his father is using to hurt me." She looked up, her eyes searching Tom's. "As soon as Craig gets home, I'll tell him I've changed my mind, that he can go white-water rafting with his father." Just saying the words frightened and exhausted her.

Tom nodded. "I think that's a wise decision. What do you think will happen next?"

She smiled, picturing the joy on her son's face. "He'll run to the phone and tell his dad to make the reservations." She smiled sadly. "I'll even hand him the phone."

He returned her sad smile. "I think that's a good plan," he said slowly. "Will you be okay with that?"

They sat quietly, both thinking about the upcoming afternoon's events at the Ruvacado place.

She spoke from her heart. "If Martin *is* using this trip as a maneuver to hurt me, he will have succeeded. Seeing Craig crushed will be the most hurtful thing he could do to me." She looked as though she were going to cry. "It would kill me."

"Let's hope I'm wrong," he said quietly. "Can we meet here tomorrow morning at eight-thirty for coffee, so you can tell me what happened before we do our treading?"

"Sure," she said with a weak smile. "I'd like that. Thanks for listening."

He nodded.

She leaned over and kissed his cheek.

"Good luck," he said simply. "Hey, I almost forgot to ask. How's the edit going?"

She smiled broadly. "It's in full swing. I'm a word-chopping pro."

His warm laughter settled around her, making her skittish once again.

"Well, I'd better go and let you get showered so you can get to work."

He reached over and squeezed her shoulder. "No rush. I'm the boss. I can do whatever I like," he said casually.

She looked at him closely, her head tilted slightly. "I don't buy your cavalier attitude, Tom Kennedy. I bet you haven't goofed off too much in your lifetime, have you?"

"You sure do call 'em like you see 'em, don't you," he said, wearing the embarrassed smile of someone who'd been caught in a lie.

"Am I wrong?"

"No. In this case, I have to give you credit. You're right on the money," he said shyly. "I'm busted."

She smiled boldly and looked up at him straight on, "Well, maybe it's not too late to learn how to shirk off some of that responsibility."

"I like the sound of that. Are you offering to teach me?"

"Maybe," she said coyly. "Maybe not."

"Do I have a vote in this?"

"Nope," she said, before turning on her sneakered heel with a squeak and prancing toward the door, moving her hips provocatively. "Now go hit the showers, soldier! We'll reassemble back here at this juncture at oh-eight-hundred!" she barked.

"Wait a minute. I thought we said eight-thirty before?"

She turned around and giggled. "We did. But I don't know how to say eight-thirty in military talk."

"I know how to say it, but now I want that extra half hour with you. How about we just make it official and rendezvous at these coordinates at oh-eight-hundred?"

She giggled. "Okay. But I have to warn you. I'm not a pretty sight at that hour."

"I'm tough," he offered as response.

"We'll see," she said, as she looked over her shoulder and threw him a wink. "I'll be the judge of that." And on that note, she left the building.

A few hours later she was sitting at her desk when the phone rang.

"Argh, I forgot to go online so this wouldn't happen!" she muttered to herself as she picked up the receiver. "Yes?" she barked into the phone.

"You're something else, do you know that?" Tom's voice came through the line.

"I try to be unique."

"You can say that again." He laughed. "I think that was the sexiest wink I've ever seen," he said, taking a deep breath and letting it out slowly.

"Yeah, right. You don't get out much, do you?"

Tom laughed.

"Wait a minute, I'm unlisted. How did you get my number?"

"I have my ways. I'm a big-shot businessman, remember?"

"And we would be business associates, how?"

"Well, I was hoping for a corporate takeover, but have to admit, in all the takeovers I've ever been associated with, not one of the CEOs had a switch like yours, Janine Ruvacado."

"Do you always look at the rear ends of your impending business victims?"

"Only when they look like yours."

Yes, they were unquestionably flirting now. She could definitely tell. "And does that happen often, Mr. Kennedy?"

"Counting yours?"

"Yes."

"Once."

She laughed heartily. "Why thank you, Mr. Kennedy."

"You're welcome, Ms. Ruvacado."

"So since I have your undivided attention, and since I am now no longer concentrating on my work, why don't you tell me a little about yourself, Mr. Kennedy?" It was easier talking to him when she didn't have to look at him. "You know so much about me, how about evening things up?"

"Let's see. There's not much to tell. I'm pretty boring, in fact."

"Boring? How so?"

"Life and work have always been synonymous for me. One can't be defined without the other. Starting at a young age, I was determined to make something of my life. Poverty had killed my mother when I was in my late teens, and my father had taken off when I was a child, leaving me with nothing but his name and hard feelings."

"That sounds so sad, Tom."

"I guess it was, but it gave me inspiration. Standing alone at my mother's grave, as the minister quietly uttered words to help escort my mother into her next journey, I silently vowed to crawl out of the impoverished life that had killed my mother and suffocated us like a damp, heavy curtain. Whatever it took, I vowed to do, to rise up from the bleak life she and I had known until then."

She pictured a proud, determined boy. "That must have been hard for you," she said gently, imagining her Craig all alone, should something happen to her.

"The world had seemed a cruel place, and for the time that I wasn't in control of my own destiny, it was. But once I was given the opportunity to better myself, I took it.

"Education. That was my ticket out of hell. My mother had worked in menial, backbreaking jobs to help us survive. She'd fallen in love with my father at a young age and had no schooling other than the minimum required at that time. She was trained to do nothing. And, sadly, perhaps wrongly, I blamed love for making and keeping her that way."

"You were just a child," she said, wondering how her son would interpret that situation.

"As a boy, I studied everything presented to me. Determined that I'd live my life differently when it was my turn to provide for myself. For one, I was not going to let love get in the way of obtaining my dream—independence. And for another, I knew from a lifetime without, that the key to my independence…was money. And to get money, you needed to be smart.

"Mastering each lesson my teachers taught—striving to better myself with each class—I meticulously acquired the mental strength and stamina it took to shine. I worked harder than any other kid I knew, and because of that, I had few friends. Not because the other kids didn't like me. I believe I was likable, and they'd try to be my friend, but I was always reading and studying, and didn't have time for playing."

She listened intently. "You were still a boy, but lived the life of a man. That's so sad."

"I didn't think it was sad. I was an intense, serious-minded kid. And after a few years, I grew to be known as the brightest boy in my high school. Although many people didn't really know me as a person, I think they liked what little they knew of me, never thinking I was a snob or a know-it-all. The few people I knew said my grit and determination were admirable, and I always tried to be friendly. I'd rarely use the knowledge I'd gained to my benefit, yet I easily could have. On the rare instances that I did, it was never for selfish reasons. Rather, I used what I'd learned in a smart way—for good reasons."

"Like what?" She was entranced in this story, and wanted to know more. She tried to imagine Craig in those shoes.

"For example, I knew the authorities would take me away and put me in a foster home had they discovered that my mother had passed, so I came up with a plan to let me finish high school without being disturbed."

"How?"

He choked out a humorless laugh. "I'd immediately called both of my mother's employers—the steam cleaners where she'd worked for a pittance in the hazardous, substandard working environment, and also the insane asylum, where she'd worked as a cleaning lady.

"Avoiding my mother's immediate bosses that she would have reported to directly, I'd asked for the owner of the cleaners and the director at the asylum, correctly assuming that they'd not ask any further questions or doubt the credibility of my falsified explanation. I'd learned a long time before that good fortune often happened to those least in need of it, and therefore hoped the steam-cleaner owner and the asylum director wouldn't question me. Whereas conversely, I also knew—from firsthand experience—that those who usually needed a fortuitous occurrence, rarely saw one. So I'd gone to the top people, knowing my mother's immediate supervisors would smell my story to be reeking of untruths, knowing it was as unbelievable as my fabricated account sounded."

"So what happened?" Janine asked breathlessly.

"I spoke with the big bosses."

"What did you say?"

"I remember it as if it were yesterday. I said, *Hello? This is Thomas Kennedy, Annabel Kennedy's son. She asked me to contact you to inform you that she will no longer be coming to work, sir. Her mother-in-law, my grandmother, also named Annabel Kennedy, recently passed and left us her entire estate, so my mother, who has already left to put things in order, will not be coming back to work.*"

"Did you get away with it?"

"Yes. In both cases, after explaining who my mother was and what she did for them, her employers muttered something to the effect of 'well, good for her,' before thanking me for contacting them. I then added, *You may send any back pay to her old address, and she will pick it up when she has the opportunity*, for good measure at the end of each phone call. I needed the money for food, and to help ward off the landlady for a while. Although thankfully, the apartment building was in such squalor, the landlady didn't make it a habit to come down monthly to get the rent. My mother had always mailed it promptly to her Fifth Avenue address, so it would be a few months before I'd be questioned."

"Oh my God, Tom. And you had no one to help you?" She was devastated.

"Luckily, long before graduation, there was a guidance counselor who took it upon herself to guide me through the labyrinth of college searches and applications. She helped me look for an undergraduate program, which I'd done with the same determination I'd attacked my years of learning. The woman had no idea that I'd been living alone for a long time, and I tried to keep it that way.

"One day she said, 'You're going to go places, Thomas. Please take this home and have your mother let me know which schools she would like you to apply for.' I didn't want to get caught living alone so I told Mrs. Abernathy that my mother pretty much left that decision up to me. I remember that she looked taken aback and said, 'Oh, well, in that case, what have you decided, Thomas?'

"I hated lying to her, but had been doing things for myself for so long I was used to the ruse. I asked Mrs. Abernathy if it cost anything to apply, and I remember how a little snort of a laugh escaped her lips before she said, 'Not with your grades, son. Maybe I should tell you, Thomas, I took it upon myself to send out a few scholarship requests. When your mother and I last met, she made it abundantly clear that you would need a scholarship to attend college, and when I told her your current academic standing in the school, she was thrilled, so I had her sign a few blank forms for me, and did the paperwork myself.'"

"What a nice woman," Janine said quietly as a tear silently ran down her cheek.

"Yes. I was thrilled at the thought that my mother knew of my academic standing before she passed away. I'd hoped she was as proud of me as I was of her."

"I'm sure she was," Janine said gently.

"Thank you."

"So what happened next?"

She heard him take a deep breath before he went on telling his tale. "I was trying to be a man, but when I heard that my mother knew I'd been doing well in school, my bravado slipped a notch and a tear slid down my cheek. I tried to wipe it away quickly, but Mrs. Abernathy had already seen it. She said, 'I'm sorry, Thomas. Did I do something wrong? I only thought your mother would be overwhelmed by the multitude of forms to fill out. No offense to your mother, Thomas. Most people have a hard time with the scholarship request forms.'

"I shook my head and stood there willing the tears to stop flowing and said, 'No, Mrs. Abernathy, you didn't do anything wrong.' And then for some reason, I leaned over the woman's paper-covered desk to give her a hug and said, 'Thank you. Thank you for everything you've done for me. I appreciate it. And I know my mother does, too.' With that said, I had to turn and leave the room, because although I'd tried, I couldn't control my tears any longer."

Janine was openly crying now for the motherless boy who wanted so hard to become something. "So what happened?"

"A couple of weeks later, Mrs. Abernathy sent me a note saying that I needed to come down to her office when I could. Never wanting to miss a moment of class, I waited until lunchtime before using the attached pass to her office."

This made Janine smile.

"I said, 'You wanted to see me, Mrs. Abernathy?' and when she looked at me with tear-filled eyes, I knew in my gut something was wrong. 'Yes, Thomas. Please come in and close the door,' she'd said. 'Am I in trouble?' I asked her. And then she made a sound that I couldn't decipher."

Janine waited with baited breath.

"She said, 'First of all, I'd like to say that I am sorry to hear about your mother, Thomas.' I remember sitting perfectly still, the blood rushing to my head. I'd survived for so long without anyone knowing, I wondered how she found out.

"I sent off the administration packets you gave me to send out. As of yesterday I've now heard back from all of the schools you applied for. I had very good news, and wanted to share it with your mother,' she said. I said, 'Let me guess. You couldn't reach her.'

"She shook her head sadly. 'No,' she said. 'So I did some calling around. I called her places of employment listed on your emergency calling card.'"

Janine gasped aloud.

"I could feel my world crashing in around me, and although I was afraid to ask, I needed to. 'And?' I asked Mrs. Abernathy. 'They told me about your mother's sudden windfall,' she replied.

"I'd hated lying to this woman who had done so much for me. Then she said, 'And when I tried to contact her at your grandmother's estate...I found out that there *is* no other Annabel Kennedy.'"

"Oh God. You poor thing. What did you do?" Janine asked.

"I hung my head in shame and apologized to Mrs. Abernathy. I tried to explain that I'd just wanted to finish school and didn't want anyone to take me away."

"What did she say?" Janine demanded.

Tom laughed softly. "She raised her ample body from behind her desk and walked around to me, putting her plump arms around me in comfort. Then she softly asked, 'How did you support yourself, son?'

"I remember jutting out my chin and saying, 'I managed,' with all the dignity I could muster. She shook her head slowly and said, 'I'm amazed by that. How did you do it?'

"Tears filled my eyes, but I'd refused to let them spill. Nor would I tell her the way I had lived those last few months. An animal deserved better, and I wouldn't upset her with the details.

"When Mrs. Abernathy saw no words would be coming forth, she held me closely to her soft, round body, and for the first time in a long time, I let myself bathe in the warmth of another human being's touch. It had been so long since I'd hugged my mother or touched another person. Or depended upon another soul," he added quietly.

"It must have felt good," Janine said in a whisper.

"It did," he whispered back.

After a few minutes of silence, Janine asked, "So what was Mrs. Abernathy's good news?"

"I'd been awarded a full scholarship at *every* school I'd applied to. As Mrs. Abernathy put it, the world was mine for the picking. Then she said something that changed my life forever."

"What?" Janine barely uttered.

"She said, 'You need only choose where you would like your future to start.'"

"What a wonderful lady!" Janine blurted.

"Yes," Tom agreed. "I remember my whisper as I asked her, 'Harvard, too?'"

"The kind, loving woman nodded with tears coursing from her eyes, and said 'Yes, Harvard, too, Thomas.' She later told me they were tears of pride and wonder."

Janine too had tears of pride and wonder flowing from her eyes. "What a wonderful story, Thomas. Thank you for sharing it with me."

"I've never told anyone this before."

"Never? It's incredible. So filled with hope and determination."

"Well," he said shyly, "now there are three people in this world who know my story."

"I'm honored that you shared it with me. Thank you." She truly did feel honored. "So that was the beginning of your long journey to now."

"Yes," he said quietly.

"You've worked hard. Have you kept in touch with Mrs. Abernathy?"

"Yes. She's the only person I've ever really had a relationship with. I seem to be always working, never stopping for anything, including a social life."

"But you've done well for yourself, haven't you?"

"Yes, it's taken a long time, but I think I can safely say I've finally arrived at my goals. And speaking of which, I should let you get back to your work. I've taken up way too much of your time with my babbling. I don't know what possessed me to tell you all of that."

He sounded embarrassed, but he shouldn't have been. "I'm glad you opened up to me and told me about your childhood. As I said, I feel honored to know the real you." Realizing that all this serious talk was making him uncomfortable, she added in a cheerier, slightly sarcastic voice, "Plus, it explains more than a few things about you. When you hear about *my* childhood, and should you be unfortunate enough to meet *my* mother, that will undoubtedly answer many, *many* questions for *you*."

He laughed lightly. "Well, have a great day, Janine, and good luck with telling Craig about the trip. I'll have my fingers crossed that all goes well for you both."

"Thank you. I'll see ya at oh-eight-hundred tomorrow morning."

"I'll be there," he said, before she heard the connection break.

CHAPTER 14

"Hey, Mom. I didn't expect you to be sitting here when I walked in the door," Craig said as he almost fell over her—righting himself as he shrugged off the heavily weighted book bag. "You're usually in your room, typing away, not sitting in the kitchen holding a huge bowl of ice cream in your lap," he observed sardonically.

"Hey, son," she said with an enormous grin. She was always amazed at the feelings that rushed through her, those first few seconds she saw him after a long day without him.

"Wassup?" He eyed her suspiciously then did the one eyebrow thing.

"Nothing," she said mock innocently. "Just having some ice cream. I combined Chunky Monkey with Cherry Garcia. It's delicious."

"Chunky Garcia," he said with a smile.

"Or Cherry Monkey," she shot back. It was their usual ice-cream banter. "You want some?"

"Sure," he said, doing the one-eyebrow thing again, but this time with the other eyebrow. Kind of like being ambidextrous—only with your eyebrows. "You must've been sitting here scarfing down ice cream for a while, Mom, 'cause you look like you're slowing down."

"I'm a couple bowls ahead of you," she admitted.

"So I suspected."

She got up and walked to the freezer, taking out the ice cream. "Both?" she asked while holding both flavors, one in each hand.

"Of course," he said with a smile.

She put the containers down on the countertop and picked up the scooper. Making perfectly round balls, she plunked two of each flavor in a large bowl. Most people used little bowls for ice-cream dishes. Their ice-cream bowls were the size of serving dishes.

"Mom, are you wearing a bra?"

"No, I was working, why?"

"For God's sakes, put on a bra once in a while, would ya?"

"What?" she asked. "Like you haven't seen breasts before?" she countered.

"Well, yeah, I have," he admitted a bit shyly.

"And mine are so different?"

"Well, no, but…"

"But what?"

"You're my *mother!*"

"So? I shouldn't have breasts?"

He rolled his eyes, "Forget it," he said, before storming out of the room.

"It's not like you haven't seen them before. Don't you want your ice cream?" she called after him.

"Yeah, I'm just putting my backpack in my room," he shouted back.

He walked back into the kitchen and slid into his chair. "So what are you celebrating, Mom?"

"Me? I'm not celebrating anything. It's *you* that should be celebrating."

He shoved a large spoonful in his mouth. "Oh yeah? Why?"

"Because I've done a lot of thinking."

"Well, let's party down!"

"Don't be fresh or I'll change my mind," she said.

He stared at her. "Something's up. I don't know what, but something's definitely up. My mother never stops working midday to wait for me to come home from school and share a bowl of ice cream." He looked at her again to see if she'd say anything. When nothing was said, he continued. "Mom, you're scaring me. What's up?"

She smiled her I-know-something-you-don't-know smile that always freaked him out. "Well…" she said, taking another bite, "I've made a decision."

"Yeah, so?"

"One I think you'll like, but we need to discuss it first." She knew she was killing him—she could see it on his face—but she wasn't too thrilled to have this conversation.

"Look, Mom, there's only one decision you could make that would make me happy, and we both know you didn't make it, so stop your teasing and tell me what your big decision is. What, are we gonna have something besides spaghetti for dinner tonight?" He looked at her laconically.

"When did you get so fresh and cynical?"

"I've always been fresh, according to you, and the cynicism is a recent addition in the last year or so."

"Hmm. I hadn't noticed. Must've been when you went goth."

"Mom," he whined like a little boy, "are you going to tell me or not!"

She smiled. Her half-boy/half-man son was fluctuating again. "Okay, okay, keep your undies on."

"That's better than *you* do, my braless mother," he muttered.

"For your information, fresh-mouth, I didn't put my bra on to begin with, so it really doesn't apply to me."

He raised his eyebrow at her, knowing how it always creeped her out. "You think you could get to the point a little quicker? I'll be *your* age by the time you tell me."

"God forbid!" she said dramatically, holding up her hands in protest when she saw he was going to start complaining again. "Okay, okay. Don't flash the brow at me again! I'll tell you."

He waited, eyebrow raised in question.

"Put that thing down. You know it creeps me out."

He lowered his brow. "Now spill it," he said as he scooped more Chunky Garcia or Cherry Monkey into his mouth, "before all my ice cream melts and all that's left are the chocolate chunks."

"Okay," she said, inhaling deeply. "Here goes. I'm going to take a chance here and let you go on that trip with your dad."

His eyes bulged open and an enormous grin swept across his face. "No way!"

She nodded, also grinning. "Yes, way."

He flew off his chair and hugged her. She hadn't expected that, but it was a wonderful surprise. "Really?" he asked.

"Really."

"You're not punking me?"

"Nope. You've not been punked."

"Damn, this is great! I can't wait to tell my friends. They're going to be so psyched!" He hugged her tightly. "You're all right, Mom. I take back every bad thing I've ever said about you."

"Thanks, son. But listen. I'm trying really hard to let go of the strings here. You know that's difficult for me," she said with a lopsided grin.

"Yeah, I know it is, Mom. Thanks for that."

"Yes, well, I need to add one other thing, Craig."

He gave her the unibrow.

"There's no easy way to say this, so I'll just come out and say it. I've got a bad feeling about this whole trip thing," she said.

"I'm not going to get knocked out of the raft, hit my head on a rock and die, facedown in the river."

"I'm not talking about something like that. I'm talking about your dad. Are you sure you want to go through with this? I may be wrong about your father—and I really hope I am, Craig—but I just don't want you to get hurt. Ever. In any way. By anyone."

"I'm not going to get hurt, Mom. He's my dad, and he wants to go on a cool trip for my birthday. How can that hurt me?"

"I'm just saying it might be a possibility. That's all," she said gently. Loving him with all her heart.

"You worry about too much shit, Mom."

She groaned. "Craig!"

"What?"

"Stop with the cursing already!"

He smiled. "Oh. Sorry. I won't say it again. It just slipped out in my excitement."

"Does it slip out when you're excited in school?" she asked pointedly.

He laughed. "Yeah, right, like you can get me with *that* lame question." He rolled his eyes heavenward. "I'm never excited at school."

"Well, it's a good thing. If the principal heard your mouth, he'd throw you right out."

"Mom, he's got more important things to worry about besides whether or not Craig Ruvacado says the word *shit*."

She gave him her evil eye. It used to work on him when he was five, but it no longer held its terror.

"What?" he asked. "The man's got teenaged pregnancy to worry about, drugs, guns, gangs, violence and illiteracy, to name a few. You think he's up nights worrying about whether I say bad words or not?"

"Well, *he* may not be, but *I* am, so cut me some slack, son of mine, and try to curb your trash mouth in front of me, okay? Plus, if your grandmother should ever hear it, she'd wash your mouth out with soap, and considering we use antibacterial soft soap, you'd be getting two squirts of the stuff, and I doubt you'd enjoy the whole sensation."

"Okay, Mom." He looked at her squarely. "So," he said as he folded his arms across his chest. "What made you change your mind?"

"What? I can't change my mind?" she asked with phony innocence.

"Well, it's never happened before, I just wondered why now?"

"I don't know. I just did. Why? You don't want to go?" she teased.

"Whoa, Nelly, now don't get all crazy on me! I was just wondering, that's all."

"Well, quit your wondering. I've changed my mind and am

now letting you go. You can call your father tonight to give him the good news."

"Hell yeah," he said, before realizing his mistake. "Sorry," he added.

She rolled her eyes and shook her head—her curls bouncing.

"You know, Mom, I'm getting used to this new look of yours. I kind of like it. It was hard enough having a hot mother, but having a hot mother with waist-length hair was even worse. This look is more...um, motherish. Although honestly, I don't know many mothers that have such wild curls. They're totally out of control, but yet, it suits you. I like the hair. Are you getting used to it?"

"Kind of."

"Yeah," he said simply. They finished their ice cream absorbed with their own thoughts, then he went to his room to work on his homework, and she went to hers to work on her edit. They met back up in the kitchen a few hours later to eat dinner.

"I'm so excited, Mom. Thanks."

She smiled warmly. "I'm glad you're happy, honey. Just don't go and get yourself hurt."

"This is so totally weird, Mom. You're so calm about the whole thing. Too calm. This isn't like you at all."

She just shrugged.

"Mom?"

"Yes?"

"Have you been smoking or drinking something that could possibly have altered your mind and attitude so drastically? I mean, I'm just wondering. 'Cause, well, hey, I don't want to delve into it too deeply for fear that you'll wake up and turn into 'momzilla the overprotective monster' again or anything."

She hid her smile. "Yes. Good that you don't delve too deeply. Let sleeping dogs lie. Don't rock the boat. Just go with the flow and thank your lucky stars that I changed my mind. Why question why? Just enjoy it, son."

"Yeah, Lord knows you usually have your claws in me so deeply I can't even take a piss without your knowing what I was doing and how long I was doing it. Maybe when you see that I've survived this trip, you'll loosen the hold a bit."

"Very cute. That's a dream worth dreaming, son. And don't say 'piss,' it's so uncouth."

Dinner was great. They actually had pork chops, French fries and canned corn, but she figured she could've served him spaghetti, and it would have tasted delicious to him. The burned chops, the slimy French fries and cold corn was probably the best meal he'd had since, well, the other night at Benihana's. Hey, he was floating on a cloud tonight, which would've made *anything* taste good, but that didn't take anything away from the excellent meal they'd had the other night. The boy was happy, not an idiot! This meal—no matter the celebration—would never beat Benihana's. Nothing she could ever make could beat Benihana's. The meal she'd serve him on the long-imagined day she'd tell him she bought him a cherry-red Porsche couldn't beat Benihana's. But this meal was up there in celebratory spirit, if not culinary reality.

She'd be the first to admit that she was culinarily challenged. She could write like a pro, wasn't afraid to try anything, and faced life like it was a contest she would win. But cooking? In all honesty, she stank big time at cooking. As her loving son would put it: her cooking would not add to the weight problem in America.

But tonight? It tasted delicious. Put enough duck sauce on the pork, and drown the fries in enough ketchup, and it was as edible as anything else. For her son, Craig Ruvacado, life was good.

Seven o'clock seemed to be the time his dad always called him, so she figured that was the best time for Craig to try. Impatiently, he waited for the clock to turn seven and he asked her if he could call Martin.

"Of course."

He'd programmed his dad's number on speed dial, so it only took a couple of seconds, but she could see on his face that those seconds lasted forever.

"Hey, Dad!"

There was a pause.

"Guess what?"

Another pause.

"You're not going to believe this."

Her son looked across the kitchen at her while she was leaning against the cabinets with her arms folded across her chest, wearing a plastic smile that she hoped he couldn't quite decipher. She gave him the thumbs-up and nodded her head, her plastic smile widening. She was worried how this would go down, and wanted to be near him in case he crashed and burned.

"Mom's letting me go."

A brief pause.

"Go where? On the *trip*, Dad!"

Janine could hear her sleazy ex scream the word *what* across the kitchen.

"Yeah, she's letting me go. Can you believe it? We can go on that trip for my birthday, Dad. You can go ahead and make the reservations. Isn't this great?"

He looked over at her as she wore her huge plastic grin, and although she was watching him with vigilance, she hoped he didn't notice how nervous she was. For a split second she saw a flash of doubt cross his face, and thought he might have wondered why she was watching him so closely. In an effort not to unnerve him, she looked away so he could focus on his phone conversation. This was about him, not her, although she was holding her breath, hoping her suspicions were wrong.

She could hear Martin's voice rise a few decibels. "Is this a joke?" came floating out of the telephone.

She watched her son as he happily replied to his father's outburst. "No, Dad, it's no joke. I thought she was kidding at first, too, but she's not. Really! She's letting me go."

"Oh, she is, is she?" She heard the little weasel squeal.

"Yeah, Dad, isn't this cool?"

His father didn't answer.

"So what happens now, Dad?"

There was a long pause.

"What I mean is, are you going to take me out to buy the equipment and clothes, and all the stuff we need?"

She could see lines of worry start to etch on Craig's face. "What did he say?" she whispered to him.

He put his hand across the phone's speaker part, and said in a stage whisper, "He said we have plenty of time for that."

She nodded, allowing herself to get a little hopeful. Maybe this *wasn't* a manipulative charade. Maybe father and son *would* celebrate Craig's birthday together. And if so, she had to then pray that maybe her beloved son *wouldn't* die out in the wilderness.

"So tell me all about it again, Dad. I can see the brochure in my head, but I can't remember all the stuff it said. Tell me again what it said."

His father obviously didn't answer.

"Dad? Did you hear me?"

Her son listened carefully, and his face dropped from what he heard.

"What did he say?" she asked as quietly as she could so Martin wouldn't hear her in the background.

Again his hand flew to cover the mouthpiece. "He said that when you said no, he threw out the brochure."

Hmm, that's not good. Perhaps Martin thought his work was done at that point.

"You threw it out! I *told* you I'd work on her, Dad," she heard her son plead.

When he saw her eyebrows shoot up, he said softly while he slipped his hand back over the mouthpiece, "No offense, Mom. I just *really* wanted to go."

She smiled and shook her head, waving her hand in front of her. "No problem, I understand," she whispered back, still eyeing him cautiously, waiting for the other shoe to drop. He was such a smart kid; she was surprised he wasn't getting what she suspected was going on here. Any minute now he might find out that his father had no intention of taking him. Not before, not now, not ever. The poor boy wanted to go so badly he wasn't really hearing what was being said. She felt her heart bleed for her son.

"Can you get a copy of it online?" Craig asked in desperation.

She watched as Craig's face grew long and sad.

"Oh," he said dejectedly. Then he brightened. "What's the name of the place, Dad? I'll look it up online from here." He looked quickly at her. She was the be-all and end-all monitor when it came to him surfing the Internet. While he was home, he wasn't allowed on the Web unless she approved it. And once she did, she always came in and out of his room to monitor the sites he surfed. Not that she thought he'd be surfing porn sites or anything, but she needed to constantly remind him (or as he put it, "rag on him") about the dangers of child molesters lurking to catch him and snatch him. If she was overprotective about things like rafting trips, she was maniacal about the computer and pedophiles.

She nodded her head to let him know he had her approval to look up the site online after he got off the phone.

"Thanks," he breathed to her.

She winked at him. Still holding out hope that she was wrong. "No problem."

"So what's the name of the place, Dad?"

Tiny pause.

"What do you mean you forgot? How could you forget? Dad, you're getting as bad as Mom!"

She looked at her son sadly and smiled sheepishly. Things were starting to become crystal clear for Janine.

Totally misinterpreting her concern, he said "I didn't mean anything by it, Mom. You're not that forgetful. Honest. So don't worry about getting older, okay? It's just that you're always complaining about becoming more forgetful as the years pass. That's all. It's not like I can tell the difference or anything."

She motioned to the phone, so he'd talk to his father. They could talk about how it's tough getting old after he hung up. But for now, if this whole thing *was* a lark on Martin's part, then this little farce needed to end, and her son needed some closure. Craig didn't disappoint her. He jumped back into the fray with both feet.

"Don't worry, Dad, I'll do some research online and see if we can't find the place again. Hey, maybe there's an even *better* place!"

Minuscule pause.

"What do ya mean, 'Yeah, maybe'? You don't sound so into this all of a sudden, Dad. I mean, where's all that enthusiasm you've had for the trip all along? How come you don't sound so psyched anymore? Don't you get it, Dad? Mom said we can go! Aren't you *getting* that?"

She watched her son's face for signs of understanding.

"Well, why aren't you excited? Did you have a bad day at work or something?"

"Or something," Janine muttered to herself, watching as Craig's eyes clouded over with concern. It looked like he was starting to get an inkling that he wasn't going to go on this trip.

But it was just an inkling, because he was still out there treading as fast as he could. She knew him well enough to know that he was trying to stay in the good mood he'd been in since she told him she'd let him go. She heard him ask, "So what do I need to pack for the trip? I want to start gathering everything and putting it together so I'm ready and we don't forget anything. Plus, there's probably lots of extra stuff I'll need to buy." He looked at her, begging her to help him continue on with his good mood.

She nodded her head and said, "I'll take you out for whatever you need."

"Way cool, Dad! Mom just said she'd take me out to get whatever I need. So we need to come up with a list of stuff to get. Since she's taking me, I'd like to get everything I need at once so she doesn't have to make a few trips. She's working on a big edit," he said to explain things, moving right next to her so he could give her a little hug.

He's such a great kid. Even in his happiest moment, he's still trying to be considerate of her time. That rat Martin didn't deserve him as his son!

Because Craig remained next to her, leaning against her, she heard Martin's reply in his most vicious voice. "Oh, so she's going to take time off from her precious work to take you out shopping, huh?"

"Yeah, she just said she would. Isn't that great? She's really being great about this," her son said, more for her benefit than his dad's. "I think she's growing up," he said, shooting her a killer smile and a wink. "You know, Dad, Mom's being *really* great about this whole thing. And don't forget, it'll be the first time ever that me and Mom won't be together for my birthday."

Oh God. She hadn't realized that. If Martin took Craig away for his birthday, they really would be apart for the first birthday ever. She could feel all the blood drain from her face. In fact she suddenly felt dizzy.

"...and at first I wondered if that was the real reason Mom didn't want me to go, but knowing her insane safety-related overcautiousness, I also knew that her primary argument—afraid I'd get hurt—was worrying her, too. You know, Dad," he said while looking over at her, "you have to realize that Mom's really given a *lot* to allow me to go on this trip. Knowing her as we do, you *know* this must be killing her inside. I mean, she can't change her thought process so easily. She's had too many years of ingrained fear and psycholike overprotection to get over it *that* quickly." He was leaning against her now. Speaking to her as well as to Martin. Damn, he was a great kid. Was he turning thirteen? Or thirty?

She smiled over at him, taking his free hand in hers.

"She's letting me grow up, Dad. Trusting me. This is more than just permission to go on a trip, this is like some huge honor," he said aloud. "All of a sudden, her intentions aren't lost on me. For Mom, this is big. Colossal. I'd say it's a redefinition of our relationship. And I really appreciate it." He looked at her and thanked her.

She smiled back, but it was still with sadness in her eyes. Sadness that he was probably about to get hurt. And sadness because she realized her little boy was growing up.

"Yeah," she heard Martin spit into the phone, "she's being really great about this! Put her on the phone, would you, Craig?"

"Sure," he said, then handed her the phone while whispering. "He wants to speak with you."

She nodded, her face suddenly losing the warm, sad smile, and in its place was a mask of indifference. That's the look she always got when she started a talk with Martin. Then soon after, the mask would shatter, and anger would replace the mask of indifference. "Martin," she said neutrally.

"I know what you're doing, you bitch!" he screamed at her.

Since he was standing right next to his mother, obviously anticipating the dates and list of things they'd have to purchase, Craig heard Martin's outburst and was shocked. He looked at her, confusion covering his face. "What's up with Dad? Why's he attacking you like that?"

She shrugged at her son's question and spoke into the phone. "Whatever do you mean, Martin?" she said calmly, innocently, since Craig was watching her and listening.

"You're *allowing* him to go on this trip?" he shrieked.

"Yes, Martin. I am. You invited him, and I know he wants to go, so after much thought, I've decided to let him go," she said calmly.

"This is total bullshit, you conniving bitch!" he shouted.

Craig's eyes shot wide-open, clearly shocked by what he heard his father saying but also amazed that his mother wasn't going ballistic. "Excuse me?" she asked evenly.

"I can't believe you're letting him go!" he barked. "This coming from the woman who would not go out alone with me after she gave birth to the kid, for fear that we'd both die in a car crash, orphaning him. This coming from the woman who always made us take separate flights if we needed to go somewhere because she didn't want to risk leaving him without parents. Your insane overprotectiveness is notorious and predictable, Janine!"

"So?" she said hesitantly. "What does that have to do with this? Those things could have happened, and I was just thinking of my son. Is that any reason to call me names, Martin?"

His voice was at the edge of hysteria now, and he was screaming so loud there probably wasn't a need to even have a telephone. They could have heard his rantings from his apartment to theirs with their naked ears.

She looked at Craig, who was clearly confused and couldn't believe his father was screaming at her for allowing him to go. Craig touched her arm and asked, "Doesn't he want to go? Why would he have asked me and caused so many fights between us if he didn't want to go?"

Janine knew the answer to that, but he needed to find out for himself, so she just shrugged.

"You're a bitch, Janine, because you know *damn well*, there is *no way in hell* you would have let the boy go on that trip, and I know it as well as you know it!"

"Well," she said smoothly, "maybe there *is* a way in hell, because I'm allowing you to take him." She looked at Craig and smiled. He returned her smile.

"You manipulative little conniving *bitch!*"

Craig's eyes went wide with astonishment. "Why's he cursing you out? And…why are you taking it?" He looked at her for an answer, but she just smiled tiredly at him and gave him another thumbs-up. She couldn't think of anything else to say or do.

"What's the matter, Martin?" she said into the phone, knowing full well what the matter was, but wanting Martin to be the one to say it. He'd started it, he needed to end it.

"Yeah, what's the matter?" Craig said more to himself than to anyone else.

"You know *full damned well* that I have no desire *whatsoever* to go on that *stupid* rafting trip! And you also knew that

I had absolutely *no intention* of going, you manipulative bitch!" he shouted before he slammed down the phone, disconnecting the line.

She didn't know if Craig heard Martin end the connection, but for lack of knowing what to do, since her son was looking at her with huge tear-filled eyes, she said, "We'll discuss the particulars another time, Martin, okay?" and hung up the phone.

After about thirty seconds of dead silence, which seemed more like thirty hours, Craig said softly, "Mom, you didn't have to say that for my benefit, or to protect me so. I heard him hang up on you. I also heard everything he shouted."

"I'm sorry, honey. I didn't mean to hurt you."

He shrugged his shoulders. "You didn't hurt me, Mom. He did."

"Well, I'm sorry for that. I've spent your entire lifetime trying to protect you from getting hurt."

He snorted a laugh. "Yeah, don't I know it."

"Well, when I started to suspect that he was just offering you this trip, knowing I'd say no and you and I would fight over it, I was upset to think he'd do such a thing. I didn't want you to get hurt."

Her son nodded solemnly. "I understand."

She wrapped her arms around him. "You're a good boy, Craig. I wish this had never happened. You were the one who got hurt in the end."

"It's not your fault."

"It's partly my fault."

"Nah, Mom. It's not. You tried to warn me."

She hugged him again, tightly. "I didn't know for sure."

"Even now you're still protecting me," he said softly. "But you know what?"

"What?"

"Now that I'm feeling the heavy disappointment and emptiness in my chest where my heart should be, I have to admit that maybe I still do need your protection." He paused a moment. "Now, since Dad doesn't want to go white-water rafting, how about you? It *is* my birthday."

He was a sarcastic little thing, but she adored him. She squeezed him tighter.

CHAPTER 15

"Janine Ruvacado, reporting for duty, sir!"

"Fall in, recruit," he said, sliding her already poured cup of coffee closer to the edge of the counter.

She hopped onto the empty stool, peering into the coffee cup—seeing blobs of melted chocolate and vanilla ice cream swirling on top. "Mmm, just the way I like it," she said with a smile.

"Just repeatin' previous orders, ma'am."

She laughed lightly. "Smart. Very smart," she said with a wink.

"Well, don't keep me waiting! Tell me how it went. Did Martin really want to go?"

She took a long sip of coffee and then smiled sadly. "No. You were right."

"I'm sorry. In this case I didn't want to be right."

"My heart aches for Craig. I know he's not a baby anymore, but he's *my* baby."

He nodded solemnly, lowering his cup to its saucer with a small clatter. "I understand. If you want to talk or vent, I'm here for you," he said gently.

"Well, I was so excited about telling Craig he could go, knowing he'd be thrilled but yet hoping we were wrong about things, I was energized and finished my self-allotted workload before schedule—"

"Good for you!" he interrupted. "How's that going?"

"You know? It's going well. I'm on a roll. I've got this well-focused drive and a different outlook, and am cutting, slicing and dicing like the Ron Popiel slice-o-matic."

"And boy, can it catch fish!" he said in his best announcer voice.

"That's the Ron Popeil Pocket Fisherman, silly."

"Oh. Sorry," he said, not looking sorry at all.

"Anyhow, so when Craig got home, I was sitting in the kitchen, eating some ice cream—"

"*More* ice cream?" he interrupted again.

"Do you want to hear the story or not?"

"Yes. Sorry," he said. This time he did look sorry. "Go ahead." He waved his hand as if giving permission.

She rolled her eyes. Yeah, like she needed his permission. "Anyhow, so I'm sitting at the kitchen counter, scarfing down some Ben & Jerry's when Craig comes home. And after a little tiff about my not wearing a bra, he—"

"Wait a minute." He held up his hands. "Just slow down a minute here. You weren't wearing a bra?'"

She sipped her coffee, licking the ice-cream mustache off her top lip. "No. I like to be comfortable when I work," she said matter-of-factly.

"So that means not wearing a bra?" He looked at her chest and winced.

Not quite the effect she'd like to have on men when they perused her chest area, but one she was familiar with, so it didn't bother her. Too much.

"Sometimes."

He smiled lasciviously, raising his eyebrows repeatedly. "Want a job at *my* office?"

She hadn't expected that, and laughed, sending bits of foamy melted ice cream to the other side of her cup. "As what?"

He shrugged. "Who cares?"

She laughed again. "If my next book is a flop I may have to take you up on that offer."

He nodded in response before barking like a drill sergeant. "Good. Now quit enticing me with your tangents, recruit, and tell me what happened when you told Craig he could go."

Her smile lit up her face. "Oh God, he was so excited! It was *wonderful*. He was so happy…he hugged me!"

"Is that unusual?"

"Lately," she admitted. "He's a teen. It's not cool," she explained. "And then we had a great dinner together, before he called his father."

"How did *that* go?"

She shook her head sadly. "Not well. He didn't even keep the brochure."

Tom looked at her with confusion, so she explained.

"It was all true that he was just trying to make me the bad guy and cause hard feelings between Craig and me. I couldn't believe it. It seemed to be stooping too low…even for Martin. He actually used my predictable overprotectiveness to assume that I'd never allow this trip. And when I changed my mind and allowed it, well, you had to *hear* the string of curses coming from that man's mouth!"

"Craig didn't hear, did he?" Tom asked with concern.

"At first I tried to hide it from him, but he was standing

pretty close to me, and Martin *was* screaming and shouting like such a lunatic, Craig did end up hearing the whole thing."

"I'm sorry for that. What did Martin say to Craig about the trip?"

"He did a whole bunch of back pedaling. He told Craig that he threw out the brochure when I'd said no, so he didn't have it anymore."

"That must have confused Craig."

"I think it did at first," she said, finishing the last of her coffee. She held up her cup. "I'm done, want a refill, too?" she asked as she hopped up and made her way around the counter to the other side.

"Sure," he said. "Thanks."

"No use calling someone over here just to refill a coffee cup," she said as she filled their two cups almost to the top, but left enough room for their special "cream." She put the coffeepot back on the warmer and turned to the freezer. Removing two huge vats of ice cream, she had to put them on the floor to get the leverage she needed to scoop out the ice cream. But each time her head popped up from behind the counter to put her newly acquired ball of ice cream into the mugs, she was grinning. "This is fun."

"You want to dive right in there, don't you?" he teased, referring to the vat before her.

"Yup," she said, "sure do."

The chocolate was almost gone and she really had to submerge herself to get the ice cream from the bottom. When she came up, she had a smudge of brown on the tip of her nose.

Putting the two vats back into the freezer, she pushed the cups to the other side of the counter and walked around again to plop back on her stool.

"So how did it end?" Tom asked her once they had both stirred the ice cream into the hot coffee. First things first.

"Well, I'm happy that the trip is off, for my sake, but Craig is miserable. I didn't want him to still think that he was going once his father put him off and then cursed me out like a raving madman—since he heard—so after I gave him a little time to himself to kind of let it all sink in, I went into his room and had a long talk with him."

"How did that go?"

She shrugged. "Not well. About as I'd suspected it would. He feels bad, he's upset and confused—which is understandable. He just found out his father is a schmuck who used him to hurt his mother."

"Sounds like he's an innocent bystander caught in the crossfire."

"He never knew that until last night. Now he certainly knows it. He's a smart kid. He may have wanted to be in denial about the trip, but he wasn't in denial about how his father used him."

"That must hurt."

Her eyes grew tired. "It did."

"And when he hurts, you hurt," he offered gently.

She closed her eyes at the reality and truthfulness of that simple statement. She felt Tom's arm wind around her shoulders. "Are you sure you don't have any kids? You really understand about them," she said with a slow, heavy sigh.

"Nope. No kids," he said gently.

"And you don't have any manipulative ex-husbands in your closet? Because you sure called *that* one correctly."

"No," he said on a long sigh, "no ex-husbands, either. And to set the record straight, I didn't call that one about Martin, Janine. *You* did when you explained his personality."

"Well, you helped me see it."

"Only by being a sounding board. That doesn't count."

"Sure it does. You helped prepare me for this whole thing and you showed me that I needed to prepare Craig."

"I think you already knew that. You just didn't want to see it. Just as I know I have a scheming ex-wife."

Her head rose with interest. "Oh? That's very interesting. I didn't know that," she said, looking at him sideways.

"Yup," he said noncommittally, smiling crookedly. "I, too, have some ugly skeletons."

"Veddy interesting," she said, sipping her coffee. "Tell me about her."

He shrugged. "What's there to tell?"

"Start at the beginning," she said, slurping loudly at the sweet foam floating atop her coffee.

"We met at the office. She was my secretary."

"Hmm. Convenient," she muttered.

"Yes, very," he responded, obviously not catching the sarcasm in her voice, or if he did, ignoring it. "I figured she of all people would understand why I had to put in such long hours at the office."

"Makes sense," she said, nodding.

"It did to me, too. At the time."

"I hear a 'but,'" she said.

"Yes. A but." He thought momentarily. "But I should have

known a young, exquisitely beautiful woman couldn't possibly have loved me the way she'd professed."

Exquisitely beautiful? That certainly knocked her already low self-image down a peg or two. "Humph," she uttered. "Why do you say that?" she asked him, wondering why he *would* say that? Did the man not own a mirror? Did he not know what good company he was? How smart and confident he came off?

"Because exactly twenty-four hours past the state-governed amount of time to qualify for half of everything I own, she told me she wanted a divorce."

"Ouch."

"Yes. Ouch. She also stated that she knew exactly how much I was worth since she *had* been my secretary, and informed me that she knew where all my assets were located—account numbers included."

"Youch!"

He nodded. "I didn't care about the money, really. It's only money and more could be made where that came from," he said honestly and without arrogance. "I was more hurt that she had manipulated me so badly. I really thought we were in love."

She didn't know how to respond. Her heart ached for the disappointed man sitting next to her. "And what was this exquisitely beautiful woman's name?" she asked, hoping to steer the conversation away from the emotional and more toward the practical. She had too much emotional stuff happening in her life right now to add more to it.

"Her name?" he asked, coming out of his reverie. "Angelina."

Angelina? It figures. What did you expect? An exquisitely

beautiful woman to have an ugly name? "I'm sorry, Tom. It sounds like she really hurt you. But if you want a woman's perspective…" She stopped there, waiting to see if he wanted to hear what she had to say, knowing that no one likes an opinion unless it's asked for or they know it's coming.

He nodded his head, interested to hear what she was about to say. "Go on."

"Well, Angelina's a half-wit. She may have thought she was playing you, but in the end, she was the idiot for leaving a man like you. *She* was the fool, Tom. Not you."

He stared at her. "Thank you, Janine. That was nice of you to say."

"I didn't say it to be nice," she said softly. "I said it because it's true."

He looked at her keenly, his eyes boring into her.

Starting to feel uncomfortable, she did what she always did when she wanted to change the mood. She cracked a joke. "I've dated, you know. I've been out there!" She grinned crookedly. "Sad to say, I probably have a lot more years on her, and therefore more experience, and am personally aware of the jerks, freaks and wimps out there. I think I've dated most of them."

He laughed as intended.

"Unfortunately for me, I married one that happened to combine all three of those lovely personality traits. A jerk, freak *and* a wimp. A triple threat!"

"A real winner," he said lightly.

"I'm a high achiever. Very goal oriented. I was going for three out of three."

She was happy to see he was smiling broadly, glad the serious, melancholy mood permeating their repartee was over.

"Looks like we both hit the jackpot," he said graciously.

"Hey, bud. Let's give credit where credit's due. In *that* race, I definitely won."

"What race?"

"The 'who could pick the bigger loser to marry' race."

"How can you be so certain you won?" he asked, curious.

"Heck, Tom, at least yours had looks. You had a trophy spouse. I already told you…mine looked like a plucked oven stuffer roaster."

"But paler and less buff," he added, laughing. "Yes, I remember."

"See?" she said with a pompous air. "I win hands down."

He leaned forward and wiped the chocolate off her nose with a napkin. "So it would appear."

"Is that how you concede all your losing business deals? By wiping their noses?"

He laughed heartily, a sound she was getting very used to hearing, and enjoying more than she knew she should. "Not all. Only the cute noses that have chocolate ice cream on them." He thought for a few seconds. "Probably about forty percent."

It was her turn to laugh.

"Now let's get on those treadmills. Time's a wastin' and the day's not getting any younger," he said.

"Clichés aside, I agree. I need to get my walking done so I can get back to that edit."

"Yes, and I have business deals to lose, and noses to wipe!"

"Better to wipe noses than to kiss butts," she muttered as she got off her stool.

He threw back his head and roared with laughter. "I agree wholeheartedly," he said when he finally calmed down.

They turned off the television sets before starting their machines, and as usual he warmed up by walking while she turned hers directly to the maximum speed she could stand. Or walk.

"I really…want to thank…you for helping…me out with the…trip thing."

"It was no problem. I didn't help much. I'm glad it worked out for you. Yesterday I was thinking of you all afternoon and evening. I was worried that it would go as it did."

"You…thought of me…all evening?"

He smiled at her, still walking calmly, still in control of his breath. "I didn't mean to tell you that. It just came out," he admitted.

So. He's thinking about you during the night, is he? That's a nice surprise. She didn't want him to know that he'd crossed her thoughts a few times yesterday, too. *More like a few thousand.* But who was counting?

He cleared his throat, bringing her attention back to the present. "The first day we met, you listed a whole bunch of problems you were having. One was your son, and that seems to be subsiding. Another was your ex-husband, and although that will never go away, you certainly held your own this last round. Your edit is well on its way from what you mentioned earlier, so what else can you fix?" he asked, turning the speed on his machine up to a brisk run.

"You know, I seem to have fixed all of those with a little help from you. Can you do hair?" she quipped.

He looked at her, already breathing hard. "I did nothing,

Janine. I keep telling you. I had nothing to do with you solving your problems. And what's wrong with your hair?"

Her eyes bulged out. "Are you blind, man? What's *not* wrong with it!"

"What does—" he panted "—that mean?"

"It's—" gasp, choke, gasp "—a mess!"

"It's—" pant, wheeze, huff "—adorable."

"You obviously…don't know…about hair."

"I know what I like," he said, making those weird phlegmy noises that she didn't mind all that much anymore now that she was getting used to them. "And I like your hair. It's cute." More sounds. "Please don't change it."

Taken aback, and a little self-conscious, she changed topics. "Well, my agent won't…return my…calls." *Where had that come from?*

"Why not?"

"Don't…know." She needed a few seconds to breathe. "Last two books…not bestsellers."

She saw him thinking. He had a wonderful mind. She could actually imagine the gears turning inside his head. "Have you looked for another?" he finally said.

"Another what?"

"Looked for…another agent."

"I couldn't!" she gasped loudly. She and Sid had been through so much together. She owed him so much. He'd launched her career. "I'd never…betray him."

"He doesn't…know that."

She looked at the man next to her. Sweat was already ringing his T-shirt, and he was huffing like the wolf of the Three Little Pigs.

"Why don't you...make some...calls, Janine?"

"But why?" she whined loudly, her voice modulation altered by her lack of air.

He waited until he could talk more smoothly. "The reason's twofold." He puffed a few times. "First, it will make...*you* feel better." He waited, trying to gather his breath until his breathing was steady again. "And secondly, it will make your agent know...that others want you."

Her face was starting to get hot, catching up with the rest of her body. "How...do you know...the others...will want me?" she said, between what sounded like asthmatic inhalations of air. She looked at him. Sweat was now dripping from his chin, and he was running hard. Never in a million years would she have ever guessed this man's opinion would mean so much to her, but for some puzzling reason, it did.

"They will," he said with confidence, certain of his answer.

They finished their walking and running deep in their own thoughts.

She was thinking about whether she should call other agents. It couldn't hurt. She wasn't being disloyal to Sid by making a couple of calls. And it would help her gauge her popularity as an author. It might even help her confidence if she knew other agents would want to steal her away from Sid. Lord knows he certainly wasn't enamored with her lately. He wouldn't even return her calls or e-mails. Maybe a bit of competition might be good for them both. Sid *and* her.

On the other hand, what if the other agents laughed in her face and didn't want her either? Then what? How would she face her career after *that* vicious blow to her ego? Did she even *want* to know? Could she handle it if they had no interest in her? There was a time every agent from New York to California had wanted her. But now? How did they feel now?

It was a horrible business—the whole literary field. A writer needed the skin of a freaking rhinoceros. It was the quintessential "what have you done for me lately?" business. There was no accounting for what you'd done before. It wasn't even a case of "you are only as good as your last book." No. In this business, it was more like "you're only as good as your *next* blockbuster."

Well, she'd think about it. She didn't have to make her decision right then. Whether she made the calls or not was her choice and was in her control. Just then she realized that *she* was the one to decide what to do with her future. She held the cards, and that alone made her feel empowered.

CHAPTER 16

That day she placed three calls to agents who handled her style of writing and her kind of work. All three were attentive and showed definite signs of interest.

"I didn't know you were thinking about leaving Sid," the first one said.

"I'm not sure I am, I just wanted to see if you would be interested in handling my work in case I made that decision."

"I certainly would! I *love* your stuff. I've been reading you for years."

That had been a nice boost to her ego, but thinking the woman was falsely leading her on, Janine tried another.

This was a man who had the reputation of being a shark. Well, worse than a shark. A shark that ate sharks. She'd never considered him before, because she didn't like the way he did business, or at least how he was rumored to do business, but she was curious and called him.

"Janine Ruvacado. Excellent to hear your voice," he said smoothly.

A shiver ran down her spine, and a sense of mistrust raised the hair on the back of her neck. She felt sullied already. "Yes, well, I was wondering if you'd be interested in possibly representing me should I decide to reconsider my contract with Sid."

"You work on a contract basis? I'd never hold you to a contract. I'd want you to want my representation, whether we negotiated a contract or not." Oh yes, he was a shark, all right.

"Well, to be honest, Sid and I haven't had a contract in years. I was just wondering if you were interested."

"There is no contract?" he asked with abundant interest.

"Well, no. But I haven't made a decision yet until I consider all of my options."

"Keep this option open, Janine dear. I'd love to have you as my client. I also think you'd be much happier with me than you've been with Sid."

Feeling disloyal, she admitted, "I've been very happy with Sid, it's just that recently I decided to consider my options, that's all."

"Well, consider me as one of them, Janine. Please."

The third call went the same way. So obviously she hadn't lost it completely, and was still considered a good risk by agents, even if her last two books weren't heavy hitters.

Feeling lucky—and confident, thanks to the realization that she was still a wanted commodity—she decided to call the IRS without hearing back from Sid, thinking that if God forbid she decided to move to a different agency, she wouldn't have Sid to help her out anyhow.

Dialing the number listed on the letter, she was connected with a man that she would bet *anything* was sitting in his colorless office wearing brown corduroy pants and a matching brown knitted argyle vest with a clashing polka-dot bow tie to complete the entire ensemble. His voice held the excitement of an announcer giving a blow-by-blow description of grass growing in three-second intervals; his inflection and tone were without any animation whatsoever. He probably lived at home with his mother, too, which was sad because he sounded as if he was in his late thirties.

"We need to see proof of income, ma'am."

"Do you want me to send you copies of my check stubs?"

"No, ma'am, we won't know if you are sending all of them."

"Oh. Good point. Well, I *have* all of them, I can send them all. Or I can send you a copy of the fax from my agent listing all moneys I've earned last year. It's some kind of tax form, I think. I can send you that, too."

"Just the fax, ma'am." His monotonous voice made her uncomfortable. Was the man alive? Was he even human? The monotonic drone was unnerving.

She laughed a bit hysterically. "That's funny."

"What's funny, ma'am?" he intoned like a robot in a B-rated movie.

"What you just said. You know, 'just the fax, ma'am' like in, 'just the facts, ma'am.'"

"It wasn't meant to be funny, ma'am."

Obviously, this man had the sense of humor of smallpox. What a catch! "So I'll send you the fax from my agent."

"Yes, ma'am."

"And I guess you'll call me if that settles things?"

"No, ma'am. That's not company procedure."

"So how will I know if this is settled?"

"You won't, ma'am, until you get a letter."

"A letter saying what?"

"Saying that you've met the required proof of substantiation, or you still owe us back taxes."

Her stress level had just shot up again. "So, this won't settle it?" she shrieked.

"I don't know, ma'am," he said calmly in that annoying monotone. So calmly, he sounded bored. He was making her life a living hell, and he was *bored?*

Before she got herself riled up and started screaming at the nerd at how he was one of the prime reasons her life was a screwed-up, frustrating mess, she smartly decided to put a sock in it and hang up the phone before she ticked off the mama's boy, causing him to do an all-out witch hunt on her finances. Her limp, sagging finances.

This was maddening! How was *she* supposed to know what they wanted? How was *she* supposed to guess what would make the IRS stop hounding her? She was certain there were papers out there that could easily prove to them that she was not trying to rob them of their precious share of her income, but for the life of her, she had no clue what those papers were! She was a writer, not a businesswoman, damn it. A high-strung, creative, hardworking schlub whose cut of the profits couldn't even put enough food on the table lately! And the realization of that was hard enough for her to deal with without having to somehow prove her financial unsuccessfulness to the powerful bunch of bloodhounds nipping at her heels!

"Thanks," she muttered into the phone, hoping the venom behind her single word wasn't heard by the dolt in the death-job. She hung up the phone gently. Calmly. Professionally. Then she picked it back up, slowly lifted it to her ear, listened for and heard the dial tone, then slammed it down with as much force as she could muster. "And screw you, you little sniveling virgin!" she shouted. "Thanks for *nothing!* Thanks for making my life a living *hell!* Thanks for adding one more straw to the camel's friggin' *back*, you little ball buster! You weasel! You…you…*virgin!*"

She smiled, and sighed quickly. *Feel better?*

"Yup," she said aloud, before pulling up her book to work on the rewrite.

She was still at it when Craig came home.

"Hey, Mom. How's it hanging?"

It was obvious he was trying to forget last night's disastrous phone conversation with his father, because based on his tone, she was once again the good guy. "Everything's hanging," she quipped. "Well, except I'm wearing a bra for you. So there are actually two less things hanging today."

He came into her room and rolled his eyes before he kissed the top of her head. "Thanks for sharing, Mom."

"No problem, son." She beamed up at him.

"You're in a good mood. Anything happen I should know about?"

She shrugged, feeling sorry for him. She knew deep down he was secretly hoping the trip would be back on. "I called the IRS to try to straighten things out with them."

"Did you?"

She shrugged again and made a face. "Who knows?"

"That's it? You seem pretty chipper for someone who may or may not have handled her problems with the gov."

She smiled. "The *gov?*"

"—ernment. You know, the government."

"Yeah, I figured it out. I'm broke, not stupid," she said with a lopsided grin. "And yes, there was something else that happened."

He did the eyebrow thing at her again.

"I called a couple of agents to see if they'd be interested in representing me."

His face registered shock. "You're leaving Sid?"

"No." She shook her head quickly, waving her hands before her. "No, no, no. I just wanted to see if they were interested, figuring if they were, my career wasn't shot."

"What makes you think your career's shot?"

"My last two books."

"What about them?"

"They weren't bestsellers."

"So?"

"So I figured Sid's not returning my calls or e-mails because my fame is fading."

"Who said your fame is fading? Everywhere I go, I see some lady reading your books. Today on the school bus I saw this girl, Margaret, with her nose in one of your books."

"You did?"

"Yeah."

"Was it one of the new ones?"

"How should I know? I just saw your name printed across it in big blue letters, and hid behind the seat."

"Big blue letters? Was the background coral?"

He stared at her blankly.

"Like a peach color," she explained.

"Yeah, I think so."

"Oh, good! That *was* one of my latest."

"Well, she seemed to be into it. Every time Hector Rivera tried to talk to her, she ignored him completely."

Spirits lifted, she said, "Oh, that's nice," and then added, "except for Hector."

He waved a dismissive hand at her. "Oh. Not to worry. Margaret always ignores Hector."

Talk about a buzz kill. "Oh."

"But she was really into your book, Mom. I could tell."

It was her turn to roll her eyes. "Thanks for trying."

He looked at the broken treadmill, which now housed a pair of shorts, some limp socks, and a brassiere draped over its arms. "So what's up with the treadmill?"

She shrugged. "Guess the part's not in yet."

"Want me to go down to Ben Franklin's and see if I can get him to hurry it up?"

She looked at the treadmill, which still looked like it was flipping her the bird, and then thought of Tom Kennedy. She was getting used to their little talks and would miss those. Just being able to talk to him and unload some of her emotional baggage had helped her out a few times already. And the man's adamant approval of her out-of-control hair helped endear him to her, too. In a way, she hoped that Ben didn't get the part too quickly. Tom Kennedy was growing on her.

"Are you sure you want to go down there?" she asked her son, hoping to get him to take back his offer.

Sighing as if he needed great patience, he said, "Not everyone thinks the basement is haunted, Mom."

"First of all, it's the sub-basement. And I don't think it's haunted, just creepy. And you'll think so too when the entire building collapses on it one day."

She watched her son shake his head and sigh. "Mom, has anyone ever told you, you're a trip?"

His comment didn't deserve an answer.

"So you want me to go ask, or not?"

She shrugged. "No, you don't have to." Thoughts of Tom Kennedy won. If it hadn't been for him, she'd be on the phone 24/7 with Ben, hounding him to fix that machine pronto!

Craig did his homework, so she kept working, and stopped only to make and eat dinner. Afterward she didn't even bother doing the dishes, just piled them in the sink and rinsed them quickly, figuring they weren't going anywhere and she'd get to them when she wasn't as caught up in her work.

It was after midnight when she looked up from cutting and hacking at her bulky manuscript. Stretching up from her chair, she took a deep breath and yawned. Tired, she wandered down the hall to her son's room and kissed his head, whispering her usual "Mommy loves you," before pulling off his heavy, black boots.

Tucking his blanket around his body, she stood for a few minutes to watch him sleep. His breathing was hypnotic, and for a second she wanted to crawl in there next to him and cuddle with him as they'd done when he was a small boy, but as tired as she was, she'd probably fall asleep the minute her head hit his pillow and she didn't want to freak him out when he woke up in the morning.

Her thoughts turned to Tom Kennedy. She was surprised at how pleased she was that he liked her horrible hair. And not just her hair. She was self-conscious of a few things about herself and his mentioning them, and complimenting her, surprised her. She had a few sore spots that might possibly set her off if they were prodded, targeted, or she were somehow inadvertently provoked. Like for example, her thunder thighs, or her crazy hair, or her huge butt, her spindly legs, her inept bookkeeping skills, her large nose, her thick waist, her small breasts, yes—definitely her small breasts, her flabby arms, her ugly feet, her bad taste in men, her stumpy fingernails, her microscopic eyes, her uneven ears, her volatile temperament, her thin lips, her impossible mother, and did she mention her small breasts?

Well, maybe she was a little oversensitive.

CHAPTER 17

Tom was already on the running portion of his workout when she finally arrived.

"Hey, stranger," he said between huffs.

"Hi," she said unenthusiastically.

"What's wrong?" he asked.

She looked at him as he struggled with his run and smiled. "What makes you think something's wrong?"

"Can…just…tell," he said between huffs.

She watched him in the mirror as she bent over and piled her stuff next to her usual treadmill, the one adjacent to his. She smiled to herself at the thought that people are such creatures of habit. Humans are so predictable. Once they sat in a chair the first time, they found their comfort zone, and for every future time they were in the same room, they would automatically sit in the same chair. It was almost always so.

She was thinking these thoughts because she didn't want to think too much about her impending doom with the almighty IRS, and how in the near future she might be doing her little doctor-prescribed walking at a little day room in Sing Sing. She wondered if the other ladies in the prison would be dangerous or more like, say, Martha Stewart. Her chances of being surrounded by a jailful of ladylike sorority sisters who could write a book on etiquette seemed pretty remote, and she shivered at the thought of ending up being some jailbird's "woman."

This thought had coursed through her mind since she hung up with the guy at the IRS, and knowing she'd need a diversion before she started crying, she packed a tape in her gym bag. She knew herself well enough to know that keeping her mind busy was the only way to keep her active imagination under control.

She didn't realize she was presently mooning Tom as she sifted through her stuff, looking for the tape. "I brought a tape of *Family Feud*, thinking they might have a VCR around here. I've been taping it right along and have about five days of show to watch. Wouldn't want to get too far behind," she said, as she turned around with a flourish and produced a cartridge. "It beats the Muzak, and *is* kind of fun," she said, hoping he'd never know of her pending possible brush with imprisonment. "I thought you'd get a kick out of it," she said as cheerfully as she could while waving the black rectangle around, searching for a VCR.

There wasn't one in sight, so she laid the tape on top of her pile of stuff, and hopped aboard the treadmill. "Hmm, doesn't seem to be one here," she said glumly.

"So, what's going on?" he asked, breathing heavily. He obviously wasn't the type of person who could just let things drop.

And she, obviously, wasn't the type of person who could just keep shoving things down. She caved instantly. "I called the IRS yesterday and asked what they wanted to get off my back with their stupid claim that I owe back taxes, and the nerd on the other end of the phone said I needed to fax over a document that I'd gotten from my agent, Sid. So I sent it right away. But I don't know if that's what they want, so I'm waiting and trying not to think too much about what my cell-mates will be like, although I keep getting visions of two-hun-dred-pound biker babes with greasy hair, missing teeth, and cat-o'-nine-tails," she blurted out as she turned the treadmill up to her usual speed. *Yeah, there you go, girl! That's the way to not let him know of your possible brush with future imprison-ment. You've got a real hold over those loose lips! Whatever hap-pened to the woman that wouldn't let anyone in? The cautious, guarded, walled-in woman!*

"And?" he huffed, obviously ignoring the latter part of her diatribe but focusing on the main, rational part of her ver-bal tirade.

"And, the guy said the fax machine was somewhere else so he couldn't see what I sent right away, but I would hear from them one way or another eventually." She was starting to get winded.

"So, what happened?" he said efficiently.

"So, I didn't want to let it sit—" she paused for breath "—because I just want to solve this—" more breath "—and get it off my mind…"

"That's perfectly understandable," he said without a smile or grimace that could be interpreted as a smile, so he was probably referring to the financial troubles, not the room-mate possibilities.

"Yeah." She huffed a little, both with annoyance and breathlessness. "So I called the little nerd bastard this morn-ing." She paused for a few deep inhalations. "That's why I was later than usual," she said between wheezing gasps of breath, "and he said…that the thing I'd sent was not—" she was getting agitated again, which only added to her inability to get air into her lungs "—what he needed." She felt like she was going to burst out in tears, and probably would have, if she could breathe.

"What does he need?"

She gasped a few times before answering. His simple question made it sound so easy. Like if she'd just give them what they needed, they'd go away! "I don't know. He gave me some examples—" she made some choking sounds "—of what I should send. I wrote them down."

"Do you have the list?"

She looked at him and made a face as if to say, *Yes, I always carry around the list of what the IRS told me I need to send them for proof that I am not a criminal who is trying to cheat them out of the back taxes they insist that I owe them.* She said, "No." It was easier to say, and took less air.

But he was smart with people, and he read her face. "Janine," he said with a laugh, "your face told me what I'd needed to know *without* your monosyllabic response." She frowned appropriately. "But I could look through your papers if you'd like—" he took a few ragged breaths to get air into his lungs "—to help you find something that would appease them."

She looked at him with surprise and gratitude. "Thanks."

"Actually, I'm hoping you'll permit me to do anything that would allow me more time with you. When you were late this morning, I'd been worried that I'd never see you again. Hell, I'd reduced myself to praying that you hadn't gotten your treadmill fixed before we could spend some quality time together." He stopped talking for a second and looked at her directly. "It's been a long time since I've prayed for anything, and although I don't attend church often, I'd hoped I still had a connection or two, or at the very least, one prayer left to be granted."

What a sweet thing to say. She was speechless.

"When I saw your reflection in the glass mirrors as you came in this morning, I first thought you were a mirage, but when you plopped down your stuff, and I saw your, ah, bottom, I knew you weren't an illusion. No illusion of *mine* ever had such a cute butt."

Of course she realized he was just trying to coax her out of her bad mood with his comment, but his words made her mind wander to the whole "being a jailbird's woman" thing, and she quickly wanted to do anything—*anything*—to make sure she didn't end up in jail. "My papers…are a mess…but you…can look through…them if you'd…like," she said. "In fact…I'd…appreciate it…greatly!"

He was walking now, doing his cooldown, so his voice and breathing had become strong again. "I'd like that," he said, smiling at her as he wiped the sweat off his chin with his shoulder.

She nodded.

Regrettably, he finished much sooner than she did today. But that was because she'd gotten there so late thanks to the time on hold waiting to get through to the IRS guy.

"I have a couple of calls I'd like to make, Janine, but I'm not leaving yet. I'll be back in a little while," he said with a smile.

"Okay," she said, not minding the way he was looking her up and down. By now it was no surprise to him that her backside jiggled like Jell-O as she stomped away her miles on the treadmill. Of course it would be wonderfully fortunate if he found it sexy as hell and got him hot, but she doubted it. If he did get hot over her rolling cellulite, he'd need a psychiatrist more than she did! And she needed one desperately.

"I love the way you hang on for dear life, and go at it aggressively," he said with a deep, smooth voice.

"What?" she said, shocked by his provocative words.

"You're a woman to be reckoned with, Janine. And I'd love to be the man to do the reckoning." He stared at her boldly. "I'd reckon you for hours!" he said, before turning to leave.

She watched him walk away with her mouth hanging open. Was the man insane? Her eyes flicked to the mirror in front of her. She was blotchy and sweaty. Her short-cropped hair was matted and wet, plastered to her scalp. She had on no makeup, and her thighs were reverberating with every step she took. *Was the man insane?*

He was sitting at the front desk, using the phone. A better word for it may have been "commandeering." Based on what she saw, he was clearly barking in orders to someone. Not in an obnoxious way, but in a way that indicated to Janine that he was used to giving instructions. And used to having them followed, too. She watched him—his facial expressions, his body language—and had to admit that she liked what she saw. She liked commanding men. Admired them. Martin would probably say it's because she was one herself.

She laughed at the thought. Yes, she was a bit domineering, but that was because she'd needed to be. Her mother would have eaten her alive had she been a shy, soft-spoken girl, so in self-defense, she toughened up. And once she left home and was fascinated with and enchanted by Martin's lack of force and his go-wherever-the-wind-blew-him temperament (never having seen or experienced anyone like that before), she married him before realizing that he was just an indecisive man with namby-pamby ways. It was hard *not* to take command once she realized his previously delightful, spineless demeanor now meant they wouldn't have enough money to feed, clothe or house themselves. When she became pregnant and had Craig, she realized *someone* had to take charge, and things sort of went downhill from there. She lost any piddling amount of respect she tried to hang on to for him, and Martin saw her as a backbreaking, hair-scaring, guru-souring shrew. Oh yeah, who made him ejaculate prematurely. She always forgot that one!

Not wanting to think about Martin for a moment longer, she switched gears as she looked at Tom on the phone and thought back to their conversation where he had described his childhood. She tried to picture him as a boy: lost, motherless, fighting to survive, struggling to make something of himself. He had certainly done well. Not that she knew how well his business was doing, but he was a strong man who seemed to have made a pretty good life for himself. At least he wasn't a wimp who blamed everyone else for his shortcomings.

She saw him say thank you into the phone before he hung it up, nodded his head tersely, and looked over at her. Embarrassed to get caught spying, she quickly turned her head, which explained why she didn't see him walk to her.

"Do you have much longer?" he asked, making her jump.

"Any amount seems like 'much longer' to me."

He laughed as he sat down on the floor next to her treadmill, and regaled her with a story about an IRS audit at his business that made her problem with them seem as small and imperceptible as a single leaf in the Brazilian rain forest. It made her feel that maybe, just maybe, her problem with them wasn't so bad.

"So did you work it all out?"

"Sure! You just have to give them the exact little form in the exact little way they need to receive it. Once you do that, and they can process your paperwork in the manner to which they're accustomed, your problem will be over."

"It's as easy as that?"

"As easy as one, two, three," he said as he clapped his hands together three times, punctuating what he said.

It was then, about five minutes after they'd started their conversation—or it could have been seven minutes—that the gym's door opened, and a man carrying a VCR walked through.

"Hi, Bill," Tom called to the man, waving his hands overhead to get the man's attention.

"Hi, Mr. Kennedy," he called back, walking over to the bank of treadmills.

"Tom, please," Tom insisted to the man when he'd arrived nearby. Tom turned to Janine. "I don't know why people insist on being so formal, I've never understood that. Bill, this is Janine. Janine, Bill."

This had to be an unusual occurrence at a gym, but being new to the whole gym experience, she wasn't really sure. "Pleasure to meet you, Bill."

"Likewise," he said politely before turning back to Tom. "Okay. I've got your VCR here. Where do you want it?"

"I'd like it installed here, by the treadmills. Attached to the right-hand television," he said aloud.

"Are you allowed to do that?" Janine asked Tom.

"I don't see why not? It improves the gym, doesn't it? Why wouldn't they want something that improves the gym?"

He had a point. "But shouldn't you ask Matt first?"

He nodded brusquely. "Good idea. I'll go ask him now. Can you wait a minute?"

Bill shrugged. "Sure. No problem."

Janine kept walking, trying to ignore the chaos going on around her. When Tom returned with Matt in tow, she now had an audience of three men watching her fat, jiggly thighs and butt.

Okay, so in reality, no one was even paying the slightest bit of attention to her. Not even remotely. Until Tom said to Bill, "And when you're done, will you please give the remote to the lady on the treadmill?"

Bill shrugged as if to say he didn't care who got the remote. "Sure thing. But I'll need a ladder first."

They walked to the rear of the gym and Bill came back carrying a ladder under his arm. Tom followed with the VCR and watched as Bill set up the VCR quickly and efficiently. He was a good mechanic.

"Do you...fix treadmills?" Janine asked him.

"Why, is one broken?" he said, looking at the treadmills.

"Not here. I...have a broken...one at home."

Strangely, Bill looked at Tom before answering. She couldn't see Tom because he was beyond her peripheral vision, but she found it strange that Bill would look his way before responding.

"Sorry, Janine, I'm more electrical than mechanical," was all he said.

"Too bad," she said. "Looks like…you do good work…and you have the…nice habit of…cleaning up after…yourself. A trait…I've grown to know…is not always…a part of someone…in your…line of work."

"Thanks," Bill said, a smile making his face glow, "I appreciate that. I like to take pride in my work." He packed up his stuff and left with a casual "See y'all around."

Tom turned to Janine. "Mind if I pop your tape in?"

"I can't believe…you just did that…for me." She waved at the VCR.

He shrugged. "It was nothing."

"Well…thanks—" she paused to catch her breath "—anyhow." She tried to smile, but it probably didn't come off that way.

He turned to get the tape and she noticed his broad shoulders again.

"You'll have…to hit…rewind," she muttered, annoyed with her reaction to him.

"Okay," he said as he rewound the tape. He stood there watching her as the tape slowly rewound. "To the beginning?"

"Yes," she puffed. "And kindly…stop…watching me," she said with a smile.

"I'm trying not to watch as you tread along, but I can't seem to tear my eyes from you."

"Like…looking at…a car wreck."

That brought a hearty laugh. "You're so funny. I don't think you see yourself as others see you."

"Let's see… My hair's…drenched with sweat…" she said, unable to continue for lack of breath. "My face is…all red." She tried to catch her breath. "My shorts are all…"

"So? You're working out. What do you think you're supposed to look like?"

She snorted with self-repugnance, shaking her head in disgust. "Better than this."

"You think so? That's not very realistic of you," he said, while looking her in the eyes as she pounded away.

She didn't know what to say, so the seconds ticked by. "I just really hate this," she said.

The tape still hadn't clicked at its start, it was still whirring. "So tell me, Janine, what's on this tape?"

"*Family Feud…* One hundred people…are polled."

"What are they polled about?"

"Anything," she grunted.

"Like what?" he asked.

"I don't know. Just…anything. You'll have to…see it to get…what I mean."

He sat down to watch her tape with her as she clumped along on her treadmill.

"*What household pet can you leave alone for a couple days?*" Richard Karn asked the two people standing at his desk area.

One person hit the buzzer quickly, got to respond first, and said, "Cat." That got a ding, and was the number-one answer, so they walked to his family on the right to ask them the same question.

The next person said, "Dog."

"Who would leave a dog home alone for a few days? Just picturing the mess the animal would leave is enough to not say 'dog,'" Tom said as he looked at her. She was shaking her head negatively. But wouldn't you know, it was met with a bing—a couple of people had voted for dog.

"Now *that's* stupid!" she spat out.

"I agree. I wouldn't leave a dog home alone for a few days," he said.

"Me neither," she said between huffs.

The next person said, "Hamster." She figured that was a safe bet, and watched to see if hamster was on the list. Surprisingly, it wasn't. That got a buzz noise.

"I'd leave a hamster home alone for a few days before I'd leave a dog home alone for a few days," Tom said to her.

She looked at him and nodded. "Yeah…me too…. People…are idiots!"

He laughed at her concise retort.

The next person said, "Snake."

"Snake?" he asked aloud. "Who has snakes as pets?"

She made a face. "You'd be…surprised."

And he *was* surprised. Surprised that snake was one of the listed answers. "Hey, now wait a minute. Hamster wasn't up there, but *snake* was up there? Is that supposed to mean that more people have snakes as pets than hamsters? I know I'm sounding foolishly incredulous, but I am. Who are they polling?" he asked with a sputter. "Have I been working so hard and out of touch with reality for that long that this could be true?"

Janine laughed. Then choked. Then lost her footing and almost fell off her machine.

"I'm sorry. I didn't mean to make you try to kill yourself," he said with concern.

"Now you see why I hang on for dear life? I'm not too coordinated."

"Perhaps," he countered, "you're just not used to it."

When she was once again centered on the treadmill, she answered. "Hopefully, no one in...my building prefers snakes...to hamsters."

He laughed. "I'm having a great time sitting on the floor watching *Family Feud* with you. I may just give up my day job to do this permanently."

"No..." she choked out. "Don't give up...your day job."

He laughed as the next person said, "Bird."

"Okay, I can see that," he said distinctly, turning to catch her nod of agreement.

Then that family said a couple of things that were not up there and ran out of things to say.

"What happens now?" he asked.

"Each family...is allowed three...wrong answers...before the other...family gets a chance...to steal all...the points."

He nodded and turned to watch the show.

Meanwhile she forgot where she was and started screaming at the television. "Fish. Fish! FISH!" as if they could hear her.

When it came time for the second family to get their shot at stealing the points, she was screaming "fish" so loudly, Tom must have gotten caught up in the excitement and he started to scream, "Yeah, fish!" at the TV, too.

They must've heard all the screaming and yelling even in California, where the show was taped, because *that* family said, "Fish," and ended up winning the round.

"This is so exciting!" Tom said, smiling like a young school kid who had just gotten a hard question right. The show went to commercial. "How come gerbil and hamster weren't good? I'd leave them alone for a couple of days. A hell of lot more so than I'd leave a dog!"

She was done with her walking and stepped off the treadmill, heading straight for a towel. She patted her face and swiped at her neck, pulling her sweat-soaked T-shirt from her skin with a pluck. "That question only listed the top five answers from the people polled." She ran the towel over her arms and draped it around her neck. "Sometimes they have the top-polled four, five, six, seven or eight answers. But Richard always tells you how many answers there are. And he also tells you if they polled, say, one hundred married men, or one hundred single women, or one hundred people in general."

He nodded. "I get it."

The game was back on. *"One hundred people were polled and the top five answers are on the board. What do you do more of around Christmastime?"* Richard Karn asked.

"Eating," Tom called out.

Janine patted his leg as she sat down next to him on the floor. "Good answer! You're pretty good at this," she said, and flashed him a big smile. "Shopping," she screamed up at the television.

Tom laughed. "I bet that's up there!" he said.

"Hey! What's all the screaming about?" Matt came over and asked. "Oh good. I see you're watching the *Feud*. I was worried for a while there while I was spotting Brian. You two were screaming 'fish' so loudly we thought you guys had suddenly simultaneously come down with some kind of culinary Tourette's."

They all laughed.

"Nope. No Tourette's. Just the *Feud*," Janine said to Matt.

Tom was already watching again, and cursed when his "attend office parties" wasn't one of the top answers. "Hell," he muttered, "at Christmastime, that's all I seem to do!"

She patted his cheek and said, "Well, 'parties' was on the top five."

"Yeah, but it only got two votes," he whined.

"Remind me not to compete with *you*," she said with a wink. "You're very competitive, and a sore loser!"

"I'm used to getting what I want," he said with a leer and a wink.

"Should I be afraid?" she asked coyly.

"Very afraid," his deep voice rumbled.

And suddenly, she was.

CHAPTER 18

Luckily, *Family Feud* wasn't the type of program that prolonged or sustained her state of fear. How could one possibly think of a scary future together with someone else when they'd spent the past half hour playfully bickering over possible answers to inane questions? After they'd watched two shows, she turned off the VCR.

"Hey, I was getting into that!"

His childish outburst made her laugh. "We'll watch two more tomorrow."

"Good. I can't wait," he said.

She looked at him sideways. "If I didn't know better, I'd think you meant that."

"I do," he said, sounding sincere. "Not to be a downer—or change the subject—but would you like me to stop by your place to look at those IRS papers?"

She pictured the mess in her room and quickly said, "Maybe some other time."

"Ah. Shot down," he said quietly. "I understand."

"No. No, you don't," she said, putting her hand to his chest. *Hmm. Hard.* "I wasn't trying to shoot you down, I was just thinking of my messy room."

"Oh," he said, looking cheered. "That really wouldn't

bother me, but if you're shy about stuff like that, how about I give you a fifteen minute head start, so you can clean up?"

She thought of the dishes still in the sink from last night, then thought of the reason they were still there and got angry all over again.

Tom laughed.

"What's so funny?" she huffed, reminded that she had no reason to be in a good mood.

"You," he said. "What were you thinking about just then?"

"My sinkful of dishes and pots from last night's dinner, and the dweeb that I spent all morning on the phone with, which is *why* I never got to do last night's dishes." She made the executive decision not to mention to him that she'd decided against doing the dishes after the call, because the call had already made her late for her usual gym time and she didn't want to miss seeing him. It sounded a bit too needy, and she wouldn't want him to think that she was, even if, well, maybe she *was*. She also didn't think this was a good time to tell him she was a complete slob and let him know how infrequently she cleaned her room. The last time she'd made her bed, disco was all the rage. She had the feeling that she'd disappoint him if he knew all this about her, and she didn't want to disappoint him before any relationship had even started. There'd be plenty of time for disappointment once a relationship was formed. There always was.

"Dirty dishes in a sink won't bother me," he said earnestly.

"It would bother *me* if you saw them."

He nodded. "Okay. It was just an idea."

Aw. He looked so dejected. "How about tonight, after you finish work?" she suggested, wondering where *that* invite had come from. Yes, she liked the guy—he was nice, good-looking, smart, easy to be with, and although she'd tried, she couldn't find anything wrong with him. Yet. But even with all that, she'd just committed herself to cleaning her apartment for him. *What were you thinking?*

She looked at him to see what he'd just done to get her to make that outrageous offer, and saw nothing strange. No voodoo dolls, no magic box, nothing. Just a guy who looked thrilled. Which was flattering, of course, but she wondered why anyone would look thrilled to review someone else's business letters and forms for the IRS. It was anyone's guess. Especially hers.

"That would be great, Janine. I'll see you tonight." He stood and offered his hand to help her get up. She took it, thankful for the assistance. Once she was sitting somewhere for any length of time, rigor mortis set in and it was hard to get her aching bones upright.

"Hey listen," he said, as if he'd just thought of something. "Since you're already doing one set of pots, pans, and dinner dishes today, how about if I bring dinner tonight so you don't have to do two?"

"Are you kidding? I'd be an idiot if I said no to that!"

"And?" he said.

"And I'm not an idiot," she said with a hearty laugh. "Sure, Tom, that would be lovely. Thank you for offering. That was very thoughtful of you."

"I'm a thoughtful kind of guy. Plus, it'll be my pleasure." He beamed. "Is it just you and your son?"

She looked at him slyly. "Let's see," she said, counting on her fingers. "There's me, my son, the gerbil, the hamster, the bird and the fish."

"I guess fish and chips is out then," he said with a grimace. She'd been kidding, of course, but he didn't know that. Any animal that was unfortunate enough to reside in the Ruvacado apartment—be it a wanted critter or not—usually ended up the same way. Lying on its back with its feet in the air, wedged under something until she or Craig smelled the decomposing carcass and had to flush it down the toilet or call Mr. Franklin to remove and dispose of it. But again, it was way too soon for him to know that.

All her maternal instincts and any nurturing aspects she had within her were expended on her son. So, as far as anything else was concerned, she considered it on its own. And it usually ended up dead. You know what they say, you come into this world alone and you die alone. If an animal wanted to come into her home, it was on its own, and it needed to take its chances.

"Yes, sorry, you can *not* bring fish and chips. My fish aren't cannibalistic."

He laughed.

"Oh yes, and I forgot to mention one other thing."

"What?"

"The snake."

He threw back his head and laughed again. "Okay. Now I know you're just yanking my chain."

She winked at him.

"Do you have *any* pets?" he asked.

"Besides my teenaged son? No. So fish and chips really can be an option. I was just playing with ya."

"What does your son like?"

"To eat? Anything but spaghetti."

"He doesn't like spaghetti?"

Might as well give him a little peek at my wonderful culinary skills and my efficient housekeeping ways. I wouldn't want to shock the guy completely! "Well, he *used* to like spaghetti, until he ate it four times a week for eight years straight because I can never remember to take anything out of the freezer."

He didn't laugh at her, although she'd expected him to. "How about if I call you later or you can call me if you think you'll be too busy working. I'd hate to interrupt you. You must need to concentrate when you're working on editing a whole book. We can arrange what I'll bring then."

She liked that he qualified his offer with attention to her work. It was for that reason that she told him he could call her anytime. "And thanks," she added.

"What for?"

"For understanding that my work is meaningful to me, and that I work hard, and that it's tough to be disturbed, sometimes. No one else in my life seems to understand that. Besides Craig, that is," she noted.

"I understand. It's the same in business. Sometimes you're in the middle of writing up a proposal or planning a strategy, and getting interrupted can really throw off your game. So when should I call you? What's a good time?"

"There's no particular time. Every day's different depending on what I'm doing. If you want Craig's input, he gets home about three forty-five."

"How 'bout if I call you at five minutes to four?"

His preciseness made her giggle. "Why not wait until four?"

"It gives me five more minutes with you."

Wow, was he a keeper! If she didn't leave right away, she'd melt in a puddle before him. "All right. I'll speak to you then, Tom."

He nodded, "Okay. I'm heading to the showers," he said.

"I'm heading home," she countered.

They stood there staring at each other, neither moving to leave. Until Bunny came through the door and headed straight for Tom.

"Hi, Tom," she cooed, as though Janine weren't also standing there.

"Hello, Bunny," he responded without taking his eyes from Janine.

"Are you going? Or coming?" She said the word *coming* slowly and with deliberate sexual innuendo.

"I was just leaving," he said, still not removing his eyes from Janine.

"Oh, too bad," she pouted prettily, striking a pose.

Without any indication that he was going to do it besides first flashing a slightly apologetic look, he leaned into Janine and kissed her full on the mouth. Sweetly at first, then hungrily. "Goodbye, love. I'll see you tonight at dinner," he said to a shocked Janine, who was taking in a shocked Bunny. "I'll call first to see what you'd like me to bring home," he added for good measure.

Bunny was clearly stunned, which was probably what he had intended, and little Miss Bunny hopped off their trail in an instant, her breasts bouncing before her as she went.

"Do I have a cloak of invisibility to that woman?" Janine asked Tom.

He licked his lips and groaned softly. "Sorry about that,

but I wanted to let her know I'm not the slightest bit interested in her, and to please stop her incessant coquetry with me."

Janine laughed. "Coquetry? There's a word I haven't heard since reading historical bodice rippers back in my high school days."

He looked at her lips, "Don't be a smart aleck."

"Or what? You'll kiss my socks off again?"

He smiled goofily. "I kissed your socks off?"

"Maybe," she said as she sashayed her way to the door. "Call me tonight, *love*, to discuss what to bring *home* for dinner."

"You are one crazy hot woman."

As she reached the door she crouched temptingly and said in her best Marilyn Monroe voice, "Am I *crazy*? Or am I *hot*?" She gave him a seductive look, not missing his obvious approval.

"Both!" he said as she slipped out the door.

The phone rang as she unlocked her door. Thinking it was probably her mother, she let the answering machine get it.

"We can't come to the phone right now, please leave a message after the beep." BEEP.

"You know," she heard a deep, male voice murmur into the phone, "you really shouldn't be so seductive. A man might get ideas and…"

She picked up the phone. "And what?" she asked boldly.

"And you might get burned. You're playing with fire, Janine Ruvacado."

"Maybe I'm a pyromaniac," she said with thick, latent sexuality.

He laughed throatily. "Then in that case, light my fire!"

"Who is this?" she demanded. "José Feliciano? Is that you again?"

Tom chuckled. "José Feliciano is your stalker?"

"No. Are you?"

"José Feliciano? Or your stalker?"

"Both." she said.

"I'm not José Feliciano, but I wouldn't mind being your stalker."

She laughed. "What size women's shoe do you take?"

"I haven't a clue."

"Well, my last stalker could fit in my shoes, and I had to throw out my best, most *favorite* black pumps thanks to him."

Tom laughed. "Are you kidding me?"

"I kid you not."

"Well, unless you have the equivalent to a man's size-thirteen shoe, I'd have to say your pumps are pretty safe with me as your stalker."

"Good! I've had to give up too much for my last stalker."

"Besides the shoes?"

"A pair of panties, too."

She heard him choking back a laugh. "That's just weird."

"Yeah, I know." she said drily. "The police said something about how he kept muttering to himself about how beautiful my hair was." Then she figured she should explain. "I used to have long hair. I recently cut it off to give it to Locks of Love."

"I think I heard about that on the news once. That's the organization that makes wigs for kids who lose their hair due to medical procedures, right?"

"Yes," she said, not really knowing what else to say. "Okay,

I'd better go now. I've got some major cleaning up to do before I get to my real work. I've got some hot guy coming over for dinner tonight to look at my forms."

"You sure he doesn't want to look at your briefs?"

"I don't know, he doesn't seem the type."

"Be careful, looks are deceiving."

"How do you know I don't want to get a peek at *his* briefs?"

"Do you?" he asked.

"Maybe," she said, letting it sink in during the long pause that followed. "I'd better go now."

"Okay. It was nice 'stalking' to you."

A giggle bubbled from her. "Very funny, Tom. It was nice 'stalking' to you, too."

"I'll call you later."

"I'll be looking forward to it."

"Oh, and Janine? One last thing. You know how I said I was sorry for the kiss when Bunny left?"

"Yes?"

"I wasn't."

She heard Craig come in, and started counting to see how long it took until he noticed the place. One, two, three, four, five… "Wow, Mom what's going on?" he called from the living room.

She laughed. Only five seconds. That's not bad. The place must look pretty good. "We're having company for dinner," she called, listening to him clomp his way to her bedroom.

He looked around and was shocked by what he saw. "Who? The Queen of England?"

She laughed. "Funny, son."

"Well, who else would be given such a clean house? It hasn't looked this clean since the first day we moved in."

"It's cleaner. Check the freezer."

She watched her son as he ran to the freezer, threw it open and stared. "Where are the lumps?"

"I got rid of them."

"Wow. I can see that. What were they?"

"One was—I think—a hamburger patty."

"Cool. Did you save it?"

"No!"

"Oh, okay. What was the other?"

"I couldn't make it out. It melted down to nothing in the kitchen sink."

"Maybe it was a lump of ice cream, or something?"

"We'll never know. I didn't feel like wasting my hard-earned money to get it analyzed."

"Why not?"

"It's not a covered or standardized deduction for the IRS."

He smiled at her crack. "Oh yeah, I forgot to ask. How'd that go? Did you call this morning?"

She sighed loudly. "Yep. That's the reason we're having company tonight."

"You're going to sleep with the IRS guy?"

She laughed. "No way! What, are you kidding? If I *did* he'd probably hit me with more fees and back taxes. Plus, I wouldn't want to be the one to take his virginity."

"Ha! Good one, Mom."

"Thanks."

"So if it's not the IRS dweeb, who's coming for dinner? And what are you going to make? Please tell me not spaghetti."

The phone rang shrilly and her eyes fluttered to the clock. It was exactly five minutes to four. "I'm not making anything," she said, before swiping the phone from his hand.

"Hello?" She smiled. "You're right on time. He just got home."

"Is it Dad?" he asked hopefully, trying to grab the phone from her fist.

"Hang on a second, Tom," she said into the phone.

"Oh, Tom. He's the gym guy, right?" he said loudly.

"Yes. He's buying dinner for us tonight. What would you like to have?"

"Anything but spaghetti," he shouted toward the phone.

Tom heard her son's reply and laughed. "You know him well."

"Yes. We're both kind of sick of spaghetti," she said into the handset.

"What *would* you like?" Tom asked.

"I don't know, let me ask Craig. What would you like?" she asked her son.

"I've been jonesin' for some Chinese. Moo Shu pork would be tight."

She nodded. "What about Chinese?" she asked Tom.

"I'm fine with that. Did he say Moo Shu pork?"

"Yes. That's his favorite. He likes to play with the little burritolike flour shells and the umiboshi plum sauce."

"He's a kid with great taste," Tom said easily. "So I know what Craig wants, but what would you like?"

"Oh, I don't know. Anything. Surprise me," she said. "I'm easy, as long as its not spaghetti."

"So Lo Mein is out?"

She snorted. "No, Lo Mein doesn't count as spaghetti, but now that you mention it, good point. Forget the Lo Mein."

"It's forgotten."

"What time should we expect you?"

"Five-thirty sound about right?"

"That's perfect if it's okay with you. Don't you usually work late?" she asked.

"Yes, but I've never had a family dinner planned before, so this is a special occasion. I'm leaving early."

"If you have stuff to do, please don't reschedule it on our account."

"There's always 'stuff to do.' Going to your house, having dinner with you and Craig, is my top priority today."

"Well, thanks. I'm honored."

"You shouldn't be," he said.

She heard some woman's voice in the background, and he asked Janine to hold on a moment. Coming back quickly, he said, "I'm just going to tie up some loose ends with my secretary, then I'm calling it a day. I'll be there at five-thirty."

"Okay, Tom. We'll see you then."

CHAPTER 19

"I've searched my memory banks, but can't seem to remember the last time I've eaten as a family. In fact, upon further review, I don't think I've ever eaten as a family of more than two."

"Really?" Craig asked, looking back and forth between Tom and Janine, "That's…well, I dunno…sad." Then he homed in on Tom before saying, "No offense, man."

"None taken," Tom said, smiling easily. "You know," he said while leaning back in his chair and crossing his arms over his chest, "I look at the two of you, laughing and talking while you eat with such pleasure and gusto, and besides seeing what I've missed, I believe I could get used to this. It feels nice."

"That's because you brought some good food and you're not eating spaghetti for the gazillionth time in as many days."

"Why thank you, son," Janine said, throwing her son a whopper of a look.

"Hey, no offense, Mom, but you have to admit, this is good," he said as he took a huge mouthful of Moo Shu pork to prove his point. "*Much* better than the China Palace up the street. And Mr. Wong's a great chef! Where'd you get this?" Craig asked, turning toward Tom.

"Over by where I work."

"Don't try to change the subject, Craig! I'm still smarting from that blow about the spaghetti." She tried to look hurt, but an incessant smile kept popping through.

"Mom." Her son reached over and patted her shoulder. "Mom, Mom, Mom. Face it! We're in a rut. The spark's gone out of our evening meal together. Spaghetti seven nights a week would put anyone in the mood for *anything else!*" He shouted those last two words, which made the adults peal with laughter.

She looked at Tom. "I'd yell at him for being insubordinate or something, but sadly, what he says is true."

She liked the way Tom laughed with them. He didn't take over and yet he didn't fade into the wallpaper. He fit in nicely and she noticed that Craig was possibly coming to the same conclusion when she heard her son say, "It's cool of you to help my mom with her tax stuff. When she said someone was coming over to help her with her tax problem, I thought she was getting desperate and was gonna sleep with the tax guy."

Tom laughed at the stark comment Craig made. "Lucky for me she's not *that* desperate," Tom said smoothly.

"But don't worry, Mr. Kennedy, Mom said she's not going to sleep with the IRS guy because he'd probably hit her with more fees and back taxes, and she wouldn't want to be the one to take his virginity."

"Craig!" she screamed at her outspoken son.

"What?" he said with mock innocence. "Well, that *is* what you said, isn't it?"

"Yes, but I never thought you'd *repeat* it!"

"Well, you thought wrong, Mom. Aren't *you* the one who's

always telling *me* to watch what I say because it may come back to bite me in the ass?"

"Don't say 'ass,'" she muttered under her breath in Craig's direction. It's not like Tom couldn't hear everything they were saying, and she was afraid that they weren't giving the best first impression they could possibly give, so she did what she needed to do to get things back to some semblance of order. She gave Craig her fiercest evil eye. But he ignored it completely. She had to do something—anything—to get him to behave, so she hauled off and belted him on the arm.

"Hey! What did you do *that* for?" he said, while rubbing his arm. As payback, Craig turned to her and arched an eyebrow in her direction.

"Eewww, knock it off. I hate when you do that," she complained before turning to Tom in embarrassment. "You'll have to excuse us, as you can clearly tell, we're not used to having guests."

"Yeah, the only guest we ever get is my grandmother," Craig added while raising the other eyebrow at his mother playfully.

"Attila the Hun dressed as Betty White," Janine clarified.

"Yeah, she's a strange old lady." Craig laughed out loud. "You know the story of Little Red Riding Hood, Mr. Kennedy?"

"Yes," Tom said slowly, cautiously.

"Well, my grandmother is like the opposite. Instead of the wolf eating Little Red Riding Hood's sweet, old grandmother, she's more like…well, the grandmother that ate the wolf."

Janine hooted with laughter. "Very good," she said to her son before turning to Tom. "Sadly, he's right, but it's an excellent analogy. She *is* like a sweet, old grandmother casing with a mean, cranky wolf inside."

Tom laughed at their antics. "She sounds, well, horrible."

"Don't feel bad for saying that, Mr. Kennedy. In reality, she's worse than horrible."

Janine and Craig high-fived, laughed, then went back to inhaling their Chinese food as Tom sat back and watched them devour enough food for eight people. Eight sumo wrestlers, really. She was sure it was astounding for him to observe, but figured he'd see their ample appetites eventually, so they might as well not waste the good food. And Craig was right! It was much better than Mr. Wong's. Not that she and Craig didn't attack the food at the China Palace heartily, but this was amazing Chinese.

"I couldn't decide what to get to 'surprise' you—and I didn't know your tastes or want to disappoint—so I chose a variety of dishes, hoping you'd like one," Tom said to explain his overabundance of choices.

"Turns out, I like them all," she said past a mouthful.

"I'm glad," he said as he sat back comfortably in his chair, watching with amazement as Janine and Craig proceeded to polish off the remainder of the food. They were no longer being polite by adding portions to their plates, but now were just forking the stuff straight out of the white cardboard containers, handing the boxes back and forth between them. As one was emptied, they tossed it on the table, out of range. The non-empty boxes were kept either in hand or within arm's reach. Tom was grinning at them.

"Having fun?" Janine asked.

"Much. You?"

She waved her present container of shrimp in lobster sauce at him in recognition and gratitude and said, "I'm in heaven."

"Yeah, this is good. What there is of it," Craig said, looking at his mom in a private joke.

Janine laughed and said, "You'll have to forgive my son. He doesn't mean to be *rude*." She gave him a toned-down version of the evil eye. "It's a private joke. He's a growing boy and eats anything not nailed down. He even takes the food right out of my mouth," she said as he grabbed the shrimp in lobster sauce box from her hand.

"Quit hogging, Mom," Craig muttered.

"See?" she said to Tom, making a face.

Tom laughed. "I'm impressed by the easy and open rapport between you two. You're like a team. Even in marriage, I never shared the closeness you two have."

"Yeah, we're pathetic, huh?" Craig said as he took his mother's glass of soda and took a swig, emptying it.

"Hey, do you *mind*?" she said to her son. "That was all I had left, and I was saving it!" She turned to Tom. "I'm sorry, we must appear to be knaves." She gave her son a poke.

Tom shook his head. "No. You're enchanting."

Janine and Craig both laughed, figuring he was kidding.

"So," Craig said, "You have any kids?"

Tom shook his head. "No," he said sadly. "I never had any children."

"Why didn't you?" Craig asked simply.

Tom shrugged and grimaced. "I was too busy building up a business. I didn't marry when everyone else was getting married."

"But now you have your business, right?" Craig asked, always trying to find the good.

"Yes, I have my business. But I look at you two and wonder what I was working so hard for? *Whom* was I working so hard for?"

"You did it for yourself," Janine said gently. "To prove to yourself that you could do it."

He shrugged. "Yes, that was the original goal. But watching you guys, I realize that maybe I missed out on something."

"Isn't your business doing well?" Craig asked.

Tom looked at Craig, and Janine could see he was analyzing something. Weighing something. "My business is quite strong. But all this time I thought money mattered. That it made a difference. Made things better. Easier."

"And has it?" Craig asked.

"I really don't know. I thought it would, but money for money's sake? I don't know."

"Dang! I'd like to find out. I'd *love* having a lot of money!" Craig said with the enthusiasm of a teen with dollar signs in his head.

"It would sure help me out of this IRS bind," Janine added.

"Or possibly get you in further," Tom said knowingly. "If you could buy anything in the world, Craig, what would it be?"

She watched her son think about the question.

"Ya know, I don't know what I'd buy. Maybe some CDs. What about you, Mom?"

She thought about what she most longed for and knew her answer. "A fashionable yet comfortable pair of black pumps that go with everything."

"Neither one of those things take a lot of money," Tom pointed out.

"Yeah, you're right. Crap. Here I always thought if I had

a lot of money, I'd have it made. Turns out, I don't even *want* anything!"

Janine laughed at her son. "Don't look so disappointed. And watch your mouth, please." She turned to Tom. "And you? What would you buy if you could buy anything in the world?"

"I've spent a lifetime thinking exactly like Craig. But now I've just found out that it's not like that at all, because honestly, I have nothing of value anymore. My ex-wife took anything worth anything when she left, and I haven't replaced a thing. To be honest, I work so much I barely noticed that anything was missing."

"Your ex-wife sounds like a real piece of work," Craig said, his responses oscillating from those of a child to those of a grown man.

Tom waved his hand in dismissal. "She had the wrong priorities, just as I always have. But here—eating with you two—spending time with a mother and her son, I realize I just may have missed something."

Craig laughed cynically. "This? You've missed all of this?" He moved his hand around to encompass his domain, and laughed again.

"Have you ever heard the old expression *You can't miss what you never had?*"

"Yeah," Craig said.

"I've always thought that expression was true, but suddenly I realize how untrue it really is. I never had this—" Tom imitated Craig's hand movement of moments before "—a loving family—but all of a sudden, now I miss it."

Janine watched her son sit there, thinking about what Tom had said. She, too, was listening intently to the man.

He was smart and articulate, and she liked his honesty. He wasn't open in a weak, vulnerable way. His openness was intense, almost brutal. She liked that. He didn't play head games and had no secret agenda. He put his cards on the table and apologized to no one for doing so. She liked that, too.

She let herself admit that she'd been attracted to the man physically for a while now, and she was beginning to see that she was attracted to him emotionally, too. She was frightened by that because she couldn't trust her instincts when it came to men. Look at the disaster her last choice was. Martin Ruvacado!

With the food finally finished and all the containers piled haphazardly on the other end of the table, Janine said, "Anyone for dessert?"

Tom groaned at the thought, but Craig was game.

"You'll never guess what Tom brought," she said to Craig with excitement.

"What?" the boy asked, looking at Tom.

"Is this another family ritualistic joke or should I tell him the answer?" Tom asked Janine with a laugh. "I wouldn't want to step on any toes, here."

"Nope. Go ahead, tell him," she said with happy anticipation.

Tom rolled his shoulders. "It was an afterthought," he said to the entire Ruvacado family in explanation. "Is this a good thing or bad thing that I've done?" He hesitated.

"Just tell him!" Janine said with frustration. "It was hard enough for me to sit through the entire dinner without spilling the beans once I knew."

Tom smiled, now understanding that it was a good thing. "I bought a dozen Krispy Kreme doughnuts for dessert."

Craig's face lit up. "I *love* those!"

"They're his favorite," Janine added.

"Yeah, except I'm not allowed to keep them in the house because Mom has no willpower."

"Sharing all our dirty laundry tonight, huh, son?" she said as she passed him the box she'd hidden inside a cabinet.

He seized the box, opened it, took out a doughnut, and shoved it—whole—into his mouth. "This is great!" he said around the doughnut. It's real fresh. What are you guys gonna have for dessert?" he said, clutching the box to his chest.

Tom laughed, and Janine threw *him* a dirty look. "Don't encourage him."

"Sorry," he said quickly, but not looking the slightest bit remorseful.

"You should be," she teased. "How the hell am I going to get one of those doughnuts out of his greedy little fists if you don't make him share with me?"

Tom laughed. "What should I do?" he whispered conspiratorially to her.

"Tell him to share," she said in a stage whisper.

He cleared his throat loudly. "Um, Craig?" he asked.

"Yes, Mr. Kennedy?" the boy asked, clutching the box closer to his chest, putting his free hand in front of it to protect it. Or possibly attempt to hide it. One couldn't tell which.

"Would you please share with your mother?"

The boy rolled his eyes dramatically and sighed heavily. "Do I have to?"

Tom scratched his chin. "Well, no. You don't *have* to. But it would be nice."

"Humph."

"If you share this time, next time I'll get you each your own box."

Janine slapped him on the back. "You're a fast learner and a fantastic businessman, Tom."

"How do I know you'll keep your promise?" Craig asked boldly.

Janine gasped in horror. "That's rude, Craig!" she yelled. "Quick! Give him the pad so he can put it in writing," she said to her son from the side of her mouth, her hand "covering" her words.

Craig slid the ever-present pad over to Tom and handed him the pen that was always lying on top.

Tom bit back his laughter. "You two are clowns. You know that?"

"Just write," Janine said, pointing to the pad.

"And I'm having the time of my life," Tom added.

"Just write!" Janine and Craig chorused.

He threw back his head and laughed before writing in a bold hand.

I OWE YOU TWO SEPARATE BOXES OF
KRISPY KREME DOUGHNUTS.
TOM KENNEDY

Janine dragged over the pad and read. "You forgot to mention how many would be in each box," Janine said, pointing to the note.

Craig leaned next to her and read the note. "Yeah!" Craig said confidently. Then with more shyness, he said, "I'm only protecting my mother's interests, you see."

Not being able to hold back the laugher any longer, Tom patted the boy on his shoulder. "You're a good son, looking out for your *mother's* interests like that," he said to Craig. "What a crock!" he said to Janine, rolling his eyes.

"Just write," she insisted, pushing the pad toward Tom again.

"You're a pushy little family, aren't you?" he said, laughing as he pulled the pad back before him to add an addendum.

I OWE YOU TWO SEPARATE BOXES OF
KRISPY KREME DOUGHNUTS.
TOM KENNEDY
ADDENDUM: EACH BOX WILL CONTAIN
ONE DOZEN DOUGHNUTS EACH
T.K.

"Better?" he said, pushing the pad so the two Ruvacados could see.

"Much," Janine said.

"I guess," Craig muttered. "It really didn't matter," he said as he stuffed the last doughnut from the box into his mouth and folded up the box.

"Hey! Where's mine? I thought Tom told you to share."

Craig laughed and produced a doughnut from under the table. "A word to the wise, Mr. Kennedy—she gets nasty if she thinks she's been cheated."

"Oh be quiet," she said to her son over her big bite of doughnut.

After she swallowed, she looked at Tom. "Feel like handling some business now?" she said with a wink.

"Sure. Just lead the way."

"On to the bedroom," she said as she rose from the table. "And in case you were wondering, I was referring to business business. Not funny business," she said as she walked to her bedroom office.

"Oh. That's a huge disappointment," he said with a deep chuckle.

"Sorry, Charlie," she said as she entered her room.

He was right behind her. "Whoa! That's some treadmill," he said, looking at the machine whose front bar was still sticking up at a ninety-degree angle.

"It's broken."

"Is it?" he asked with a sparkle in his eye. "I didn't notice."

She threw him a look and said, "Looks like it's flipping you off, doesn't it?"

He looked at it again and laughed. "Now that you mention it, it does."

"Well, don't take it personally," she said lightly, rummaging through her desk. When she found what she wanted, she handed him a sheet with handwritten notes to herself…and a shoe box.

"Nice filing system," he said drily.

"Thanks. I've used it for years." She watched as he looked at the old shoe box.

"I'd hope so. Unless either you or Craig are the closet wearers of a children's size-ten pair of Teenage Mutant Ninja slippers."

"They were Martin's," she said flippantly.

"Really?"

She looked at him and smiled.

"I'll have to be on my toes with you. I'm not used to some-one with your acerbic wit," he said, while opening the shoebox.

She didn't know what he'd expected to find, but she'd bet anything it wasn't a complete, unorganized mess consisting of many irregularly sized scraps of paper, faxed sheets that were fading from time, and nonsensical check stubs. In no apparent order.

She watched as he patiently looked carefully through each piece.

Forty-five minutes later he said, "I've found a few sheets, forms and scraps that I think will satisfy the IRS based on your handwritten list of what they want to review. Send them these." He handed her the small, neat pile he'd care-fully laid on her desk. "It should do the trick."

"Is that all I have to do? Just mail them these?"

"It might be best if you enclose a letter, explaining every-thing. I've found that when dealing with the IRS you have to always assume you're starting from square one each time you approach them. It makes things easier for you."

"I'd love to enclose a letter, but haven't a clue what I'd say to them that they'd want to hear."

He laughed. "A business letter. Not a personal letter, Janine."

She smiled.

"Oh, there's that wit again. If you'd like, we can write up the note together and you can type it up and sign it and get it to the man you spoke with."

"You mean the thirty-eight-year-old virgin in the brown corduroy pants, knitted argyle vest, and polka-dot bow tie?"

"Really?" he looked disgusted.

She laughed. "No, I have no idea what he looks like. I just like picturing him that way."

"Well, in that case, give him some acne, too."

She nodded. "Good idea. Large, swollen, angry pustules."

Now he was really disgusted. "Ugh, that's so graphic!"

"I'm a writer, remember?"

"Yes, I've been meaning to tell you, my secretary is reading one of your books. I saw it on her desk the other day. And then I realized that Angelina bought *all* of your books. I thought I'd recognized your name from somewhere, but didn't realize where until I saw it in print. That must be pretty cool, seeing your name printed on a book like that."

"You get used to it," she said modestly, but was secretly delighted that he was impressed. She was also delighted to hear that his secretary and his ex-wife were avid readers of her work.

"I'll have to pick up some of your books so I can familiarize myself with what you do for a living."

This made her blush. The thought of him reading her innermost thoughts made her embarrassed. She didn't mind women reading them, obviously, but the thought of a guy she might be interested in having a...well, relationship with, reading her personal thoughts and desires, well, that was just...discomforting. "Oh, you won't like them, they're written for women."

"That's a pretty sexist thing to say," he said distractedly before turning his attention to the pad before him. "Okay, let's see. We need to sum up the problem and then write what we're enclosing so they'll have it all concisely together on one easy-to-read sheet. Any suggestions?"

"Me? None. I'm a writer of fiction. You're the business-

man. Why don't you compose it, then I'll type it up and
sign it."

He shrugged. "Okay, no problem." When he was done, he
ripped it off the pad and handed it to her. "Here. This should
do the trick."

"Let's hope."

"It probably will, but if not, remember, try not to get too
bogged down with this IRS fight. I've learned the hard way
that when you have troubles with the IRS, it's best to keep
in mind that it's a marathon, not a sprint."

She looked at him blankly.

"That means…don't expend too much energy too soon,
or you'll be exhausted for the long haul. I'm hoping this settles it, but it *may* be a long haul."

She looked at his handwritten note.

Dear Mr. Pimply faced Virgin,
Enclosed please find my W-4 form and the payment
stubs that correspond.
Blah, blah, blah…

"I'm assuming you want me to substitute his name for Mr.
Pimply faced Virgin?"

He nodded. "Yes, that would probably be best."

"And you think this might solve things?" she said, waving the sheet at him.

"I think it will, but one never knows."

She nodded. "Thank you, Tom. I'll type it up later. I appreciate your help."

"Enough to return the favor?"

She looked surprised. "Ex-ca-*use* me?" Surprised, but not all that offended or repulsed by the offer. In fact…

"Not like that, smarty-pants," he said, interrupting her thoughts.

She looked at him suspiciously, but truthfully was certain that she wouldn't have minded any suggestion he made.

"Help me with decorating my apartment."

"What?" She laughed. "Have you looked around this place? I have no eye for decorating."

"I was immediately struck by the homeyness of your apartment. It feels warm. Lived in. I like it. My place, even before being just about emptied by Angelina, never had a warmth to it. I like your home. It's much nicer than mine."

"I doubt that."

"It is! Come to my place and see for yourself. It's bare, it's cold, and what little furniture is left, is really not my style."

"Whose style is it?"

"Angelina's."

"Oh."

He held his hands out. "Please. I would appreciate it. Just help me out a little by making some suggestions."

She smiled slyly at him.

"Not the suggestion you're thinking right now," he said adroitly.

She winked provocatively. "How do you know what I was thinking? You might have liked my suggestion."

"I probably would have *loved* your suggestion! But, now is not the time or place," he said, looking out her doorway and down the hall.

"Okay. This weekend?" she offered. "For the decorating," she added, not wanting to appear as desperate for sex as she was.

"How about tomorrow after the gym?" he said, looking behind him at the fractured treadmill.

She was kind of hoping he was talking about their little sexual innuendo more than the decorating, but she'd be damned if she'd let on. "Don't you have to work?"

He shrugged. "Work can wait."

"What about my shower?"

He groaned. *Good! Maybe he was thinking about both!* "You can take it at the gym," he offered.

Her face looked like she had just smelled stinky cheese. "I don't like to shower in public places."

"There's nothing wrong with the gym's facilities, but if you're more comfortable showering at home, let's say you can run home, shower, and I'll pick you up after I shower and dress at the gym. Then we can go together to my apartment and you can offer some *decorating* suggestions."

Bummer. He had to be a gentleman! Great. "Okay. It's a deal." She held out her hand, and he grasped it firmly. Not wanting to let go, she didn't. Neither did he. They both held on, staring into the other's eyes.

Like a splash of cold water, music suddenly blared in the next room. Horrible music. "What is that?"

"Sorry," Janine said, raising her voice to be heard, "that's Craig's music."

"That's considered music?" he wondered aloud.

She nodded. Any romantic mood that might have developed came to a screeching halt with that audible dampening. *Thanks a lot, my son. You're killing me here!*

"It's like nails on a chalkboard," he shouted in her direction despite being only a foot and a half away from her.

She nodded. "You get used to it," she shouted back.

He stood there, cringing. "It seems the perfect time to call it a night. We've already confirmed our gym time and arranged an…ah…arrangement for afterward, so there's not much left for us to accomplish, I guess," he screamed over the atonal din. "I'd better go now. Unless you need help with the dishes or something?"

She smiled and put her hand to his chest. "No, the disposable plates and plastic utensils you brought saved me from that chore, thank you very much," she said, sounding like a screeching buzzard as she rubbed his chest idly.

"I had a great time," he screamed. "Thanks."

She nodded.

"This was nice," he screamed again.

Her hand stilled on his chest and she leaned forward on her tiptoes to give him a kiss.

When it ended, they stared at each other. If his fake, Bunny-ridding kiss at the gym had moved her, this one should have knocked her unconscious.

CHAPTER 20

After he'd left, she typed the letter Tom had written for her, and immediately faxed it to the IRS office with the attached papers he'd recommended sending. Figuring they didn't work at night, but kept their fax machines turned on, she'd added a note that she'd call the next day to find out if they needed anything else from her.

The next morning, the gym was uncrowded, as usual, and Tom and Janine enjoyed their walking and jogging while hollering at the television to the new family members of *Family Feud*.

"Thanks for a great evening," Tom said before he got too winded.

"Thank *you* for a…great meal and…the IRS help." She was already winded, within mere minutes of starting.

"I hope it was a help. From what I could tell, it should do the trick, but one never knows."

She nodded. "You know…more than I do."

The commercial was over, and they focused on the show.

"Hey, why are…we watching…commercials? This is… taped," she said between gasps.

"Good point," he said, offering her the remote.

"No, you," she said efficiently.

By now it shouldn't be a surprise to him that she had no coordination and couldn't aim the remote at the VCR without falling off the treadmill. At home she had the VCR on top of the television so she could just press the remote button while it sat in the crevice designed for remotes without having to lift her hand from the hold-on bar. Or whatever the handlebars were called.

He was running now and she noticed he turned up the volume, which was considerate, because he was making his usual noises. Funny, but they didn't annoy her or gross her out anymore. That was weird. Just shows, she thought. You could get used to anything.

She looked over at him and smiled. Yes, his face was now red and blotchy, and he was sweating just as much as he was that first day she saw him, but it didn't seem to matter to her anymore. She caught her own reflection in the mirror and realized that she was no athletic beauty queen either.

She enjoyed his company; he was easy to be with. He didn't demand anything of her, yet he was so self-sufficient and competent that she didn't have to do or be anything for him. Thanks to Martin, she wasn't used to that. But she liked it. Could get really used to it.

"The house!" he screamed at the television.

Her attention flew back to the game show. "What was…the question? I…missed it," she said.

"What can't a husband and wife split after a divorce."

"Damn, Thomas…too bad we're not…really playing…. We could have…aced…this question!"

"Yes, indeed!"

"The kids," she shouted.

"The pets," he added.

"The car," she offered.

"Too bad the bank accounts split so easily," he said with a chuckle.

She rolled her eyes, feeling a line of sweat drip down her cheek. "What bank…accounts? Martin and I…didn't have any!"

Tom laughed good-naturedly.

The rest of the morning workout went smoothly. Matt came by to see if he could help them solve one particularly troubling question, but they must have asked one hundred Martians for the answers because not one of them could guess any of the top six answers. When Richard Karn read off the answers, all three people standing there were as baffled as Richard Karn seemed to be.

"There's no accounting for people's opinions," Tom said as he waited for her to finish her walking. "Which you'll see for yourself when you see my furniture."

"How bad…can it be?" she asked.

"You'll see. Ready to uphold your end of the bargain?" he said as she finished.

"Sure. Just let me run home quickly and shower," she said, huffing for breath and hating the hot stickiness of her sweaty clothes plastered to her skin.

"Okay, I'll meet you there," he said, "after I shower and dress."

Expecting to see him show up at her door in one of his kick-ass Armani suits, she slipped on a casual black dress. Nothing too fancy, but it did fit her nicely and managed to conceal some of her not so wonderful parts. Getting lost in the excitement of the prospect of their sort-of date, she also sprang for a bit of makeup. Again, nothing too fancy, just a bit of color and some mascara. After all, she wanted him to recognize her.

The phone rang just as she finished applying her lipstick. She wondered if it was Tom, calling to cancel.

"Hello?"

Nothing. Silence.

She waited a few seconds, said "hello" one more time, then hung up.

The phone rang again. "What?" she barked into it.

"What did you do to your hair?" a soft, male voice croaked.

"Who is this?" she demanded.

A slight pause passed before the soft voice said, "It's Heubert." Her stalker. He made a little sad, sighing sound. "What did you do to your hair?" he repeated softly.

It was almost a wail, but was said so gently and sadly, it sounded pitiful.

"I cut it, and gave it to Locks of Love," she explained mildly. Normally she'd be defiant in her retort, but Heubert sounded so wretched—as though he were truly wounded by her action—that she didn't have the heart to be defiant.

"Yes," he said, sounding on the verge of tears. "I saw you. I couldn't believe my eyes."

Her mind flashed to her mother's comments. *Your hair was one of the only appealing things about you.*

"Believe them," Janine said, starting to feel defensive. Plus, who was *he* to be disappointed in *her* actions? The last time they'd had any contact, he was found in her closet wearing nothing but her pumps and panties, her most garish red lipstick, and helping himself to her Chunky Monkey! And no offense, but red wasn't his color. She was *still* ticked off about the shoes, and his big, hairy body could have lived without wearing silk panties, not to mention the extra serving of ice cream.

There was a long silence.

"Heubert?"

"Yes?"

"You okay?"

More silence.

Finally he spoke. "I'm sorry, Janine. There's no easy way to say this, but…I'm leaving you. You just don't do it for me anymore."

She knew she should be happy and relieved by his words, but she wasn't. She was shocked. And upset. And pissed.

"Why, Heubert? Is it my writing? I'll have another book coming out soon. I promise. And it'll be good. You'll see." She sounded pathetic even to her own ears.

"It's not that. It's your hair," he said sadly, simply. "Goodbye, Janine."

She heard him hang up, and stood there holding the phone to her ear, shocked, listening to a dial tone. She couldn't believe it. She was actually getting dumped by her stalker…over her hair.

She couldn't believe it, but she was upset—and realized her reaction to this situation was probably not typical. There was a therapist's couch out there somewhere with her name on it.

The doorbell rang, knocking her out of her stupor. She

hung up the phone, ran her hands over her dress and took a deep breath, letting it out slowly as she walked to the door.

"Wow," Tom said as she opened the door. His approval was flattering, but maybe he was just comparing what she looked like now to what she looked like at the gym. Sure it was a step up, but his admiration could also be construed as an insult too. As if he was shocked she could clean up so well. Or perhaps she was just overreacting because she was reeling from her still-stinging dismissal. Hey, if Heubert could dump her in a flash, this guy could too.

"Wow, yourself," she said back, admiring his casual look. He stood before her in jeans and a light blue polo shirt, which brought out his gorgeous eyes and blended nicely with his gray hair. They stood like two statues—two *old* statues—staring. Then he kissed her.

It started gently but quickly burst into flames. They finally broke apart—breathless.

"Ready to go?" he asked in a choked voice.

Bummer! She was surprised that he'd want to leave and go anywhere after that. Lord knows she didn't. But if he wanted to leave, she wouldn't force him to stay. "Sure," she said, grabbing her bag as they left her apartment.

Conveniently, they found a cab waiting right at the entrance of her building. "That's strange, it takes forever to find a cab around here," she said, looking around the cab's interior. "And this one is so *clean*." She sniffed the air. "And doesn't smell." She was amazed. "It's like winning the trifecta," she said excitedly.

Tom laughed. "Because it's there, clean and non-smelly?"

"Yes. Obviously, you have no idea how rare that is."

"Obviously not." He laughed again. "Then I guess I shouldn't disappoint you by telling you that I called the cab company last night, making a reservation for a 'new' cab to be waiting by your building."

"Really?" She didn't know if he was kidding around or not.

"First off, do you actually think I'd opt to leave your apartment after that kiss if I didn't have a cab waiting down here? And secondly, I figured it was too soon to have you see my personal car and driver."

Now she *knew* he was kidding, but was immensely pleased by his "first off." *So, he had liked that kiss, and would have wanted it to continue. Okay. Maybe I've still got it!*

He was watching her intently. "Yeah, babe. You've got it!"

How did he *do* that? It was truly like he really was a mind reader.

He laughed at her surprised look before he continued speaking. "Considering the dark, dank stench of some cabs, I'd put in the call so we'd have a nice ride to my apartment and then hopefully—after seeing how desperate my situation is, and trying to persuade you to spend the entire day with me—to the furniture stores."

The cabbie started pulling away from the curb, and Tom leaned forward to give the driver the destination. "One-eleven East Sixtieth Street, please. Between Park and Lexington."

"Yes, sir. One-eleven East Sixtieth Street."

"And the driver speaks English, too," she whispered to Tom. "That's a rarity. You must have made quite the impression with the dispatcher to get a clean cab with an English-speaking driver. There's—what?—*three* of those in all of Manhattan?"

He laughed before putting his arm around her, "For safety's

sake," he said as she looked up at him with pleasure and cuddled next to him. "Thank God for New York City's potholes. Usually I curse them, but today I'm elated by them. I like the way you keep getting jostled next to me."

"Yeah, those damned potholes," she said as she sensuously rubbed herself against him.

"You smell nice," he said quietly, after a few minutes of silence.

"Thank you, so do you."

"Thanks." He blushed slightly. "It's new. By Ralph Lauren. It's called Silver."

She buried her face in his neck and took a deep breath. "I like it. It's sexy."

His blush deepened.

"Don't wear cologne much, do you?" she asked mischievously. *Either that or the man wasn't used to compliments, which would be a huge surprise.*

"No," he admitted. "I can wash it off at my place if you don't like it. Like I said, it's new. A gift from a business associate."

"I like it," she said breathing against his neck again. "You know, from what I know about you already, it's not like you to get flustered, Mr. Kennedy. So what *aren't* you telling me about this cologne?"

He smiled. "You're good. Ever think of becoming a detective?"

"A private eye? No. But Sid's mentioned a time or two that I should try writing a mystery."

He nodded. "What I *didn't* say was that it was a *female* business associate who'd bought it for me."

"So? Should I be jealous or something?"

He snorted a laugh. "No. Not at all. The aftershave's real name is Ralph Lauren *Romance* Silver, and the woman who gave it to me tried to seduce me the night she gave it to me, saying that she'd 'hoped we could have a *romance* while in my *silver* years.'"

Janine laughed. "She sounds…schmaltzy."

Tom chuckled. "Yes, I guess. I disliked the woman, but I liked the smell, and am embarrassed that I kept it. I was hoping to get better olfactory memories of the scent with you."

"I like it, too," she said simply. "And we'll see what kind of 'olfactory memories' we can produce for you later."

He groaned. "I need to change the subject or I'll never let you out of my apartment."

She nodded, looked out the window, and said, "Don't you love knishes?"

His laughter rumbled through the cab. "I didn't need that drastic a change of subject," he said, while nuzzling her ear. "You smell nice, too. What is it?" he asked.

"I'm not wearing anything."

"Hmm. You mean you smell like that naturally?"

She laughed. "I don't know, maybe it's my shampoo you're smelling." She provided her head to him, so he could catch a whiff.

He sniffed. "Nope. Nice and kind of coconutty. But that's not what I smell."

She tilted her head back, offering her neck to him.

With a groan, he immersed his face against her smooth, warm neck. "Yup, that's it. You smell clean and very, um, womanlike." His nose caressed her neck, sending shards of electricity to her stomach.

"It's all me, buster. And, for the record—" she sidled up next to him "—I *am* clean, and very...womanlike."

"You're playing with fire again, Janine," he growled.

"So you keep saying. But what I can't figure out is—is that a warning or an invitation?"

"Both," he admitted warily.

She nestled into him. "Good. I've never shied away from a challenge."

Just as she thought he was going to kiss her, the cab driver interrupted. "We're here, sir."

Tom groaned and held his finger up to Janine. "Hold that thought," he said with a wink.

He paid the cab fare with what appeared to be a one-hundred-dollar bill, and leaned his head into the driver's window to say something.

"Nice neighborhood," she said, looking impressed as they got out.

He shrugged. "I couldn't liquidate easily, so I gave up the penthouse on Fifth, the brownstone off Park, and the loft in SoHo to Angelina."

"Oh. So I guess this is slumming it for you," she said easily.

He kissed her forehead. "Has anyone ever told you you're a wiseass?"

"Never," she said impishly as they walked to the door. "What? No doorman?"

As if he heard her words, a man in a red coat and navy slacks appeared before them at the door. "Good morning, Mr. Kennedy."

"Good morning, Clarence."

"It's a surprise to see you back so soon. Are you all right?"

"Yes, fine. Thanks." Then Tom laughed. "I just realized, you've never seen me come back *in*, have you? You only see me going *out*."

"Yes, sir. Geoffrey always sees you coming in."

Janine laughed. "You're kind of predictable, aren't you, Mr. Kennedy? Let's hope we don't find an illegal craps game going on in your apartment, or worse, a temporary room for hookers."

Tom laughed, but she noticed Clarence was mortified.

"That would never happen, sir. No one goes in or out of this door that we don't know about," Clarence assured.

"She was only kidding, Clarence. She knows that's not going on in here."

"I'm sorry, Clarence, I was just teasing."

He smiled at Janine, and she knew she was forgiven. "That's okay, ma'am. Not many people in this building have a sense of humor. I'm so used to being here, I forget that some people do." Then he looked at Tom, and apologized. "I didn't mean you, sir."

Tom laughed. "It's okay, Clarence. Now everyone's even."

"No we're not!" Janine insisted.

Both men looked at her. "First I mistakenly insulted Clarence. Then Clarence mistakenly insulted you. Now for us to all be even…*you* have to mistakenly insult *me*."

Tom looked at her sardonically. "Sounds good in theory, but do I look like an idiot?"

Laughing, she said, "No, you're not paying attention. It's *your* turn to insult *me*, not the other way around. If I agreed with your question of whether you looked like an idiot, then we'd all have to reverse the order of our future mistaken insults."

Clarence nodded. "She's got you there, Mr. Kennedy."

Tom shook his head. "I'm so confused."

"For simplicity's sake, let's just call it even, even if it's not," she suggested.

"Deal," Tom said.

"I'm okay with that," Clarence added.

"Okay. And I can live with it, too," Janine agreed. "It's a threeway tie."

Clarence winked at Janine. "You have a nice day, ma'am."

"You have a great day, too, Clarence," she called back as they headed for the elevator.

"Will do," she heard as the elevator door closed.

"I think my doorman is smitten with you," Tom said, cornering her in the elevator.

"He won't be the first doorman to swoon before my enticing ways."

"I think I'm swooning before your enticing ways," he said suggestively.

She shook her head vehemently. "No, that's probably just hunger."

He nodded his head, looking at her lips, "Yes, probably just hunger." His last words were smothered on her lips.

The strong hardness of his lips unnerved her. His kiss was at first giving, then demanding. When the elevator's bell rang, signaling their arrival at his floor, her lips were still warm and moist from his kiss.

"Home, sweet, home," he said as he unlocked the door and motioned her in.

"Behave yourself," she said before entering, wagging a finger at him.

"You're the one who started it, little Miss 'Clean and Very Womanlike.'"

As if on cue, his only neighbor, nosy Mrs. Stippledorf, came out of her apartment. "Oh, dear," she said, tightening her robe around her zaftig figure. "I thought I heard voices out here, and I was right," she said, eyeing Janine suspiciously.

"It's only me, Mrs. Stippledorf. But if I don't get this lady out of here in an hour, you may want to send in reinforcements."

"Well," she harrumphed, "I'll be!" She turned on her slippered heel and went back into her apartment. They heard her fasten three security locks.

"With such a nosy neighbor, you'd think she would have notified me the day Angelina came in here and took everything that wasn't attached."

"Is her name really Mrs. Stippledorf?"

"You can't make up stuff like that!" he joked. Then he thought about it. "Well, *you* can, but *I* certainly can't. And wouldn't." He was babbling. He must be a little nervous.

"Am I the first woman you've brought here, since your ex-wife?" she asked gently.

He nodded, looking down at the hallway's tile as if he'd never noticed the intricate pattern before. "Yes," he said simply. "Please, come in."

They stepped inside, and Janine felt like Alice falling down the giant hole in Wonderland.

"Oh, my God," she said with a gasp as she looked around. "I can *not* believe this!"

CHAPTER 21

"**It** looks like Barbie's mansion," she said with a combination of awe and disgust. "Only…supersized."

"I told you I needed help with this."

"Oh my God," she said, looking around in disbelief.

"You already said that," he noted.

"It deserves repeating," she insisted.

"I guess I'm used to it. I've lived with it for so long."

"You poor thing." There was only furniture in the place. Nothing else. Just couches, chairs, and a huge lamp sporting some sort of ostrich-feather lamp shade. "Where the hell did they find a pink ostrich?" she muttered to herself.

"Pretty weird, huh?" he asked.

She looked around at the bubblegum-pink, frilly, lacy couches and matching chairs. They weren't overstuffed. Instead, they were…understuffed. "What, did you have a life-size anorexic Barbie doll living here?"

"That about sums it up," he said with admiration.

She shook her head and started rubbing her temples. "Please tell me you didn't choose this furniture."

"Does it look like my style?" he said good-naturedly.

"God, I hope not. I'd lose all respect for you if it were! I can't believe it's *anyone's* style."

"I know. And you'd think that something that looks like this would have to have some redeeming quality—like to at least be practical or comfortable, right?"

"I can see it's not practical. So is it comfortable?"

"No. It's as uncomfortable as it looks," he said with a chuckle.

She went closer to it, walking around the gathered set of furniture with caution—as if it were a strange animal to be observed yet avoided. "That is some ugly furniture."

"Why do you think I want to get rid of it?"

"Well, you can't sell it. It's got a Pepto-Bismol stain on it."

"Where?" he asked.

Was he *serious?* "All over it! It's one gigantic Pepto-Bismol stain."

He laughed. "One *lacy*, gigantic Pepto-Bismol stain," he clarified. "I was hoping to give it away. I had no intentions of selling it."

"Where did you *buy* this stuff?"

He shook his head, rollicking laughter starting to rise up within him. "You're never going to believe this. She had it specially made."

"No!"

He nodded, wiping the tears from his eyes. "Really!" He looked at her incredulously. "I can't make this stuff up."

He rolled with laughter and put his arm around her for support. She too started to melt with a case of the giggles. "This is the ugliest furniture I think I've ever seen," she said, around peals of laughter.

"Me too, but I've never admitted it before. At first I didn't want to insult Angelina, so I kept it bottled up inside. Then, when she left me, taking everything I owned—all my beautiful antiques—leaving just this—" he motioned to the collection of cotton-candy furniture "—I was so depressed, I couldn't even look at it."

She took in the couch and chairs and the hideous lamp, and roared with laughter, setting him off again. They fell on the couch together. "Ow, this ugly thing just pinched my butt!"

"Yeah. Welcome to my world," he said before plopping down on the spring-loaded couch and pulling her onto his lap. "This'll be more comfortable for you," he murmured.

"Thanks," she said. "Such a hero. Yes, this couch *is* much better when it's 'once removed.'" She turned to smile at him, but was instantly uncomfortable with their closeness. Or, more accurately, her reaction to their closeness. "So, giving it away," she said as she jumped out of his lap. "That's a great idea."

She walked around the room, taking in the floor-to-ceiling windows that connected the hardwood floors with the high ceilings. "You can give it to Goodwill Industries or possibly donate it to that organization that gives furniture to people who have lost everything to fire."

"That's a good idea," he said slowly, rising from the couch.

She looked around and motioned at the hideous furnishings. "I've changed my mind."

He groaned aloud. "Please don't tell me you like it now."

"God no! On second thought I realize that people who've just lost everything they owned to the devastation of a fire do *not* need further punishment."

"Yes. I agree. Seems they've suffered enough. Okay then, we've decided. Goodwill it is. I'll call them today to come pick it up."

"You'd better play it safe and have it delivered. That way they can't refuse it."

He laughed again. "You may be right." He nodded seriously. "Listen to you. Janine Ruvacado—problem solver! Okay, so now that that's solved, we need to move on to the acquiring aspect of this job. I bought some house magazines and have some furniture brochures in the kitchen. I've been looking through them in my spare time to see what I should get to replace this awful stuff. The only problem is, I can't make up my mind. Maybe you can help me."

"You can't buy a couch from a magazine, silly. You have to sit on it, see how it feels."

"Yes," he said, "I guess you're right. If you don't test it out, it could be lumpy," he said with a wink.

"Usually I hate a lumpy couch, but yours—that second one, the one 'once removed'—wasn't so bad," she said as she sashayed out of the room to inspect the rest of the house.

The kitchen was bare but beautifully set up. There was a lot that could be done with it. It was so striking and inspiring, even *she* felt she could cook something edible in there. Down the hallway, past two empty bedrooms, the master bedroom was immense—and gorgeous. Crown molding and a beautifully classy cherrywood chair rail circled the room. His bed was a huge, king-size bed, made up in a great dark print, but without a bed skirt or added pillows.

"I like your bedding," she said.

"Thank you. It's the only thing I picked out myself. I bought it after Angelina left. She even took the sheets and pillows. As I said—anything that wasn't nailed down."

"We have similar taste," she said. "I like this a lot. It's, I don't know, solid…and warm. I'm not the pink frilly, lacy type."

He shook his head. "Me neither."

She started picturing him in his big, inviting bed and needed to get out of there. Turning, she clicked her way down the hardwood hallway until she was once again safely in Barbie's life-size living room. It could've also passed for the inside of Jeannie's bottle.

He followed behind her, easing his wide shoulders into a sports coat. "Want to go furniture shopping now?" he asked. "We still have the cab waiting."

"Sure." She shrugged. "We might as well get to it."

When they got outside, the cab was still sitting there. "Thank you for waiting. I'm sorry we took so long. Can you take us to this address please?" Tom said, handing the cabbie a slip of paper.

"Sure thing, sir."

Tom turned to Janine. "I'm not certain, but they should probably have everything I'll need. If not, we can go elsewhere. I made some calls, and this place we're going to said they had an entire floor of furnishings that could be taken immediately. Their usual furniture needs to be ordered, and would take several weeks or months to receive. I figure it can't hurt to look at what they have ready and available."

"Lord knows the stuff you special-ordered and waited for wasn't worth the wait. How much worse can it get than what you've already got?"

"Right! My sentiments exactly. And remember, if we don't see anything to our liking, there are a couple other places that have the same setup. I'm willing to run around to a few different stores, thinking that the sooner I can get it all, the sooner I can get rid of the pink stuff," he said with a grimace.

"That's understandable. Good plan," she said. "Very practical." Then she smiled. "This'll be fun."

He looked skeptical.

"You'll see," she said. "You really need to lighten up. You know, play things by ear."

"I don't think I've ever lightened up. I think I was born intense." He laughed at himself.

She didn't laugh. "You had a reason for that. Now, you've accomplished what you set out to do. It's time to lighten up."

"I agree. Teach me everything you know."

She smiled coyly. "Now that might take all day, Mr. Kennedy." She batted her eyelashes playfully. "Possibly longer."

He smiled. "That wouldn't be a problem," he said as he leaned in for another kiss.

"We're here, sir," the cabbie said.

"Is it me? Or does this guy have the worst timing?" he asked. "I'm starting to get really cheesed off at him!" he added good-naturedly.

"Don't worry, Tom. There'll be plenty of time and plenty of days."

"Good," he said, looking pleased with her comment.

She was pleased that he was pleased, because today she wasn't feeling so self-confident about her womanly sex appeal. *After all,* she thought to herself, *I'm a woman who can't even keep her own stalker interested.*

They got out of the cab and went into the store, heading right for the basement where they knew they'd find the immediately available furniture.

"It probably won't look or feel like a basement, so I won't freak out," she said as they pressed the B button on the elevator.

"You freak out in basements?"

"A little."

"I didn't know one could freak out 'a little,'" he said, raising his eyebrows.

"One can."

"Why do you freak out—a little—in basements?"

"I'm afraid they're going to fall in and crush me."

"Has that ever happened to you?"

"No."

"Anyone you know?"

"No."

"Ever read about it happening?"

"Not that I'm aware of."

"Oh," he said.

"Aren't you going to tell me I'm being ridiculous?"

"Why should I?"

"Because it *is* ridiculous!"

"Not to you, I suppose."

She grabbed the lapels of his jacket and tugged him to her, rising on her toes to capture his mouth with hers. Her tongue dove into his surprised mouth and she took that opportunity to taste him.

Wrapping his arms tightly around her, he returned her kiss with passion, crushing her to his solid chest. She could stay like this forever. Unfortunately, in the distance, she heard a bell and the whoosh of elevator doors, and felt Tom pull back, leaving her mouth burning with fire.

"Damn," he cursed. "Will we ever *not* get interrupted?"

She licked her lips, "You know, I think you may be right." She put her fingers to her lips to cool them down. "I just may be playing with fire."

"Yes," he said simply, before clearing his throat, taking her hand and stepping out of the elevator.

They walked hand in hand throughout the maze of couches, chairs, end tables and wall units. They both stopped abruptly at a tall cherry entertainment center.

"I love that," she said.

"So do I. And look—" he pointed across the room "—there's another piece that matches it."

"This looks tempting," Janine said, her gaze caressing a big, comfy-looking black leather couch.

"Sure does, " Tom said as he turned her to face him, held her shoulders and dragged her to him, kissing her senseless. They ended up falling onto the leather cough and making out like eighteen-year-olds.

"Ahem." Someone cleared his throat loudly. "Can I help you folks with anything? Or couldn't you find a vacant hotel room in all of New York City?"

Obviously he didn't work on commission.

Janine jumped up and wiped at the corners of her lipstick-smudged mouth with her thumbs. She gasped and stared at the salesman. She didn't know if her mind was playing tricks on her, but the sniveling, hairy, beer-bellied man reminded her of Heubert.

Tom remained seated. "This is nice," he said, "but it's not as supple as I'd anticipated," he said with authority. He was all business once again.

"Keep in mind that it will start out stiff at first but after a little time and use, it will soften up," the salesman said, taking a cue from Tom's businesslike demeanor.

Janine stared at him, then looked at Tom, then threw back her head, and laughed. "It *does* usually work that way. But thanks for reminding us. In case we forgot."

This tossed Janine and Tom into fits of laughter.

The salesman shook his head and walked off, muttering to himself about how he should have listened to his parents and stayed in college.

When they stopped laughing, Janine muttered, "I can't believe I've chased another one off."

"Salesman? You do that often?" he asked, still wearing a huge smile.

"No, another Heubert," she said.

"What's a Heubert?" he asked.

"My stalker," she said.

"You're on a first-name basis with your stalker?"

"Well, I *was*. Until today."

He was obviously expecting the punch line for the joke. "What happened today?"

"He dumped me."

He looked confused. "I don't get it."

"What don't you get?"

"The joke."

She tilted her head and looked at him. "I wasn't joking. My stalker—Heubert—called me up today and told me I didn't do it for him anymore."

"That's not funny," Tom said, starting to look serious.

"I know! I can't tell if I'm more upset or pissed off about it."

Tom was staring at Janine, and she could see a muscle in his jaw flexing wildly.

"What's wrong?" she asked.

"What's wrong? Your stalker—whom you have a restraining order against—contacted you today. That's what's wrong."

"It's Heubert, Tom. He's harmless." She couldn't believe she got dumped by her stalker with a "dear John" phone call. It was humiliating. What kind of famous VIP was she if she couldn't even keep her stalker interested?

"I'm calling the police," he said, whipping out his cell phone.

She was shocked. "Why?"

"Because you have a restraining order, and he broke it," he sputtered as though she were nuts for not knowing that.

"Lighten up, Tom," she said, swiping the phone from his hand and ending the call so it wouldn't go through.

"Lighten up? Are you kidding? You obviously can't take care of yourself, so *someone* has to do it," he said caustically.

That ticked her off, and scared her. More so than being contacted, then dumped by her panty-wearing, shoe-stealing, hair fetished, fat, hairy stalker.

"Oh yeah?" she said. "Well, look, I've been taking care of myself my whole life. And I don't need your high-and-mighty attitude." She faced him square on.

"Let me get this straight. You're actually mad at *me*? I don't get it," he said, shaking his head while he raked his hand through his perfectly spiked hair.

"Obviously," she spit out before turning on her heel to leave.

He watched her walk away. "Let me at least take you home," he called to her retreating back.

"Despite what you may think, I don't need your help finding my way home," she shot back as the elevator doors closed shut.

CHAPTER 22

The phone was ringing as she unlocked the door. The kitchen phone was the closest, and she ran like a maniac to answer it.

"How come you're never home anymore?" the woman on the phone demanded. "What's going on, Janine? These past few weeks I can hardly get you anymore."

Pity. She might as well tell her. "I've been dating someone, Mother," she said with resignation into the phone.

"Who?"

What kind of stupid question was that? "I doubt you know him, Mother."

"Probably so," she said, her distaste audible. "Where did you meet him?"

"At the gym."

"A gym? What on earth were you doing there?"

What do you think I was doing there? "Walking."

She tsked multiple times before demanding, "When can I meet this man that's monopolizing all of your time?" Then she muttered to herself in a stage whisper that Ethel Merman would have envied, "He's probably a bum! Met him at a gym."

Janine chose not to respond.

"It's over now, Mother."

"Hmm. So soon? Why did he leave you?" she demanded.

"It was probably because you don't help yourself with your appearance. You just don't care. A man doesn't like a sloppy woman, Janine."

Janine rolled her eyes.

"Have you done anything with that hair of yours, Janine? You should never have cut it!"

Janine sighed heavily. It was too much. She couldn't handle everything lately. She needed a break, and this conversation wasn't helping.

"Mother, listen, I have to go. I've got work to do."

"For one of your little books?"

"Yes, for one of my 'little books.' And by the way, Mother, just for your information—" Janine knew this would get her goat "—*I left him.*"

Janine could hear her mother's horrified gasp, but hung up before she could hear anything else.

The phone rang again immediately.

"I don't have time to discuss this now, Mother," she yelled into the phone.

"Hello? Is this Janine Ruvacado?" a toneless male voice asked.

She smiled. Well, that was embarrassing. "Yes, this is she," she said, trying to come off as less of an idiot than her opening greeting made her sound.

"I'm calling from the Internal Revenue Service. I just wanted to inform you that we received your paperwork, and everything is now in order."

"What does that mean?" she asked.

"It means that for now, we are satisfied with your documentation, which confirms your claimed income."

She didn't know if she should be thrilled that she'd won her argument and proved her point, or embarrassed and sad that she'd earned so little. "Well, thank you for calling. I appreciate it."

"You're welcome, ma'am." *Ma'am.* She hated that.

She was about to hang up when something popped into her head. "Oh, one last thing. What did you mean by the words 'for now'?"

"Once your name has been flagged by the system, ma'am, our computers take a closer look at your return for approximately five years after that."

It figures. But there was nothing she could do about that.

After she hung up, the phone rang again. This time she was smart enough not to assume she knew who was on the other end. "Hello?"

"Hi, Janine, dear. It's Harvey. Listen I want you to get another bone scan so we can see how you're doing. It's been a while now, and I'd like to see how you're progressing. You've been walking routinely, right?"

"Right, Harv," she said, thinking about Tom, her *still* broken treadmill, and panicking at the thought of what she'd do now. She'd be embarrassed to see him at the gym, but it *was* convenient. She still couldn't walk at home, and she *had* prepaid for another two weeks since it didn't seem that Ben Franklin was electrically charged to get her treadmill fixed anytime soon.

"Taking the meds?" Harvey asked.

"Yes, Doctor. Every Monday like clockwork."

"Good. Good. You're taking calcium supplements, too, right?" he asked.

"Was that on the list?" she asked innocently.

"Oh no, don't tell me I forgot to write that down," he said, sounding flustered and upset.

She laughed. "Don't worry, Harvey. It was on the list, and yes, I'm doing that too. I'm also eating lots of dairy products."

"Just get the bone scan. I'll call you with the results."

She hung up the phone and waited for it to ring again. When it didn't, she reached behind herself and unzipped her dress, stepped out of it, walked to her room and draped it ceremoniously across the handle of the treadmill.

The next morning she decided she could probably skip one day of walking. She'd been doing it religiously for so long how could skipping one day hurt?

She really didn't want to see Tom. At first she'd thought he'd held such promise, but it ended up he was as bad as everyone else she was stuck with in her life. Except Craig, of course. He was the best thing to ever happen to her.

She spent the day working and stopped only to talk with Craig when he came home from school. Looked like work was her number-one friend again now.

That thought surprised her. She hadn't really thought of Tom as a "friend," but she now realized that somehow, somewhere along the line, that's exactly what he'd become.

She also realized that she'd miss him. Uptight, repressed and controlling as he was, he was a good friend to her. And she really shouldn't be angry with the fact that he was controlling; if anything, she was a *major* control freak.

As far as being "uptight" and "repressed," well, he'd shown an interest in trying to change that. For himself, not for her. And you had to respect that in a person.

* * *

The next day was day two without walking and she felt a tug of guilt at two consecutive days without doing what she needed to do. It wasn't like her to not tackle things head-on, and by afternoon she knew she'd have to go to the gym.

She was happy to see she'd be alone at the treadmill.

"Hey, Janine," Matt called from behind the reception desk.

"Hi, Matt." She needed to know. "Was Tom here already?"

"Yeah, this morning. You missed him," he said, looking away.

Good, so that would be the plan. It worked out perfectly. She'd come in the afternoon and avoid Tom completely.

She was halfway through her walking when she heard a familiar voice behind her.

"Look, I'm sorry, Janine. Please forgive me."

She kept walking and said nothing.

"I was frightened and worried, and I got all he-man on you."

She kept walking, but smiled slightly at his use of the word *he-man*.

"I'm used to being in control," he continued, "and your having a stalker scared me."

Still walking.

"Please, Janine. Don't leave me over this. Give us a chance. Please. I'll do anything to prove to you I'm in this for the long haul."

The long haul? *That's* what every woman wanted to hear a relationship with her being compared to. She still didn't budge.

"I love you," he said softly, but still loud enough to be heard over the whirring of the machine.

That surprised her and she stopped walking for a beat, and

ended up shooting off the back end of the treadmill. Right into his arms.

She twisted her hot, sweaty body around and looked him in the eye.

"You'll do anything to prove you're in this for the *long haul?*" she emphasized "long haul," showing her displeasure with his choice of words.

He laughed. "Sorry. I'm not a writer like you. I'm a businessman. And prospective partners want to hear that you're committed to being there through the long haul."

"So I'm a prospective partner?" she asked, liking the sound of that.

"You are," he answered shyly. "Am I?" he asked hesitantly.

She shrugged. "I don't know. Maybe. We'll see," she answered.

"So what do I have to do to prove myself to you?"

Two weeks later, the three of them were waiting in the Ruvacado apartment for their invited guest.

"You guys are so screwed," Craig said to Tom and his mother while shaking his head.

"Don't say 'screwed' please," Janine said to her son.

Tom laughed then wiped his hands over his face. "I'm sorry. I know. Don't encourage him." He winked at Craig. "Plus, how bad can she be?" he asked.

"Let's just say, she's not the most kind or generous person in her apartment. And she lives alone." Janine paused for effect. "She likes to think of the glass half-full," she continued, trying to keep a straight face. "Of sour milk," she added for illumination, before cringing.

"Wow. She's, well, unique," Tom said shaking his head. "And what's with all her cracks about your hair? I love your hair and I love that you're not vain and into looking like a…"

"Barbie doll?"

"I was thinking more like 'super model,' but in my eyes, you *do* look like a super model. Or at least what a super model *should* look like."

How did he always say the sweetest thing? She immediately forgot about her mother as they kissed like kids under the bleachers.

"Oh, jeez! Do you two have to go at it again?" Craig said with disgust as he plopped down on the couch next to them.

It was amazing how the three of them got along. Janine couldn't be happier if she tried. "I like sitting here with my two favorite guys," she said, smiling like a fool.

"I like sitting here with my two favorite people," Tom said, mirroring her goofy smile.

They looked at Craig, who rolled his eyes. "God, I hope I don't get this sappy when I fall in love."

"You will," Janine and Tom chorused.

"Jeez, I've got the two sappiest parents around!" he uttered before realizing what he'd said. He slapped his hand over his mouth and looked at Tom. Janine thought Craig looked paler than usual, and it wasn't due to the goth outfit he was wearing.

Tom took over like a pro. "Thanks, Craig. Even if you didn't mean it, I liked that you said it."

"Sorry, man, it's just that, well, I'm so comfortable with you. I feel like you've been around forever."

"I wish I had been, Craig. Any man would be proud to call you son."

Craig's face turned crimson, but he smiled at Tom. "Yeah. Ditto, Tom. I mean, you know, any kid would be proud to call you Dad."

Tom nodded, also turning scarlet.

They were a lot alike, her two guys.

"Oh, God. Here she is," Craig said with a loud groan as the doorbell pealed.

A tiny, well-dressed, harmless-looking woman stood in the entrance hall.

"Mother? This is Tom Kennedy. Tom? This is my mother, Elizabeth Black."

Her mother's usually pinched face mellowed as she looked him up and down with unhidden appreciation. "Nice suit," she said, not bothering to cover her surprise.

"Thanks. I left my lime-green leisure suit at home today. I'm saving that for a special occasion."

Janine and Craig laughed, but based on her Prunella face, Janine's mother didn't find his comment all that amusing.

"He doesn't own a lime-green leisure suit, Mother," Janine clarified.

Relieved, the woman looked at Tom again, assessing the cut and make of his tailored suit. She must not have found it lacking, because she said, "My friends call me Betty."

"It's a pleasure to meet you," he said easily. "I've asked Janine not to bother cooking tonight, and took it upon myself to make reservations for dinner. I hope you don't mind."

At her sour face he added, "They wouldn't take my reservation at McDonald's, so I was forced to get one somewhere else."

Although Janine giggled under her hand, Craig laughed

loudly, without pretense. "As long as I can get something other than spaghetti there, I'm down with that," Craig said, going along with Tom's joke.

"I think that can be arranged," Tom said to Craig with a wink. They got along so well, it sometimes amazed her. Once again she said a tiny prayer of thanks that her two favorite guys liked each other so much. Now if Tom could only survive the wrath of mother-Khan without running to the hills with his hands covering his vulnerable parts, she'd be thrilled.

Knowing she couldn't soften her mother—thousands had tried, not one had succeeded—she implored the almighty powers that be to let Tom find the strength to handle the vicious vulture otherwise known as "Mom."

"My car is waiting downstairs to take us there," he said in his quietly commanding manner. Janine was used to his understated, powerful personality, but her mother was not, and was obviously taken aback by his authoritative demeanor.

"Thanks for not bringing the car up to the apartment again. I hate when you do that! Besides getting too crowded, it always leaves so much dirt for me to clean up."

Before anyone could react to Janine's silly playfulness, her mother loudly stated, "My daughter considers herself a comedienne."

Tom replied with a chuckle, "I do, too. She's a laugh riot in my eyes."

Craig, also laughing, said, "Yeah, she's hilarious. Like she'd *willingly* clean up the apartment."

Tom and Craig did a high-five followed by their secret handshake. From what she could pick up—the multitude of times she'd seen them do it while she was in the room with them—it consisted of some kind of weird series of hand grips and finger play they'd developed together. They did it every time they said or did something together that they found particularly amusing. And they were amused often—not that she was complaining. She was thankful they were so compatible.

"Please excuse me while I get a jacket," Janine said. "Tom, would you please help me pick one out?"

Her mother was quick. "She has no fashion sense at all. *Someone's* got to help her."

As they got out of earshot, Tom said, "Betty Black? That nasty woman—who is the *spitting* image of Betty White—is named Betty Black? That is totally amazing. She's like the anti Betty White."

He laughed, making her realize she wasn't in this alone. Unlike Martin, who shriveled up and all but disappeared when her mother was near him, Tom could hold his own against her. He didn't seem intimidated at all. That was a good sign. "It's ironic that she's named Elizabeth Black. Isn't it?"

"It's scary!" he said.

"Wait a while, you'll soon find out that *she* is, too."

"Who is too, what?" Craig said as he came into her bedroom. "Grandma. Is scary."

"Don't you know it! I came in here because I hate being alone with her. Besides being one of the nastiest people you'll ever meet, she's got her allergies again or something, and she's coughing and spewing all sorts of gross stuff. She said it was yellow, so she's not contagious. I thanked her for sharing, but she didn't get my sarcasm." Craig looked at his mother and shrugged. "Mom says sarcasm's wasted on Grandma," he said to Tom.

"The woman doesn't know what funny is," Tom said with unhidden disbelief.

They returned to the living room, a team of three.

All four left the apartment and bustled outside as three of the four were shocked to see a chauffeured limousine waiting at the curb.

"Is that it?" Craig asked. "Your car?"

"Yup," he said to the boy.

Janine watched as her mother's eyes got round. Hers weren't all that blasé either. When they got to the car, the chauffeur opened the door for them. After piling in, they settled in their Corinthian leather seats and Tom offered them a drink. Craig took a Mountain Dew Code Red, which Tom had stocked, knowing the boy's penchant for the beverage.

"My favorite!" Craig squealed, looking at Tom when he discovered the many cans stacked in the tiny fridge.

She saw Tom wink back at her son.

"Where did you say we were going for dinner?" her mother asked Tom.

"I didn't," he said.

Janine squeezed his hand. He was handling her mother perfectly. He stayed in control, letting her know who was the boss. It was an unfamiliar experience for her mother, who looked uncomfortable. Most likely from the alien sensation that she was no longer the absolute dictator. Two points for the home team. Janine squeezed Tom's hand again. He squeezed back.

"Nice wheels," Craig said, slurping from his soda can.

"Thanks."

Janine's mother was looking out the window wearing a dour expression that would have spoiled milk had some been present.

"'Betty Black,'" he whispered directly into Janine's ear. "I still can't believe it."

"Believe it," she whispered back. "And people wonder why I don't understand the expression 'Everything's not black and white, there *are* shades of gray.'"

He laughed, then covered it with a cough, and excused himself when he drew the attention of the elderly woman.

Once she was looking out the window again, Janine leaned back into his ear and continued. "Look at her. *Listen* to her! If there were ever a better case—living proof, if you will—that the theory of black and white with no shades of gray exists…she's it!"

His laughter filled the car, and he was thankful when a metallic voice coming through an overhead speaker interrupted him. "Less than five minutes, sir."

"Thanks, James," he said aloud.

Three sets of eyes stared at him. "I usually work in the car, and James always lets me know when I'm within a few minutes of my place of arrival so I can gather up my papers and get them back in my briefcase."

"Or cram for last-minute stuff, huh?" Craig asked.

"Yeah, that, too," Tom said to the boy as they exchanged their secret hand thing again.

"I do that on the school bus," Craig said, taking this all in with the ease of a child.

Janine had no idea he lived this comfortably, and obviously her mother hadn't expected it either.

On Spring Street in SoHo, they pulled to a stop in front of Balthazar's, and her mother gasped. "When did you make your reservations?" she asked Tom, as he helped her out of the car. "It takes months to get a table here."

"I called yesterday. But if you don't like the place, I can give a quick call to Le Cirque and we can go there, if you'd prefer."

The older woman stared at him. "No one 'gives a quick call to Le Cirque' and gets in unless they're someone special. Tom Kennedy," she said slowly, "where have I heard that name before?" Her eyes suddenly protruded. "Thomas Edward Kennedy the *Third?*"

"Yes, that's me," he said with a cockeyed grin, as he walked her from the car to the door.

"Who is Thomas Edward Kennedy the Third?" Janine asked, stepping onto the sidewalk from the car.

"That would be me," he said to her, walking her to her mother.

"You can't lift up the *Wall Street Journal* without seeing his name plastered on just about every page, dear!" her mother admonished her.

"You can't?" she asked Tom, obviously baffled. It didn't seem to fit the man she'd been dating for the past few months.

He shrugged, embarrassed.

"But you're so easygoing, so relaxed and, well, *normal*."

"Don't let that fool you, dear. He's a barracuda in the business world," the old woman said as she looked at him like a starving woman gazing at a prime rib. "How did you two meet again?"

"At the gym, Grandma. They met at the gym," Craig said as he opened the door to New York City's hottest, hardest-to-get-into restaurant.

"From the moment I saw you climb on that treadmill and start aggressively stomping the miles away, I was attracted to you. But that first evening when I went to your place and sat in your kitchen, with you and Craig inhaling all that Chinese food I brought, I realized that I could love you dearly. Both of you. That night I'd looked at Craig and knew I already loved him. He was smart, funny, warm, open, honest, unique, obviously loved his mom, and I could see a side of Craig that was hurt and needed protecting. I wanted to be the one to protect him. His comic indifference shelters that vulnerable part, and I could see right through it. I could see through it because I had worn the same armor myself as a boy."

Tears streamed down Janine's cheeks. "What did I ever do to deserve you?" she said as she kissed him wholly. Then she excused herself to visit the ladies' room to fix her makeup.

When she came out, she looked for Tom.

The room was beautiful. Elegant, tasteful, and filled with friends, family, and a large number of the most influential business people from all over the country. She was still just meeting many of them, but their admiration and respect for her brand-new husband was evident.

"Pleasure to meet you, Janine. You've done wonders with

Tom," a portly man in an expensive suit said while reaching up to slap Tom's shoulder. "He's so distracted with you lately, he let one slip by and for once gave me a good deal a few weeks back."

"Nothing slipped by me, Ed. I just don't have the hunger I used to have," Tom said with a laugh and a wink in Janine's direction. If she had any idea who Ed was, she might've answered Tom's witty response with one of her own. Tom may have lost his hunger for business, but what he had lost in one department, he made up for in another. His hunger in the pleasure department was more than abundant! Not that she was complaining. At all. The man was as skillful in the bedroom as he apparently was in the boardroom.

The man named Ed turned to Janine. "He's lost his killer instinct."

That she could respond to. Looking at her gorgeous husband, she said, "Displaced, not lost."

The man chuckled and patted Tom on the back again. "Congratulations, again, and good luck to you both."

As soon as she said thank you, Sid appeared.

"I hope they're getting plenty of good pictures, dear. This is great PR. A posh wedding at the Four Seasons? Your readers will love it! And to have all the tables adjacent to the magnificent marble pool in the coveted Pool Room? It's the coup de grâce, dear, a grand coup!"

She laughed at her agent. "I did it less for the public relations and more for the private relations, Sid."

"Your charming humor always makes me laugh, dear. Your readers, too. By the way, your latest book was just sold at auction. I think it's your best yet."

"Wow. It did? That's great news. Thank you, Sid," she said warmly. "Now please go sit down. You shouldn't be standing around," she said with concern.

When the man was out of earshot, she said to Tom, "Turns out, he'd had a mild heart attack and had been hospitalized, which was why he hadn't returned my calls or e-mails. His office was told not to let *anyone* know of his illness for fear his clients and contacts might portray him as weak or—worse—at death's door, and would go elsewhere. That's why I never heard from him."

Tom kissed her forehead. "I told you something was wrong. Your writing's fantastic."

Before the glowing smile left her face, Matt came over to shake Tom's hand and kiss the bride. "I guess you can have shower privileges now, Janine," he said with a laugh.

"Why's that?" she asked.

Matt looked at Tom. "You *still* haven't told her?"

Tom shrugged and laughed, then turned to Janine. "I own the gym, too."

"You do?" she said with surprise. Her brow knit together before she spoke again. "You mean all this time you could have *paid* someone to do your walking for you?"

Both men laughed at her comment, and her new husband said, "That defeats the purpose, my little smart aleck."

"Well, now that we're married—and your money's my money—can we pay someone to do *my* walking for *me?*"

From behind her, Dr. Harvey Rogers said, "I heard that, young lady." He feigned annoyance. "Just because I told you your latest scan showed you're rebuilding bone mass, it doesn't mean you can stop your regimen. Understand?" he challenged.

"She understands, Doc." Tom kissed her nose lightly. "Plus, if you're not there, who'll keep me company?" he asked his new wife.

"Richard Karn?" she offered.

He laughed the deep, warm laugh that always molded over her. "Nice try, but I like having you with me, calling out the answers."

"You never needed help with the answers before," an older buxom woman said to Tom as she joined the conversation.

Tom smiled. "Honey," he said to Janine, "this is Mrs. Abernathy."

"Mrs. Abernathy, I've heard so much about you," Janine said, taking the older woman's hand in her own.

"And I've heard wonderful things about you too, my dear."

"We'll have to have you over for dinner soon, when we get back from our honeymoon." Janine turned to Tom. "Don't worry, I won't cook. I'll order in."

He laughed.

"Time for some parting words," someone called to Tom and Janine.

Tom cleared his throat. Holding up his glass of champagne, he said, "Finding my way to you, Janine, was a long, lonely, winding road. In my lifetime, there have only been two women before you who have loved and trusted me as you do. My mother, God rest her soul, and Mrs. Abernathy," he said, saluting the woman standing next to him with his glass.

He'd never explained to anyone who she was, but by his toast he made it clear Mrs. Abernathy was an honored guest. From the look of pride in the elderly woman's eyes, it was evident to Janine that she admired and loved him deeply in return.

"Thank you, darling," Janine replied with tears in her eyes. "And before you wreck my makeup by making me cry again, I'd like to note that yes, I do love and adore you, and yes, I also must trust you. Otherwise we'd be going to Paris for our honeymoon instead of where we're about to go."

The crowd roared with laughter, giving her a standing ovation, immediately after Craig made "Whoo, Whoo, Whoo" noises as he pumped his fist in the air with each utterance.

She saw her mother walking over to where they stood. "Brace yourself. Here she comes."

"We're going to have to tell her eventually," Tom said softly.

"Maybe she won't ask," Janine whispered back.

Tom chuckled. "Keep dreaming, babe."

The moment the woman reached their sides, she said, "Where *are* you two going on your honeymoon? I don't see what all the secrecy is about! Tom, now that you're married to her, you'll have to teach her how to act like a grown woman."

Tom braced Janine by his side. "Sorry, Betty, but I've got to tell you, you're all wrong about your daughter. She's the *perfect* 'grown woman.' I'm hoping she can teach *me* how to act like a teenaged boy."

Janine laughed, loving the way he stood up to her mother. "You already know how to do that," she said to him.

Betty sputtered, ignoring the negative response just received and squaring her small shoulders for the next wave of battle. "And since you're both going to be gone, I don't know *why* my grandson can't spend his birthday with me!"

"There are so many responses for that question on so many

levels, Mother, but since we're at my wedding, surrounded by people, I'll answer you with just the facts." Janine stood tall as she looked down at her mother. "First of all, as to where we're going for our honeymoon? We're going to Colorado."

"Colorado?" her mother spit out in disgust. "What is in Colorado?" she said, her eyes boring into Tom. "A business trip? A spa in Aspen?"

"There's a lot to do in Colorado," Tom said, smiling guilelessly. "But you tell her, Janine. I know your mother would probably prefer to hear it coming from you."

Janine grinned. "Craig's coming with us."

"On your honeymoon?" She looked appalled.

Craig clomped over in his tux and his big, black boots and said, "Yeah, Grandma. How cool is that? Who woulda guessed that my mom—that maniacally overprotective, cautionary to the point of phobic, unathletic, sworn city woman—would end up spending her honeymoon—and my thirteenth birthday—" he looked between Tom and Janine and grinned before turning back to face his grandmother head-on "—white-water rafting."

She gasped aloud and clutched her chest before regaining her usual stiff-backed composure. "Probably the same people who would have guessed she'd marry a Kennedy," her mother said with haughty disdain.

Some things never changed.

Dear Reader,

Like Janine, I always thought osteoporosis only affected much older women in their seventies or eighties. In reality, though, it can strike at any age. Also like Janine, I was completely blown away when my doctor told me (when I was in my early forties) that I had osteoporosis. Shockingly, osteoporosis can be found in fifty-five percent of people fifty years of age and older.

It's often called the "silent disease" because bone loss occurs without symptoms. People may not know that they have osteoporosis until, like me, their bones become so weak that a sudden strain, bump, or fall causes a fracture or a vertebra to collapse. Collapsed vertebrae may initially be felt or seen in the form of severe back pain, loss of height, or spinal deformites (aka: "a humpity back"), but can also be painless.

No, I don't have a humpity back. But yes, I now have to eat more cheese and ice cream (I force myself), take a pill once a week (every Monday like clockwork), and I *do* coerce myself to walk most days (which—I'm sorry but I'm being honest with you here—I *truly* hate doing), but my bones are miraculously becoming denser, which is the ultimate goal. And if *I* can do it…you can do it.

Although women are four times more likely than men to develop this disease, osteoporosis affects more than forty-four million Americans. And that's only counting the people who *know* they have it. Personally, I hadn't a clue until I went to the doctor with a backache and found out I'd fractured a vertebra. Sadly, the cold, hard facts are: One in two women over age fifty will have an osteoporosis-related fracture in her remaining lifetime. But fortunately, osteoporosis is not only treatable, in many cases it can be *reversible!* And the sooner you find out you have it, the better. So talk to your doctor today about scheduling a bone scan. It's painless, only takes about fifteen minutes, and you don't even have to take off your clothes! (But I'm sure they'd let you if you *really* wanted to.) For more information, please visit:

The National Osteoporosis Foundation (in the US) at http://www.nof.org

The National Osteoporosis Society (in the UK) at http://www.nos.org.uk

The Osteoporosis Society of Canada (in Canada) at http://www.osteoporosis.ca

Osteoporosis Australia (for our friends down under) at http://www.osteoporosis.org.au

And lastly, the International Osteoporosis Foundation (for everywhere else) at http://www.osteofound.org

And feel free to write to me anytime at Elise.Lanier@gmail.com or visit my Web site at www.eliselanier.com.

Please take care of yourself, stay well, and be happy,

Elise

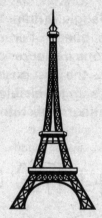

Mothers, sisters and other passengers

Novelist Maggie Dufrane's mama is the Mississippi queen of drama. When her sister Jean drops a shocker on the family, Mama thinks it's the best gossip she's heard all year. But it's up to reliable Maggie-the-family-chauffeur to fix things...again.

Driving Me Crazy

PEGGY WEBB

A woman determined to walk her own path

Joining a gym was the last thing Janine ever expected to do. But with each step on that treadmill, a new world of possibilities was opening up!

TREADING LIGHTLY
ELISE LANIER

HN28

Available January 2006
TheNextNovel.com

REQUEST YOUR FREE BOOKS!

2 FREE NOVELS TO INTRODUCE YOU TO OUR BRAND-NEW LINE!

There's the life you planned. And there's what comes next.

NEXT05

Sometimes the craziness of living
the perfect suburban life is enough
to make a woman wonder…

Who
makes up
these rules,
Anyway?

BY
STEVI MITTMAN

HARLEQUIN®
Next™

HN30
Available February 2006
TheNextNovel.com

Since when did life ever tell you where you were going?

Sometimes you just have to dip your oar
into the water and start to paddle.

THE
SUNSHINE
COAST
NEWS

KATE AUSTIN

HARLEQUIN®
NeXt™

HN32

Available February 2006
TheNextNovel.com